SHETANI "ZERU" BRYAN

NEW PRAETORIANS 2

RK SYRUS

Editing:
Crystal "Godzilla" Watanabe
Taryn "Lois Lane" Lawson

Proofing/Book Interior:
Crystal Watanabe, Pikko's House

Print and Ebook Cover:
James "Tiberius" Egan of Bookfly Design

E-book
eISBN10 1-910890-07-3
(eISBN13:) 978-1-910890-07-3

Paper book
ISBN10 1-910890-08-1
(ISBN13:) 978-1-910890-08-0

THE SCI-FI TECHNOTHRILLER NOVEL SERIES BEGINS WITH:

NEW PRAETORIANS 1: SIENNA MCKNIGHT

"Wonder Woman meets Tom Clancy's Splinter Cell."

Praise for *Sienna McKnight*:

"In a world filled with crumbling governments and dangerous, out-of-control technology, Sienna learns the only way to effectively wage war is to follow her own rules."

—Samuel Morningstar, Author of the Dirk Garrick
Occult Detective Series

"…an intriguing world of futuristic technology, made more familiar by contemporary references."

"Radiant descriptions also enhance the story."

—Kirkus Reviews

"Sienna was an interesting character. I was happy that she did in fact remind me of Sarah Connor from Terminator, just like the blurb said. She only gets more awesome as the book progresses."

—Brittany S., NetGalley reviewer

Man was born into barbarism, when killing his fellow man was a normal condition of existence. He became endowed with a conscience. And he has now reached the day when violence toward another human being must become as abhorrent as eating another's flesh.

—Dr. Martin Luther King, Jr.
Why We Can't Wait, 1963

Pamir Mountains

Khorasan Sovereignty

Wandering Desert

Gulf of Oman

In certain places it is believed the body parts of albinos hold magical powers, that they can make someone instantly prosperous, powerful, or lucky if a witch doctor turns them into a talisman, or a salve, or a stew. A person who wants to quickly become rich is advised to put a set of properly prepared albino legs on either side of his/her door entrance with the toes pointing into the home.

Raw ingredients are often procured by the witch doctors' clients: powerful politicians and ascendant warlords.

A complete set of human albino body parts—all four limbs, genitalia, ears, tongue, nose, and skin—can be sold for up to $75,000 (LCU equivalent) according to the current report by Worldwide Help International.

One Swahili word for albinos is "zeru," meaning "ghost."

1

FORTY-THREE YEARS AGO
SUB-SAHARAN AFRICA

ELAHAJ

The boy ran headlong through the thornbushes at night. No moon, no stars, the thick-woven canopy above blotted out any glimmer that might guide him. Elahaj stuck one hand out to feel his way. The other held his burden, the reason for his mad dash.

Behind him, there might be lights. Only electric. No gas, no kerosene. The bush was very dry in this season. He did not look back. Turning, he might stumble. It was enough to know they were not ahead of him. He felt around, tried to be careful, tried with each step to lift his feet over roots and vines. Then he tripped anyway, slid to a stop, skinning one knee. He rose and moved on.

A long thorn pierced his palm where thumb and first finger met. The world all around was so dark that he could see the pain. It flashed red-orange, then faded to silver. Better his hand than his leg or foot.

With his mouth, he pulled out the long, needle-shaped intruder. He spat, tasting sap, sweat, dirt, and blood.

It might have gone all the way through. He could not tell. He squeezed his fingers, felt wet drip. It was not a bad wound. Maybe the dark held luck for him.

Maybe he could last till day came. In daylight he could find government rangers or strong Maasai who would not be afraid to help. Now, no one would help him. In the dull dead of night, all creatures were on their own.

He sensed a hollow space ahead and ducked left.

Somewhere, a hyena laughed.

Elahaj understood the meaning of the sound as if it had come from a person. This was how they spoke to each other when approached by something more dangerous. Hyenas laughed when they were afraid.

The weight he carried stirred but remained silent.

A minute later, Elahaj heard another hyena noise, this one was different.

"Whoop, whoop."

That sound they made to call their clan together for a hunt. If the stories have been told true, they obeyed something that was less than a spirit, yet more than a man. Something that walked on two legs and carried a hunger no natural beast could endure.

"Whoop, whoop."

Were the hyenas closer now? Or had he run toward them in the dark? No way to know.

These scavengers could run faster than any wild dog. Their ears, eyes, and noses were built for finding wounded prey. Elahaj felt his portion of luck fade. He had no chance. *They* had no chance.

Something crawled on him. It wasn't biting, so he left it.

He had to think.

The river?

Could he find it? By the sun, yes. But in pitch dark by a sickle moon that kept vanishing behind cloud and trees? How? Every turn could run him straight into the hyenas. At a full run, they were as quiet as snakes. He might not know they were there until he was surrounded.

The river!

Minutes later, Elahaj felt the maze of bramble bushes open. He felt the jabs and pricks less and less.

Left. *Ah!*

Right. *Ow!*

Left. *Gah!*

Then no more.

Even better, a boon. He saw something to guide his way.

By the meager silver light in the sky, he could make out the Giraffe's Horns. Two prongs of faraway mountaintops behind a hill. He knew where he was and the way to go.

He ran. He wasn't alone.

A ripple of silence washed through trees and bushes. The silence of insects, the sudden quiet of bird calls, the absence of these things was as alarming as panting snarls. A mute hush spread out around the hunting pack and what followed after them.

Close? Far?

Didn't matter. If he could sense the hyenas, they had marked him long ago. If they caught him, they would not kill him. These were not so merciful as truly wild things. They were cunning servants.

Once, when he was very young and watching from the low branches of a fat tree, he had seen a guard dog killed. Its neck had been broken silently and bloodlessly. Its body lay on the dirt path, hind legs twitching. The pack of wild hyenas ignored it and worked together to pull a calf over a fence.

These ones, somewhere out there, were not wild. They were sternly trained. They had been taught to hunt humans and keep the prize whole. Schooled by the lash, marked by the branding iron, they had devoured the carcasses of their brothers and sisters who did not learn quickly enough. This pack would hold them still until the real beast came: the Ghost Eater.

The side of the river he was on was the same side as his village. On this side, the riverbank was high, like the ledge of a small hill. Before he got to this ledge, he would run into a mud wallow. That place smelled very bad, was hard to cross, and dangerous. Long worms with teeth lived on the bottom. You never stepped there without good shoes, or you'd lose a toe to a biting thing. But now he hoped to feel the squish under his soles.

He did. Dry hardpack turned to sand. Sand turned to cool mud.

Just then, the sound of padding came from behind. He looked. Fickle light bounced off five, maybe six pairs of eyes.

So close. Maybe closer to him than he was to the wide flowing waters of the river.

He ran.

Hyena eyes twinkled and dipped and came on.

That second that separated them, it was enough. Enough for his foot to find the solid crest of a sand bank. The sand was firm enough for his feet to push off from. Elahaj leaped with all his remaining might.

Air rushed under his arms. He held them up high. High enough so that if he hit deep water, his baby brother would not drown, not right away.

The unnamed infant held out a hand. He seemed to be reaching up into the sky to grab for the sharply honed sickle moon. Like the moon, his little arm was bone white.

***

Sometime later, but well before the glimmer of the next day, Elahaj hid where the Ghost Eater and the hunters were least likely to look. He was on a small hill overlooking the road into the village he had just run away from. He crouched there, doing what they would not expect. He had doubled back and was watching *them*.

When he'd jumped, he had not flown across the whole river. He would have needed wings to do that. And on the other side, where was there for him to go? Only more flat country. Good for those on four feet, bad for those with two legs.

Instead, he had leaped from the near bank only as far as he needed to convince the hyenas' noses and the men with lights that they had crossed.

As he waded, he'd held the baby higher than he had to. A visitor to the village told him that in his country ghosts, albinos, were not allowed to go near deep running water. He had said it was known their spirit father came upon the earth in the form of a river. This water demon, the traveler's story

SHETANI ZERU BRYAN - NEW PRAETORIANS 2

went, would gladly take them home at the earliest opportunity.

Elahaj did not believe this. The only spirit he personally had knowledge of was the lazy one attached to the fat Kigelia trees around the village. On the other hand, why take chances where spirits were concerned?

He had made his way down river. Sometimes only the ends of his toes touched the bottom of the channel. The wind was behind him the whole way. A gurgling current covered the small noises made by his baby brother. Behind them, white cones of light darted this way and that above the dark waters.

Then he had found a spot where the river turned and a branch hung; it was thick with leaves. He grabbed it. Elahaj stayed still.

There he waited, listening. He knew enough English to be a guide. He did not need it to understand what was happening on the riverbank where his footprints disappeared. The language he overheard was universal: fear and pain.

Under a tattered safari hat, a black-lipped mouth set in a vulture-gray face snarled silently. The Ghost Eater raised his arm and the gnarled leather-bound lash at the end of it. After the first few strokes, the hyenas no longer whimper-laughed, they only grunted, feeling their master's outrage. Feeling it blow by blow.

Ten strokes each. Six hardy scavengers.

Sixty strokes in all. The last three or four were always wet slaps on thick hide as blood welled in fresh wounds. Jaws that could splinter an antelope's thighbones gnashed in agony.

Elahaj had witnessed this while standing in the river, bracing himself against its slow plentiful current. Tired, hurt, and hungry as he was, he forced himself to think.

There were spirits that clung to the trees ringing his village. These spirits sometimes helped people when their need was very great. They were lazy. If he ran too far away, they would not follow. He looked at the shapes of the Kigelia trees outlined by the hunter's headlights and lamps.

A plan, dangerous and desperate, fixed itself in his mind. Once punished, the hyenas would slink off to lick their wounds. Perhaps the weakest ones would die. What mattered was their ears and noses would be somewhere else. He could quietly go back to the village.

He left the river to do just that.

Their home was barely a lean-to. It stood away from the center of the ring of huts, as befitted the spawn of demons. Theirs was a tolerant community. A community with one traitor in it, whose desire for hard currency had overcome human compassion.

As dusk had fallen that day, one of their fellow villager's words had brought doom rolling in on four wheels. The trucks of the albino hunters still stood there in a circle, headlamp lights flaring out so the visitors had light to work by.

Clothes dripping with river water, Elahaj hid his brother in the baby's own swaddling crib. The little one was quiet. He only had to remain undetected for a short while longer. In a few minutes, if the plan went well, it would not matter. It also occurred to Elahaj that if the plan went badly, it would also not matter. With that in mind, and with much less hesitation weighing down his feet, he ducked out of the lean-to to prepare.

***

He worked silently, darting along narrow paths he had

followed since he was old enough to walk. They wound their way through the dry brush that ringed the village.

New voices came from the ring of trucks. Some were angry in the local way, the way a motorcyclist would yell at you to move your cow to the side. Other voices spoke English in very harsh, superior tones. Those were angry in way he had heard on the radio.

A scream.

From the pit of hopeless agony, it slashed out and split the night air. It was all Elahaj could do to keep still. He wanted to rush in, just him and a piece of plastic against four, maybe five, men with machetes.

"Why… why do you do this?"

A female voice he knew very well came from the doorway of a communal hut. The one used for sorting and mashing grain. He wanted to shut his ears, but the sounds carried clearly.

"You are from this village," the same woman's voice pleaded. "I knew you as a boy. You played and hunted with my brothers. We are your people, I am—"

"YOU are a demon!" the man said, backing up to the hut's doorway to give himself room to work.

The albino hunter's legs and feet came into view. He wore new leather boots with no socks. The laces were tied wrong, with the top part and tongue flopping. This was not how the foreign safari visitors would have tied them.

"The magic that gave you life," he went on, "the beast that lay with your mother and you as well. Your confession is on your skin and the zeru boy's."

The man's head swivelled around on his long, sweaty neck.

Bloodshot eyes wild with greed gazed at the trees. Looked right at Elahaj. Or so it felt. The servant of the Ghost Eater must have seen only the low-hanging Kigelia branches, because a second later, those greedy eyes darted the other way, as if they would catch a valuable zeru just strolling by.

The albino hunter turned back to the one he had trapped in the hut.

"We are taking those magics, not human people. Our boss will let the magic out, and he will use it," he said, leaning back and bracing his arm. "He will pay us. Pay us for every part…"

Thock.

"…of you."

The machete hacked through sinewy gristle and stubborn joint. Elahaj knew the sound, but it was not a bushmeat animal being cut. It was his own mother.

Her next sound was more terrifying than a scream. She gave up a wavering exhalation, one cut off by a thick wet sob of utter hopelessness.

Elahaj had to do something. He could not just sit safely in cover. He breathed in and out. Then did what he came back from the river to do. Unseen, he circled the outermost huts.

He heard everything but let none of it penetrate his mind like the thorn that had earlier pushed through his hand. If he let one moment in, he would be lost. All would be lost.

"Please, leave me one hand."

"Woman, are you *stupid*?"

The machete, now dripping, waved at the trucks and the other helpers.

"Look around. You tell me 'take one arm and go'?" The man sounded offended by this unreasonable suggestion. "Everyone has to be paid. He told us he needs all of you, and not to come back without the double-demon baby in one piece."

Elahaj was nearly done. Suddenly a white man nearly spoiled everything.

A German missionary came crashing through the trees, much too close to his hiding place. The man and his lamplight were going to reveal him.

"Mein Gott! Was machst du?" Father Rebmann yelled. He had a light strapped to his head; its beam came close to hitting Elahaj. It didn't. Elahaj remained motionless against the rough tree trunk. The older man was in such a hurry to get to the communal hut that he saw nothing else.

"What…? How can you do this? This is barbarism," Rebmann shouted. "This is against the laws of man and God. Stop! Let this woman up."

"Hands off, old fool. Or we will forget we agreed not to harm holy white fathers. I am Maasai. I will not be touched by you."

"You, a hunter? And this is your prize?" Rebmann scoffed. "You make me ill. Hack a defenseless woman? She is baptized Rachel. Of my parish. You will harm her *no more*!"

"Speak any more tonight, I will silence your nonsense tongue forever by taking it out." The man with the machete looked down the road with suspicion on his face. "How did you come here? We saw no one coming."

"You wouldn't have, would you," said another white man sharply as he entered the clearing. This one Elahaj had never seen before.

He was younger and followed by a city-dressed black man. Both came up behind Rebmann. They wore strange, long eyeglasses, like the head-light of the holy father but flashing a dull green.

"If you saw our lights you might have had time to cover up this atrocity."

A thick thorn vine snapped on the other side of the clearing.

Everyone, the holy white father, the two new men with him, looked there.

The Maasai albino hunter by the hut dropped his bloody blade in fear. It was the Ghost Eater. True to his name, he had appeared without warning.

The Eater's servant, the black Maasai brute, held out the pale chopped-off arm with both hands. He greeted his master with awe and a humble offering.

The Ghost Eater came into the light. He was large, his clothing made him look squared off at the shoulders. It was hard to tell him apart from the trees behind. When he stood, he was as still as a stone. It was a false stillness. This was like the illusion sent out by the river crocodile or the tree snake.

When the Eater finally spoke, his voice was the sound of a thousand beetle jaws rasping inside a rotting hollow log. "Now, who might you be?"

The stranger replied too quickly. It dawned on Elahaj that the newcomer might not know enough to be respectful to the Ghost Eater. Though he had expensive clothes and fancy electronic devices, he should consider his words and how he spoke them to a being that was part man, part beast, and part spirit.

"I am Delphino Everett. The leader of a bioarchaeology expedition sponsored by Linacre College, Oxford."

Everett spoke with enough pride to make Elahaj nervous. The Eater's man-face could be reasoned with as long as one did not enrage the two other sides. In a moment, he would need to speak with the man-face. These new people were making that unnecessarily complicated. At the moment, he could only listen and watch.

"My colleague is Dr. Akan, MD." Everett nodded to the taller black man. "We're tracing the matrilineal origins of sub-Saharan albinos. Apparently we are following the same breadcrumb trail of alleles as these brutes, who I assume are under your charge," he said, taking the green light from his head. "But it would appear our respective endeavours were undertaken for egregiously different purposes."

The Ghost Eater's purple-black lips made a sucking sound. "Well, cover me all over in 'don't give a shit.'"

The Eater moved forward, closer. If Elahaj had blinked, he would have missed the movement, so sly it was, deliberate, and quick.

"You may give a... uh, a care... about this: Dr. Akan is employed by Worldwide Help International." Everett spoke more carefully but again with all too much boldness. He reminded Elahaj of a tourist trying to take a picture with a lion.

"We are all witness to your barbaric assaults. This country enthusiastically administers the death penalty for poaching." He looked with disgust at the severed arm. "Technically, that includes human as well as animal trophies. Of course, if we don't return safely to the WWHI compound, the government gibbet will be the least of your worries."

The Ghost Eater wore a long coat made of stiff cloth, like

that of safari tents. The ends dragged through the ashes of the cold village campfire as he walked forward. He chuckled. It was not a pleasant sound to hear.

"Every time I get a death sentence, a demon sprouts its wings," he said softly and smoothly, like the noose of an oiled rope closing fast.

The Eater added, not softly, "Tie them. And find me my *shetani zeru!*"

One of the Eater's men knocked away some kind of electronic device from the doctor's hands, but they did not have time to tie them. Elahaj stepped out into the lights.

"Hello, Sir Ghost Eater. I am Elahaj of this village."

"Little kijana, I'm kinda preoccupied."

The Eater called him "boy." He felt the need to speak with authority, though he was small for his age.

"I am taking my marks of manhood after the next great beast walk. I must speak with you."

He drew himself to his maximum height. His upper body was in full view, his feet and other items hidden by a log. Maybe it looked like he was leaving the option of running again open for himself. He could not. No matter how things turned out between him and the Eater, that was not an option. Another reason to start with flattery.

"You are very old," Elahaj said. "Yes, very powerful, and wise. Women sing songs of you. No man and no beast willingly invites your anger. But, we must ask you to stop chopping my mother. We ask you: Please leave this village."

The Ghost Eater had a gun. Maybe he was deciding if a normal-colored boy was worth a bullet.

"Who's 'we'?"

"My friend, the Tree Sprit has a message: Let everyone go. Leave."

Elahaj searched for the other's man-face. The Eater looked at him. Black-rimmed lips peeled back from sharpened teeth.

"Boy, is there an 'or else' that comes with that?"

Elahaj was unsure. The Eater was equal parts mindless animal, wicked spirit, and evil man. The evil man could be reasoned with. If the other aspects dominated, the Eater would kill everyone in a rage.

Elahaj was not sure which aspect ruled the mind behind the hooded eyes set deeply in vulture-gray skin. He said it anyway.

"It is a big world, and I do not know many things. But I know the one thing the Ghost Eater fears… is fire."

The last word hung in the air.

With that, Elahaj threw forward a large plastic jug that had once held gasoline. It was empty.

"You wouldn't…" A hundred thousand beetle jaws gritted and vibrated their anger from the deep pit of a dark throat.

"Sir, Tree Spirit says to go and never come back. All the ghosts will be gone. Nothing for you here."

The Eater's helpers looked around as though they expected the encircling thorn brush to erupt in a blaze and the fat Kigelia trees to start belching flame at them from hollows in their trunks.

On their own, the trees would do nothing. He and the villagers knew from a long history that they would just sit and watch people do as they would. The trees were lazy. In response to the terror and pain brought here by strangers in the dead of night, what did they do? Only filled him with small power, and even that for only a short time. Then again, it was better than no help at all from the world of spirits. He must make the most of it.

Before he could be shot, Elahaj took the precaution of igniting a butane torch. He had found this in the back of one of the visitors' trucks along with the gas cans. It was much more reliable than the plastic lighter he had planned to use. A solid finger of blue flame sprang out. He held it above the dry grass.

Some moments of quiet followed.

The blue flame hissed.

The city people watched.

Father Rebmann muttered a prayer.

The severed arm dripped blood.

People were clearly thinking about what would happen next. The holy father broke the silence.

"Leaving out the unholy aspects," he said, "the young man has a point. There is a drought, *ja*?" He took his hat off and fanned his bearded face. "The brush is very dry. With this much fuel spread around us…"

"And four more cans, even bigger than this one," Elahaj added.

After a few seconds, the Ghost Eater reached his hand back. It swept past the ivory handle of his gun. He pulled his coat closed. His hollowed-out mouth aimed right at Elahaj. "You're smart. Something my guys should be but ain't."

He flicked his thumb at his helpers. They murmured, frozen by their own fears.

"And you're not a coward," the half-demon concluded. As he blinked, the Jeep's headlights reflected off his retinas. Purple-rimmed lips pulled back from the points of dark, filed-down teeth. "If you want to be rich and powerful, come see me. I'll be waitin', Elahaj."

The taste of sudden, and in truth, unexpected success was soured a bit in his mouth by two things. First, the Eater now knew his name. In his haste, he had forgotten that. One's right name was a thing to keep hidden from all but guaranteed friendly sprits. Second, all the while he spoke, the Eater was looking past him, past the trees, as if he could see the lean-to where his baby brother was.

Very quickly, it seemed, the Eater and the albino hunters drove off. They kept his mother's arm but took little else to show for their troubles.

With the stressful minutes past, the Tree Spirit's power drained out of him. It flowed back up into squat trunks and drooping branches. Elahaj collapsed, cross-legged, to the ground.

He remembered only some of the things that happened next. The black doctor putting blood back into his mother and sewing the end of her arm. The German father leaning over him, his thick tobacco-stained fingers cleaning the thorn jab in his hand. The dull ache of the other injuries he didn't remember getting.

"*Ja*," the missionary said through his sparse yellowing beard. "I have seen a wildfire go from lightning strike to taking a whole mountainside, all before a man can empty his bladder. The poacher who survives, he is one who has learned when to run."

He looked closely at Elahaj. Perhaps the holy father was trying to give him comfort, or admiring him for his bravery, or curious about the ways of the Tree Spirit. At the best of times, it was hard to figure out what was on a foreigner's mind.

"Ach, poor Rachel."

The strange white man, Everett Delphino, held his baby brother.

"Kofi," he said to his friend the black doctor, "WWHI has a high-risk relocation division, don't they? We've got to get everyone who carries the albinism gene to the capital."

The scientist was a most strange man. With delicate long fingers, he put a small cotton-tipped stick into his brother's mouth and kept some of his spit as though it were most precious.

"You're a unique little achromian, aren't you?" The baby grabbed at Everett's large complicated-looking wristwatch. "Yes, you are."

Elahaj sat on the empty gasoline jug. Men talked and ran and spoke on expensive phones to places far away. He stared at the edge of the forest. He stared until he saw the blush of dawn. He did not really believe the Ghost Eater was gone until birds started singing.

***

"Me and the missus been talkin'," the American man who wore glasses said. "We'd like to help your fine organization in some way."

The couple were speaking to the parish office secretary, but Elahaj's ears pricked up immediately. By the looks of their clothes, their watches, and the keycard of their hotel, they were certainly wealthy.

He had to get them away from the holy white father's office before they were talked into donating all their money to buy goats and chickens for poor farmers. It was needed for something more important.

A week ago, before the sun was fully up, he, his mother, and brother—who had no name by baptism or tribal name ceremony—had left the village. They rode inside Dr. Akan's official WWHI truck.

All the way, his mother fussed with her newly bandaged stump, trying hard not to get blood on the expensive leather seats. Dirt roads turned to gravel and then to smooth blacktop as they drove to a truly terrifying place: the capital.

As they inched along, he had looked out through thick, tinted windows. The narrow jam-packed streets were a new experience. He thought all of the cars in the world had come together to annoy one another. They coughed and barked and honked like the worst kind of irascible animals around a small watering hole. But here, he was told, ghosts were safe. Laws written in books by educated people protected the weak. Most of the time.

Dr. Akan had a stick. Elahaj asked about it. It was decorated with the WWHI symbol. He was naturally interested in any kind of beneficial magic, especially after his experiences. He asked about it. The symbol represented some sort of snake that lived in the sky and the giant who carried it, the doctor tried to explain. Elahaj decided this shiny metal stick was like the spirit wand a witch doctor would carry.

"Oh, no," Akan said, "*hakuna uchawi*. No. It's not magical at all."

It was called a "scroll," and he had trouble believing it was not magical. It opened into a shockingly large flat piece of plastic paper. This, in turn, opened into smaller rectangles through which one could see other places. With it you could see and speak to the whole world. One wave of this stick got them past the guards at a modern hospital. Most definitely uchawi.

All three of them were well cared for. However, after a while, Elahaj sensed the two foreigners' attentions fade. Everett and Akan had many interests beyond protecting a few albinos. He had to find others who would help him do what he needed to do.

The German holy father took them to his boss's office. No one seemed pleased to see the bearded minister. He had been in the bush for many years. The city had grown too big for his mind. He seemed lost. Elahaj knew how he felt.

In his pocket he had only the few coins they'd given him. In the capital, he had no idea who was who or what was what. His one certainty was his belief that his baby brother could not stay. Not after he heard the Eater say his name. Just like an animal will tell you what it intends by growl or bark or roar, he sensed unquenchable hunger. Not here, not in the capital, not anywhere in Africa would a prize shetani zeru baby ever be safe.

He put on the clothes the missionaries offered him and spent a few coins on a Coke. It was sweet, good, and fizzy, but didn't last long or satisfy. The city might be the same. He had to take what he needed and go.

From street kids, he learned a few things.

From the "document man," he learned more.

Documents and government decorations were like spells. People saw a mark and had to do what the mark said. This was good magic to counter the bad; that he understood, but not much more. He could read nothing. Yet the Eater himself had told him he was smart and not a coward. That was something. So he acted more confident than he truly felt.

Elahaj knew when was the time for patience and also when to seize an opportunity. Like the one that had come in the form of this well-fed foreign couple who had dropped by the parish office. They were offering to help—he had to accept before someone else did.

Speaking as fast as he could, which he knew impressed Americans, Elahaj convinced them he was the most reputable tour guide in the capital. He got the man and his wife away from the office. He had to get out of earshot of the nosey secretary to do this thing properly. He had to convince them to kidnap his brother.

Elahaj realized the type of people who would quickly and with no questions just take a child away across the sea were not people you would want taking your helpless infant brother away.

He watched this couple.

They were kind to each other but cautious. They avoided the fake beggars in the street. The parish secretary had told him they had been on charity missions in many places. They had good jobs and owned some land where they lived. They had a son, but he died of cholera while he was studying for ministry.

These were very fine people with high morals. A kidnapping, even for the most wholesome reasons, was not something they would ever agree to. They would have to be tricked into stealing his brother.

His story, when he finally settled on the best one, was

very convincing. It was much more believable than the truth. His tale involved two orphaned boys fleeing from tribal wars. Elahaj said he was the baby's only living relative. He added in a long trek across the savannah while being chased by leopards. He felt the couple would like stories featuring picturesque drama.

With half smiles on their faces, they gave him money. It was enough to start the document man working. In all likelihood, they did not expect to see him again.

The next day, he surprised them at their hotel. They seemed more interested in the boerewors—a round sausage he brought them as a present—than the barely dry papers fresh from the printing machine. He had been right to invest some money in food. These folks liked to eat.

After that, they trusted him. Getting Mr. and Mrs. Bryan to believe they were an orphan albino's last hope of survival was not hard. Nearly all of the ghosts in the capital were missing some part of their body.

Elahaj told the Americans that getting the right magic onto pieces of paper and plastic would be expensive. They handed him more cash than he'd ever seen. It was more than all the livestock in his village was worth. They gave it to save a poor orphan albino. There was only one place the Eater would not find him: America.

His brother—and this made him jealous for a moment— even got his photo taken and put onto the most priceless paper of all. He took a picture of the document with a flip phone he'd found in the trash and charged up at an electricity stand.

A week later, in a building more impressive than the

hospital, and at a line he was not allowed to cross, he waved goodbye to the three of them.

Years passed quickly. Elahaj learned to read. In the process, he'd talked himself into an exciting new job with a literacy organization known as First Book. The work came with a new place to live. As he was deciding what to take and what to leave, he found copies of his brother's travel papers. He saw the mistake he had made back then.

The mistake had to do with his brother's name. Elahaj recalled the precise time he made it.

It was a few days before a woman in a robe gave the final blessing for his brother to join the Bryans' clan and go with them across the sea. He went to get the last papers that were needed. The document man had an office in a room underneath a halal butcher's shop. Elahaj had been there many times to shop for food gifts and arrange for his brother's travel to safety.

Down some dusty stairs, if one went left, one would find goats and lambs hanging by their hind feet, quietly bleeding into buckets from very large cuts in their necks. If one went right, one found a man with a hooked nose and a very large head topped with a round hat of crimson cloth.

The document man looked startled when Elahaj entered, though he had knocked twice. He was perhaps expecting someone else. Elahaj also noticed the pictures of the man's wife and sons were not on the shelf but now inside a bag, partly hidden by the desk. He did not know much about how things worked in the capital, but Elahaj thought he should complete his business soon.

"Do you have my money?"

"Yes, sir," he replied respectfully. Mindful of the bloody room next door and the industrial-sized meat grinder, which was always mulching meat, tendons, and cartilage into many yards of juicy sausages, he added, "It is not on my person at the moment. I will bring it to the café when everything is ready."

As he nodded, the man's mouth smiled, but his eyes did not.

"There was one last…" He checked the papers he was working on. "Ah, the child's name. I have his new parents' names. I need the rest."

His brother had no name, not from his tribe or from the holy father's water ceremony.

Before he could explain, the door was knocked open. The document man half jumped out of his seat, then relaxed. It was only the eyeless, skinless, tongueless head of a sheep poking into the room. All the good parts had been removed and were pickling in a tub of vinegar. The result would be poured into gelatin molds and was considered a delicacy with the curious name "head cheese."

The butcher's assistant mumbled, "Sorry." The flayed skull withdrew, leaving smears on the door.

"Ach!" The man shook his head, cursing his assistant for leaving the bloody mess. His fat sweating head turned to Elahaj. "So, my friend, the name we shall put down for your brother?"

Elahaj hesitated. If he gave the wrong one, the documents might not do the right magic. The man stared. The place smelled quite foul. He blurted out the first thing he could think of.

"So be it." The man wiped perspiration from the rim of his

hat. "Meet me at the café in five hours. Bring my money, or you'll regret it."

Elahaj dashed up the stairs, quite glad to never have to go back there. He was quite busy. There were other hands to fill with Mr. and Mrs. Bryan's cash. If everything went as planned, they would take his brother far away and give him a proper American name.

Years later, when he had learned to read them, he looked at a copy of his brother's travel papers. He smiled grimly. Somehow, he thought, the world of spirts had a way of marking what belonged to them.

Surname/Nom/Apellido

BRYAN

Given Names/Prénoms/Nombres

SHETANI ZERU

Elahaj had one photo of the two of them. It was a type of instant picture. It came out of the camera a glossy gray rectangle. Their images appeared before his eyes.

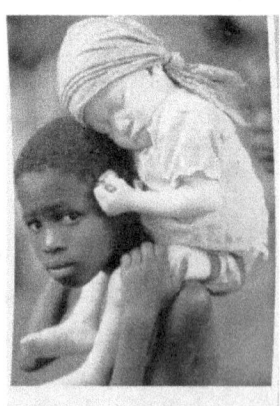

Over the years, it had become yellowed and faded, even though he kept it in a plastic case among his most valuable things. Every time he looked at it, no matter how badly things had gone for him that day, he took heart. His brother was growing up far away, free from mindless bigotry and hateful prejudice.

2

30 YEARS AGO

NEAR THE OLD REIDT MINE

OUTSIDE FAYETTEVILLE, NORTH CAROLINA

SHAY BRYAN

You know why God made albinos, don'tcha?" a boy hollered into the dark woods. "So's Africans could see how ugly they would look if they was white!"

Taddy Eddington tried to laugh at his own taunting joke. But the "haw" only came out as a short-of-breath whistle. In addition to having some kind of asthma, Taddy had something wrong with the right side of his mouth and jaw. The other kids with him were even more goofy looking. Suspenders trailing, buck teeth grinning, they supported their leader with belly laughs and catcalls.

Lungs burning, with cold sweat trickling down between shoulder blades, Shay Bryan peered out at them through a thin line of bushes. Taddy was older. The Eddingtons' oldest son had been held back from twelfth grade twice. He was huge. He had man-teats. They were the two funniest things at their high school that no one ever laughed about.

Last year, one of their high school's A-list bullies decided to have a go at Taddy. On the way to the practice field, a tall and athletic senior thought Taddy's titties would make for an easy prank target. His stunt to try and impress random girls in the hallway was now school legend, but not the way the tall muscular fellow intended. He'd jumped behind Taddy, gave him a bear hug from behind, and then tried to milk him. Big honkin' mistake.

Taddy wrestled the Colts's best linebacker down. He pinned him face-down with Lord knows what ginormous weight of blubber. Enraged and hissing, drool coming out of the sunken side of his face, Taddy whammed the football player's grill over and over down onto his own steel cleats.

Taddy only got a couple weeks' suspension, on account of it being judged more like an accident than an attack using a weapon. Shay also got the idea people were kind of afraid of Taddy Eddington, Sr. After they sewed up the football player, he looked like Frankenstein's monster and never came back to class. Shay heard he got homeschooled for the GED.

After that, no one messed with Taddy, but that didn't mean he was respected. As a bully, that is. He was still a wheezing, crater-faced boob boy, and his posse wasn't much more.

That night, while running for his life, Shay Bryan cussed his luck. As if he didn't have it crappy enough already being an albino and looking at himself with glowy red vampire-bat eyes. He just had to be set upon by the runts of the local bully litter. Crouching down further into the undergrowth, he looked skyward. A big pale moon was high. His skin felt like that reflective paint they put on ambulances and cop cars. Any bumslack moron could spot him.

"I seen him," said one of Taddy's hangers-on, a bumslack moron.

"Watch the road. It'sh th'only way outta here."

"He can't be far."

"I wish I had Ketchum. He'd sniff that pale bastard out."

"We can git him ourselfs," their leader admonished. "An' don't talk foolish. If your dog bit, they'd put her down. No sense riskin' a perfectly good dog."

"How would they know it was Ketchum who bit?"

"They got doggy CSI and such. They can match dog teeth marks to the one what bit. Shore 'nuff that damned pale creeper would fink on you." Taddy spat. He'd probably snuck his daddy's dip, which didn't help his verbal articulation any.

"Over here!" said Jeep, a kid in Shay's own grade. "The dandelions is bent here. Let's follow."

They looked where Jeep was shining his little stick flashlight and followed. Going the wrong way.

That didn't lift Shay's spirits any. The gravel road into these hills led to a dead end at the old mine. It was shut down. For some business reason, they kept the trees and bushes along the road and tracks cut back. There was no way to keep to cover while making a break for it.

His best bet was to hope the smaller kids in the pack would get whiny and tired and want to go home. There would be no point in Taddy puttin' a wuppin' on him if no one was there to see it. Everybody had come out into the hallway to watch him tenderize the linebacker's face. Pictures even got posted. Taddy was hungry for more local fame.

Suddenly something tickled Shay's nose fiercely. He bit his lip to stop from sneezing. The moment passed. Gosh-darned dandelions were everywhere. He wiped snot on his hands, trying to keep it off his clothes.

He felt hemmed in. He was faster than any of them. But for that to be an advantage he would need open ground, and around the mine there was precious little. As quietly as he could, Shay slid down the bank of a slow-moving creek. Making sure of his footing, he hopped over the dark molasses water.

Some of the rocks he saw in the moonlight were pretty good for throwing. He could stop running. If he launched a surprise attack, he could bean a few of them before they even knew what was happening. He could. But that would give away his position. And Taddy was the only one he really wanted to hit. Just his lousy luck the rocks would probably bounce off those chest udders.

By rights, Jeep should be on his side. His mom was from Egypt, which, geographically was located in Africa. Fat chance of that working for him. Shay had seen stuff online from there about how they hacked up and even ate people who looked like him. He was way too pale for his own good.

He did not personally know any other albinos. The closest people to him in stories were the elves in Tolkien's stories. At a time like this, their leader, Elrond, would have told him: "Our list of allies grows thin, Ser Bryan."

"Lord Elrond," Shay whispered, clinging close to a big boulder overlooking the scene. "If only on this, of all evenings, I had brought my shadow cloak. Yet we have not staff, sword, and sling? With these can we not defeat the Dark Lord of Chubb?"

"A wise general considers all options. Even painful ones."

The imaginary elf had a point.

Shay looked at his nice shoes and then at the rough terrain. If he continued to run, his shoes, his pants, and his nice shirt would get messed and torn. Most of these kids ran wild after school. They could keep him out way past his own absolute red-line home time.

Whatever abuse Taddy had planned, he would suffer it anyway when they caught him. Then at home he'd be punished a second time. Shay wasn't a tattler, not for his own sake. He'd have to make up a story that fit the time, state of his clothes, and any injuries.

He considered a Riders of Rohan-style surprise attack.

If he tried to isolate and fight a few of the stronger attackers at a time and outrun the slower ones, maybe they would lose interest. But that would take time and he'd still take some licks. Same outcome: messed-up clothes, missed curfew.

Also, to have any chance against the larger group, he'd have to fight sneaky and underhanded. There were smaller kids pulled along by Taddy's charisma, though he couldn't really see what charisma there was in Cheetos-smelling belches. Point was, they were in the line of fire and likely to get hurt. He'd been brought up never to hurt people smaller or weaker; it was cowardice in its purest form.

Holler out and set some kind of surrender terms? That might let him hobble back home a little late. He could make sure his clothes didn't get ripped or too badly soiled.

A gravel sanding on his ass, or whatever measly torment they had planned, might be okay. If he kept his pants on at gym, no one would see while the scabs healed. And after tonight, if he gave up, they might lose interest in him and pick another victim, one who put up more of a challenge. A scraped butt would be better than a broken leg.

That's what he'd get running around here, even with his abnormal vision. Rocks that looked steady slid right out from under you. Roots that looked flat and dry reached up and grabbed your ankles. If he didn't watch his step, he'd have to drag himself to the road and get someone to call 911. Even worse, he knew from a field trip to the mine that there were plenty of hidden air holes cut up to the surface from shafts deep underground.

If he could find some high ground, his ability to bean people with rocks might give him a negotiating advantage. Maybe they'd be happy if they beat him with some sticks and made him eat a couple bugs and worms. He wouldn't even have to take off his pants.

As Shay considered surrendering and taking his lumps, his pursuers crashed this way and that among the bushes. Their lanterns darted left and right.

"Who's got the trap?"

"Got it." Someone rattled the equipment for his planned torture.

Clink, clink, clink went the chain.

"And the padlock?"

For a guy who couldn't get a job taking out trash, Taddy's evil recreational activities sure were organized.

"Yup."

That upped the ante. Shay had seen enough animal toes and feet left in the jagged metal teeth of leg holds. Fat chance of them hauling that trap all the way out here and deciding not to spring it while they held him down. The medicine Taddy's gang was fixed on dishing out was too strong to stomach.

Gandalf whispered in his ear, *"Fly, you fool!"*

He did.

***

Around the old Reidt Mine, every rutted little roadway, every animal path through underbrush just went in circles. There was no escape, only hiding.

Around a bend, Shay saw the A-shape of a roof. On top stood a haggard cross. Moss hung down from it like a gray-green beard. The chapel. Old, abandoned. Doorless.

He wasn't that far up in the hills, but damn if it didn't seem a lot colder. If it had a belfry, maybe the other bats wouldn't mind some company for a while.

There was a plaque. He read the faded inscription easily.

*Dedicated to the 8 freed men and about 120 convicts killed
in the Reidt Mine catastrophe of May 25, 1877.
And also to all those, before and after,
Sacrificed on the altar of Mammon.*

Maybe if he hid in the chapel, Taddy's gang would get tired, get cold, and get gone. Shay decided he wouldn't come out until they were all the way down the gravel road. Back to their nasty houses and their greasy dinners. Taddy's huge helping of pork rinds—or whatever his parents fed him to blimp him up—getting all cold and disgusting.

Shay didn't have a lantern. He didn't need one to see the wrecked inside of the small wooden building clearly. He picked his way over the strongest looking floorboards. It would be hella embarrassing after all this to fall through the floor and get stuck.

Maybe there were rusty nails that would hurt and tear worse than that little old leg-hold they had. Shay imagined himself calling out to Taddy's gang for help before he bled to death. Not that they'd hear. The trees, with their swish-swaying, swallowed up all sounds human and animal.

He checked his phone. One measly bar flickered.

Besides Elrond and Gandalf, there was really no one he could call for help. He had friends he did assignments with and sat next to at lunch, but he always got the idea people either thought he was sick or were waiting for him to do something crazy. Outside his home, away from his parents' ministries and not being examined by doctors who kept writing papers on his visual abilities, he was as alone as this old chapel.

He gave it a good once-over. There was nothing much on the first floor. All the seats had been taken out or used as firewood. A cooking pit had been dug into the middle of the small room. Its sides were charred.

On one side of the chapel, most of a crooked staircase was still standing. He picked his way up over missing steps. At the top landing, something fell over with a couple of small thumps. It started smelling bad.

It was a group of opossums. Stiff as week-old roadkill and just as gamey. They weren't dead, just playing.

They fainted like that. Hag Glantzer had shown him a while back. The crazy one-eyed woman was related to the Bryans in some way. Glantzer had called him out one day, told him she'd show him something more educational than anything he'd find at the library, where he'd been headed. The woodswoman snuck up on an opossum and barked, imitating a hound perfectly. The critter fell over, stiff as a board.

Hag Glantzer was delighted. She picked it up and put it into Shay's schoolbook knapsack. Said it would wake up in an hour or so, and he could show his classmates.

"What you kids need is real, practical education about wildlife and such," Glantzer said, zipping her satchel closed. "While you're studyin' the opossum—that's the proper name for this marsupial in the Americas, by the by—you might let it slip to who's ever in charge that I'm open to teachin' a class here and there."

Glantzer patted the knapsack and handed it back.

"Nothin' formal, mind ya. I cherish my ad hoc schedule. And I take cash only, in advance. Tell 'em Darina Hofer Glantzer, bachelor of science, magna, is willin' if they are."

Shay had left the stiff body of the educational opossum by a tree, but he did convey the message. The administration of the high school was not willing to take her up on the offer.

In the dark, cobwebbed recesses of the miner's chapel, each member of the opossum family at his feet was spewing nasty stuff from both ends. Five jaws were frozen in snarls, their pointy little teeth bared. He left them to sleep off the fright he'd caused.

What an undignified way to avoid predators, he thought.

Peering out the broken window, he saw his own predators were still there, in a sort of huddle. They were not moving.

He slumped down against moldering wood. Was he any better than an opossum? According to Glantzer, they couldn't help fainting when they were scared. Why the heck would the Lord make them that way?

He looked at his hands. Their white skin shone like phosphorus. The tips of his fingers blazed hotly with his uncanny heat-sensitive vision. They looked like extremities of something less natural than an animal.

"Look at me," he said to the catatonic opossums. "Who am I to make fun of you?"

Down below were torn-up pews. He guessed only about eight or ten people could have fit in the place. The church he and his parents went to was a hundred times bigger.

Opposite the entrance doorway, on the high wall, was a space. A big cross had hung there. They probably took it when they closed the place. But the wood remembered. For decades, the crucifix had blocked light, leaving a permanent shadow on the planks. For him, it was the perfect icon. A zeru cross, one only he could see.

His adoptive parents, Mom and Dad, were so filled with Spirit, so busy with ministry, that he was determined not to add to their burdens. No matter what Taddy and his gang did, he would just say it was an accident. He couldn't let his parents down by telling them he felt out of place and picked on. How ungrateful would that be?

He'd recently exchanged messages online with his natural brother, Elahaj. He'd gone to the cyber café in Fayetteville to play *Moats and Monsters*. That was not an approved game for him, on account of the demon and undead toons being the preferred choice of guild champions due to their racial buffs. But just try explaining that to lay preachers who ran an appliance shop.

His brother in Africa played on a different server, where they spoke French. It would have cost too much game gold to move their main toons. So they had created level-one avatars in each other's domains so they could chat when they were both online. Best of all, it was free from any chance of parental monitoring.

Some of the things Elahaj told him were pretty crazy. Shay could tell he was holding back details of how and why his brother and parents got him away to America. Then it kinda started to make sense why the Bryans never tried to change his first name.

They were lay preachers, and their kid was named after Lucifer. That was odd, even if the language was Swahili, which nobody he'd yet met in North Carolina spoke. Opening up the paperwork on his adoption was probably as risky as opening a can of wriggly worms. If something was wrong with those papers could "the Man" (who Shay always pictured as an older version of Taddy who worked for the government) send him back? He didn't know. He suspected his parents didn't either.

Elahaj had other stories too. Ones about warlords and tribal gangs and all the stuff he'd endured because he'd stayed put there. It all made Shay grateful to his brother and his parents. Most times Shay Bryan tried to do right and live by the gentler parts of Scripture.

Sometimes, though, the Old Testament parts suited a situation. Heck, there was even a biblical time that might have suited him even better. Suited him for the way he was, for how people looked at him.

Shetani Zeru Bryan seemed out of place in a world where dawn could be counted on. Sometimes he imagined himself more fitted to a time before light was invented, when everything was "formless and void, and darkness was over the surface of the deep." If that was the way it was now, then who'd be running, and who'd be chasing?

Wind blew down the hill. The old building creaked. Gusts came through gaps in the wood slats. The old place echoed with low, moaning flute noises. It was a pipe organ made out of the chapel's dry hollow bones.

Outside, the moon got clouded over. The last silver light trickling through the cracks in the walls extinguished. This was not a night to do right. This was a time for actions that would not bear the bright light of sunshine any better than his pale albino skin.

He knelt in front of where the cross used to hang. He reached into the pit. Someone had made a fire out of the wood from the pews. Toothpick-thin bits of bones and scraggly wing feathers were in the ash. Some hobo had had a feast. Shay needed the charcoal. The zeru needed the soot to cover his face, hands, and hair. He did that. He bathed his hands and head in the remains of a dead fire.

The Moon was hidden. He'd be nearly invisible. With darkened hands, he tore loose a banister railing. Hard weathered and milled at the end to fit his grip, it was a better club than he'd find in the woods.

He followed the road over the tracks to the mine. It was the fastest way to get close to Taddy and his posse. Moving toward them took less time than running away. Cones of light jiggled this way and that. A dozen sneakers crunched gravel.

Their flashlights were Shay's main problem. These artificial lights were also his enemy's main weakness. They had only three.

"Tad!" Jeep said. "My batteries're dead."

Then they had only two. Two small lights defended the bullies from the pitch blackness that surrounded them. The darkness he would use to destroy them.

He crept closer.

"My feet hurt," complained another. That guy must be low man in the gang. He had been put to hauling around the leg-hold trap and chain while they looked for a juicy ankle to spring it on. His juicy ankle.

"That bone-white bastard's long gone."

Closer than you think.

Shay gripped the timber. His legs coiled under him, ready to spring out. Taddy had the tactical Maglite. First thing to do was knock that out of the bully's hands and break it. The other guy just had a small LED bike light. They wouldn't be able to make sense of anything that was happening. Not with the moon gone.

Shay only had a vague plan of what to do after his tormentors were helpless. Maybe he'd trip Taddy and keep conking him on his arms and gut until he told the others to give up. Shay could make them take their pants off and walk back into town bare assed or displaying their skid-marked undies.

The group was moving away from the tree line where he was hiding. If he was going to do something, it had to be now. Shay gathered his breath and tried to think of some horrific wild-beast noise to make as he charged. One like a lion or tiger would make leaping into a herd of antelope. One that would freeze their minds and feet for the short time it would take to—

"Shut it," Taddy said in kind of a high voice. "My dad's texting me."

The humongous teenager wheezed nervously as he fiddled with his phone.

"Crap, crap, crap," he said. "My brother'sh out past his home time."

"He can take care of hisself. Ethan's near eight years old."

"I ain't where I said I'd be. Crap."

The bully sounded fretful. Shay had never seen Taddy's daddy. Rumor was he raised pit bulls outside the county line. Rumor of that rumor was he ran a roving dog fighting club. Further elaborations had it that if the dogs weren't fighting hard enough, Mr. Eddington would get bust-out mad. He'd climb into the pit wearing only a metal groin guard (to keep his man parts from being chewed off) and brass knuckles with long spikes on them. With those he'd finish off both canine contestants.

Since there was no video evidence, skeptics of these stories remained. However, in Shay's estimation, people often tried to live up to their hear-tell reputations. Mr. Eddington was probably not someone you wanted to get punished by.

Shay watched as Taddy's hand rubbed a section of blubber poking out from his shirt. There was a weird scar on the small of his back. It looked like burns shaped like letters.

"Gotta go."

His nemesis waddled away. He led his posse right quick down the train tracks, straight for the lights of town.

"NONE of you better say a WORD of where we was or WHAT we was doin'," Taddy threatened easily, "or you'll

WISH you looked as good as that football jackassh when I got through tenderizing him."

That left Shay out of sorts.

He had a fine stick and no one to beat on. He was covered in charcoal and was shivering from unspent anger and the creeping cold of night. More chill than that was the realization of what he'd done to his clothes.

How was he going to explain his state to his parents? He was no tattler, and this was not the time to start. Thing was, it wasn't like they rolled him in tar. The gang hadn't done this. He did this to himself. He sat down and felt as low as he would have chained to a tree with the jaws of a leg trap biting into his ankle.

It was no use trying to wash up. The last thing he'd thought about when he applied his crappy fake camo paint was ruining his clothes. They were new from Bonworthy's department store. They cost his adoptive parents' hard-earned money. Now they were ruined. It was not enough the Bryans had rescued him from certain death and dismemberment. Now they'd wish they just left him where they found him: where he was born.

He'd screwed everything up by running to the woods in the first place. He knew the Reidt Mine road was a dead end. He should have just ducked into the gas station until Taddy lost interest.

That would have been smartest. But he hadn't wanted to be the white-faced weirdo lurking around the convenience store asking for help.

He threw his club in the bushes and moved warily down the gravel road. He kept low in case any of Taddy's guys looked back.

With the moon barely a glow behind thick clouds, he could see better than when there was more light. That was another way he was the opposite of normal.

To one side of the trail was a little loop snare. Nearby was some pee. Shay could see stuff that was normally only visible when you shined black light on it. The experts who tested him were still working on how he did that. This pee didn't seem like it was from a scared animal. It was neatly deposited, not splattered. It smelled strong, even to his completely ordinary nose. He moved along.

His ears were normal and average too. That was why it took him a few steps past the faint sound to think about what it might be. Only when it stopped, only by its absence from between the sounds of stiff leaves shivering in the wind, did he realize what he'd heard. Coming from the dark of the woods, Shay could hear a faint weeping.

Shay stopped.

Sound could be awfully tricky in the wild. You'd hear something once. Could be miles away, from inside a cabin somewhere, or just your mind playing tricks.

"Harmmm."

Where from?

He thought about all the animal sounds he knew. It matched none. Maybe something was caught in one of the traps scattered round.

He angled his head this way and that.

"HARmmm."

Best guess led off the trail. He went.

He saw paw tracks. The newer ones were small. Bigger, older ones were made by a pig, maybe. The ground only got freshly disturbed when his clumsy feet in high-top runners snapped twigs and sent puffs of mossy stuff flying. Yet there was a faint heat trail.

Things warmer than their surroundings gave off infrared rays. Those he could see as indistinct blobs until they cooled to the temperature of the rest of the trail.

Moving ahead, he nearly had to crawl because of overhanging branches. He stopped himself short of a gap in the ground. It was a smooth-sided crevice, big enough to take in a wild pig. It was small enough on top so's you could cover it over with thin branches.

The hole was chiseled into rock. It had to be an air shaft cut upward from the old mine. It had been turned into a deadfall trap. Something was caught in it.

He could hear breathing. The stone pit itself seemed to be inhaling and exhaling.

Wary of getting his face bit or clawed by a wild creature desperate to escape, he peered over the edge. What was in there was not thrashing. It looked all busted up and bloody. Bones poked white and sharp though a nylon jacket and junior-sized cargo pants.

About six feet down in the slimy pit lay Taddy's little brother, Ethan Eddington.

***

Ethan moaned. The younger boy opened his eyes weakly from inside the pit. He looked like he was going to have a fear fit, which would send any blood remaining in him squirting out like a stepped-on packet of ketchup.

"Gwawwww!"

Shay suddenly realized what he must look like peering over the rim of the deadfall trap. Shay's first challenge was assuring Ethan that, brimstone-soot-covered face and glowing red eyes notwithstanding, he was no demon from Hades come to claim Ethan's soul for all the mischief he'd done in his eight sin-filled years on earth.

"Hang on, kid. Don't do nothing," Shay said. The sound of his non-demonic voice seemed to settle Ethan down. "I gotta figure this."

The airshaft went down several feet. At about six feet, it was covered securely by canvas and wood. This was a depth most wild things could not escape, but it was in easy reach of a hunting spear.

Shay was torn between trying to do what he could right there or calling for somebody to come. There was one evasive signal bar on his phone.

The alternative way would mean trusting that the trap platform would hold their combined weight. There was no way the kid could climb up. Not with injuries too gruesome to look at closely.

Would Ethan Eddington even live until recue came? What if he left to search for a better signal and the poor little fellow died, alone, in a gross slimy pit? Shay hadn't a clue what the right thing to do was.

Then Ethan jumped to his feet.

"Hey!" Shay said. "Be still. Your arms and legs is all busted up."

"No they ain't!" Ethan retorted.

He shook critter bones off his clothes. He bounded on the

canvas, oblivious to the fact it was the nation's most dangerous trampoline.

"I just hit my nose tryin' to get out," Ethan explained. "Would you help me, sir?"

Shay could not ever recall being called sir. It was kinda cool.

Ethan was on a much healthier diet than his sibling. Lifting him out was easy. After checking him over and finding only a few scrapes, they started back to town.

"How'd you get in that hole?"

"I dunno."

"What was you doing out here?"

"Following after Taddy." Ethan looked at him. "Why are you all sooty?"

"Escapin' from Taddy."

"Yeah," the smaller boy said sagely, "I knows all about that."

In front of the Eddingtons' house, a local deputy slouched on the hood of a cop car, so Shay led Ethan up the back way. He didn't want any fuss.

Shay stayed to watch as the kid crept around the veranda and prepared to surprise everyone by being alive and completely free of bites from bears or rattlesnakes. While walking, they had formulated and rehearsed the small boy's story. Ethan would pretend to have forgotten the time and fallen asleep in some hidey hole. That was the plan.

That strategy got squished by a humongous ass crack pushing open the back screen door.

"What the...?"

Either because of fear of his father's wrath or because he felt genuinely guilty for his brother going missing while he was supposed to be watching him, Taddy was plainly mortified and in personal agony. He reacted predictably.

"You bleached-out sumbitch. You kidnapped him!" he hissed and reached to grab rusty garden shears next to the trash bin.

Before Taddy could start pruning albino body parts, Ethan and Shay talked reason into the mutated potato head of the rotund maniac. After some hushed discussion, it was decided Ethan would go in the house while the older boys collaborated on a story.

That joint effort began with Shetani Zeru Bryan's fist hitting Taddy on the good side of his face. The sound was like a rolling pin hitting a tough steak. Besides finding Ethan and getting him out of that hole, it was the most satisfying thing about that evening.

"I don't know why God made me this way," Shay said, leaning over the beached whale with a bloody nose. "But I do know why He gave these here fists. And they gots as many sermons in 'em as you need to learn some respect and decency into your thick skull."

Cries of joy and general adult hubbub came from the house.

"Now get up and just nod when I say something."

"But... my mnose..."

"Do I have to think of everything?" Shay said, surprising himself with his alibi-making abilities. "You got hit by a branch goin' to check the tree fort you thought Ethan might be in. Right?"

Taddy's nostril dribbled blood on his T-shirt. It was from

the local Dumpty Burger and commemorated his proudest achievement:

1,000 GOBBLED
All-Star Burger Eater

Taddy nodded.

"Then you'll do just like that when I say you and I met on the road. Then I remembered the other place I'd seen Ethan sometimes. After that, I went to check it out for you because that's what neighbors in this town do."

That plan went pretty much as advertised. There was no real evidence to send the minds of the sheriff or any of the adults in any other direction. Ethan could not recall exactly how he got into the deadfall trap hole.

For a spell, there was pitchfork-and-torches talk about rounding up vagrants living in the woods. That died down when it was pointed out that had the air shaft not been slung with scavenged canvas, the drop would have been hundreds of feet. They resolved to write a stern letter about the matter to the Reidt Mining Company, which had an address in Delaware.

A few days after the story was in the local paper, the Bryans got a call from the Army. A real, live Green Beret colonel wanted to give Shay an award for resourcefulness and bravery.

That happened at the JROTC meeting hall the following month. He'd never thought of the military as any kind of career option. It just seemed too normal.

"As long as you pass the physical, we're happy to have you," the colonel assured him. The Army officer was older but still looked like he could headbutt his way through a brick wall.

"I'll have the JROTC exec drop by your house with all the information."

They shook hands. The Army officer checked him over.

"Son, they tell me you can see in the dark, like night vision that never runs out of batteries. No foolin'?"

He confirmed the absence of hogwash.

"Well. Ain't that somethin'?"

The colonel looked impressed. With him.

***

Years later, Bryan reached up to hang a stack of clothes on a bar in the hallway. He winced. Fresh stitches closed a cut on his arm. The uniforms and shirts he'd just brought in from the dry cleaner nearly slid to the floor.

It would be a shame to tear these stitches, he thought. They were really neat, artistic almost. The new hotshot Army surgeon assured him he would have no scarring. Nagging frustration would be the only memento of his latest attempt to break the Army post's obstacle course record.

Before he had time to take off his shoes, he was dispatched again into the wet falling snow on an urgent mission.

"We set a place for her," his mom said through the lusciously scented steam billowing from the kitchen door. "So no one's eating until she's here."

Private Bryan, E-1, considered the parameters of his assignment. Most importantly, if there was any leeway in the directive that no one eat Christmas dinner until Cousin Glantzer was at table. Maybe just getting her into the guest bathroom (or if she was really crusty, into the garage) would be sufficient. Letting her clean up enough to actually be decent to sit at the table might take longer than fetching her.

He decided to let Kitchen Command worry about details. His main concern was not sliding off the road. It had been decked out with Fayetteville's small annual ration of snow, which had all come down at once.

He drove past his old high school. The buildings were quiet and frosted white. Dang place looked a lot smaller than he remembered it.

Little dripping icicles hung from the sign:

CAPE FEAR
High School
welcomes you.
We're the home of the *Colts*!

At the end of a dirt road, he slid the truck to a stop. After taking a rough bearing, he trudged out.

A few hundred yards in, he came across a bait-stick snare. Near the contraption, a dollop of yellow pee had been carefully poured in the snow. It reminded Bryan of something.

It took the whole walk to Glantzer's hootch to figure out what it was. A few threads of past memories he hadn't really noticed before now seemed loose. He tugged on them mentally. Things he hadn't wondered about in years fell into place. They assumed a more devious shape.

"You were there," he told the lady hermit.

Behind Glantzer, a pot boiled, and steam was coming out from her canvas tent. The smell was anything but appetizing and made Bryan gag a little.

"Howdy ter y'too!"

"That night," Bryan said, "when Ethan Eddington fell in that trap."

Hag Gantzer's eye widened innocently. "Got some potluck opossums stewin' on account o' the holidays."

The stirring brought a chewy-looking tail to the surface of the liquid in the battered old cooking pot.

"You were on that hill by the Old Reidt Mine," Bryan said, not letting his cousin (twenty times removed) off the hook, "spoiling other people's traps with bobcat urine."

"If you've come to bring me to your folks' place for supper, I accept. Just let me make sure the lid's tight. I don't want to spill any of this stew." Glantzer patted her bowie knife. "Y'think your pa will let me carve the turkey?"

"Oh, just fess up." Bryan tried to recall details from that night. "Come to think of it, little Ethan wasn't making a sound from deep down inside that deadfall trap."

The woodswoman smiled crookedly under her eyepatch. She raised hands so permanently dirty they looked tattooed and put them to her lips. A pretty good wild turkey hen call came out. Glantzer could imitate all kinds of sounds.

"You didn't think the little feller got innat hole all by himself, did ya?"

Bryan was stunned. Yet not surprised.

That night had been the turning point of his younger years. Taddy never bothered him again. Better, he hardly noticed the absence of bullying. During the rest of his time at Cape Fear High, he was too busy with Junior ROTC and a mess of new, true friends. He rarely thought about that night of flight and fear that had him crouching down in a charcoal-rimmed pit inside an abandoned mine chapel.

There was no way Hag Glantzer could have known any of that would happen, no way in creation. But still…

Getting Cousin Glantzer fit to be at table was not that cumbersome. She had, on her own initiative, dropped in on the Seven Hills shelter. She did not like going there because she got tired of telling people she wasn't homeless. She was free, and they should try it.

When the two of them got home, their special guest was asked to leave the pot of opossum-tail stew outside along with her long all-weather coat, which had a hundred pockets in the lining. Hanging on a peg on the porch, it appeared to wriggle, but that was probably only the wind.

Bryan was about to bring the big bird to table. His father got up to help.

"Your arm must still be sore," Mr. Bryan said. "Took eight or nine stitches to fix, didn't it?"

"I hardly feel 'em, sir," he said. "I'll go in a week early; maybe they can come out. Doc used a new technique they teach at Chapel Hill where she did her internship."

"She's on base?" Mrs. Bryan said, perturbed. "You could have invited her."

"I thought, y'know, it was family only." He looked at Glantzer. The rangy widow was behaving herself, using cutlery and keeping her Bowie sheathed.

"It's only Christmas once a year."

He couldn't dispute that logic.

"Atten-shun, phone," Bryan said to his handset. The display lit up, ready to receive its orders. "Dial Captain McKnight."

3

23 YEARS AGO
WANDERING DESERT
AFGHANISTAN (TODAY'S KHORASAN)

CORPORAL BRYAN

Here, even the sky was at war with itself. Bolts of lightning lanced between clouds. They hung heavy and low over the hard earth, cracked, dusty, dry, greedy for rain. Over the centuries, these hills and plateaus had seen countless battles, human and celestial.

Corporal Bryan watched the combat. He drank coffee and waited for his watch to begin. Through pale albino eyes he saw one cloud and then another strobing with ever-increasing intensity until it let loose a jagged fork into the guts of its nearest rival.

Not everyone could see the buildup of electric charges before a lightning strike. He'd been told he was the only person ever measured whose naked eyes could see the circles of drifting ozone that followed. These were like melting auroras, gone in few blinks.

By a quirk of achromia genetics, his natural vision was highly sensitive. Charleston's top eye specialist was a supporter of his parents' ministry. Around what they reckoned was his first birthday, the doctor examined him. So did the doctor's friends from the university, more than once.

Experts found he could see a single photon of light. This was many times more sensitive than the vision of differently colored people. Bryan learned none of the other kids, not even adults or teachers, could see ultraviolet, infrared, and polarized light. They called them "butterfly eyes."

That had ticked him off.

Bryan was old enough to understand that butterflies were frilly things often seen on girls' hairclips and dresses. After some research, he discovered many albinos were the opposite of the way he was. They had vision problems and nearly normal-looking skin. He was the other way around, in ways the scientists had not seen before. He also found out other animals had special vision too. Vampire bats could sense more than average wavelengths. Vampire-bat vision was cool.

That evening, riding on top of a desert that was moving, inching along and devouring everything in its path, those old eyes of young Corporal Bryan scanned a blasted landscape. It was like pictures of Mars, only this place was more hostile to human life. He was part of an international peacekeeping mission: United Nations UNISCOM 90 CH. About three thousand men and women were hunkered down in the fortified compound they had tagged "90 Charlie."

Hundreds of tons of square-blocked HESCO bastions (collapsible wire-mesh containers filled with dirt) challenged the wind and the animosity it carried. A giant kid's deadly serious LEGO setup. Two feet would stop an AK bullet. About four feet of packed local dirt would deflect shrapnel from the average Toyota suicide bomb. And five full feet were needed to protect the bodies of soldiers from an armor-piercing RPG. There were many of those. Thousands, probably, in the hands of people itching to use them.

Locals were employed on 90 Charlie. They even had baking pits on one side of the post to make their lunches. The bread that came out was flat and tasted like naked pizza dough.

Any of the workers who shared their water and smiled at him during the day could, come nightfall, put down shovels and picked up AKs and RPGs. Anyone could be just beyond the halo of the halogen towers itching for a clear shot and a clean getaway.

There had been a change in enemy tactics—small to generals in DC and dangerous for grunts on the line. It was partly their fault. Officers had no real plan for engaging with the enemy other than driving them out and waiting to be shot at. Besides the obvious downside of ballistic perforations, they completely gave up the initiative. The ground, the time, and the intensity of contacts were never their choice. They gave the enemy time to innovate.

One of those innovations made Corporal Bryan the go-to guy for night sentry duty. Enemy snipers had started shooting at UN troops with infrared homing .50 cal rounds. It was the US Army and DARPA who invented the damn things.

Copycats! he had fumed.

Instead of following a laser line *to* the target, these guys were using their own infrared technology *as* the target. Light up a dark area with IR and you could expect to be vulnerable to deadly accurate rounds fired from up to a mile and a half away. These bullets found you in the dark by the invisible light you were shining out. Before the crack of the enemy sniper's muzzle blast came your way, your eardrums and the rest of your head would be blown into pieces the size of good-quality road gravel.

What a crappy time to be a soldier.

Rain on plywood roofs beat a steady drumroll.

"Let me guess, you want me on exterior perimeter."

"Ja, Corporal Bryan." The commander of third watch was Fänrik Lasse Jerker Björneborg. "If you would please to be on the main barrier pass duty during this storming rain. Your eyes, they can be seeing more."

True. Bryan's natural night-vision goggles did not send out electronic bullseyes, and they never ran out of batteries.

He met the Swede inside a dirt-topped Containerized Housing Unit, which everyone called the Hobbit House. It was the tidiest and safest structure inside the perimeter.

Björneborg was a graduate of Karlberg, his country's West Point. He didn't speak English well enough to be comfortable with typical base humor. The fänrik (Swedish for second lieutenant) was, however, one of the few international soldiers who took the time to learn Dari and Pashtun. He got a reputation as a hard-ass officer whose eagle eye you could not escape.

A private from Bryan's own platoon had learned that when he questioned whether fänrik was a rank or the name of a dish at the Swedish House of Pancakes. Finding out the European officer's middle name was Jerker had not helped the enlisted man find a cork for his humor bottle. By the time he came up with a limerick that rhymed "Jerker" with "berserker" and "twerker," the private's fate was sealed. He was put on all-base crapper-burning duty for a week straight.

Maybe as a result of the incident, the blond coalition officer was also extra careful not to appear prejudiced.

"I am not meaning anything irregular by this duty assignment, you must know," Björneborg said stiffly but sincerely. "About the way you are being. Your skin and your race. I am not treating you with difference. I would never do this."

"I know," Bryan assured him. "Heck, if you were any whiter, people would think we're related."

The Nordic soldier's hair was just a shade yellower than Bryan's snow-white afro. Björneborg asked him to sit a spell and became as gabby as he'd ever seen him.

"I think your men, USA personnel, they are surprised to find Swedish has armed services with much capability," he ventured.

Bryan could not deny a certain blind spot Americans had about countries they had not fought recent major wars with.

"You should know a few small things about us," Björneborg said with matter-of-fact pride. "Sweden has never been invaded. Not by French, German, or Ryssland."

"Maybe everyone's just flat scared of you Vikings," Bryan suggested. "For a while there you guys had a reputation of rolling up in your ships, killing everyone who didn't run away, and taking their shit."

The Swede thought a moment. "Yes, the raiding by ships and taking of people's shit, that lasted many years. It was done by men and our schildmaids, shield maids, whose participation was in war and loot equal to the men if they pick this way of life.

"But even recently, Sweden could put to field armed forces commanding in the number of one million soldiers. Not so small for having ten million total population, huh, Corporal?"

That was a damned impressive number for a country everyone thought was kind of laid back. After a friendly and thoughtful discussion about the comparative skull-splitting power of Viking iron axes versus Native American stone tomahawks, Bryan left for his stint on watch.

"Please let the staff sergeant know if you need anything," Björneborg said. "Extra slicker or coffee. Yes? It looks like the not-good weather is staying for a while."

"Sir, I will. Yes, sir."

He passed other CHUs. Through the slits between entrance flaps, he saw soldiers enjoying hot food and all the comforts of a UNI-SCOM outpost. The British brought food, the Aussies and Canadian brought beer, and the US Army sprung for everything else.

"Everything else" included a sophisticated mobile surgical unit mustered at his home station in North Carolina and reassembled in the middle of the desert. It was headed by the military's finest trauma surgeon, one who had stapled Bryan back together more than once, Dr. Theodora McKnight. While there had been no all-out attacks on 90 Charlie, over the past weeks, the hospital had received a steady stream of customers.

As he got to the gate, he cinched his ceramic body armor tighter. Bryan's thumb nudged his weapon's safety, confirming the mode it was on by touch. He couldn't shake the feeling that some*thing*, not just someone, was watching him from just out of range of even his vision.

He turned his head into the storm. Rain here was hostile. Droplets hit you like wet bees. Flying like they aimed to trick you up and grind you down. It was not normal rain.

On the roads leading up to their fort, streets of hardpack became rivers. Sensors were useless. MechBrain ears were deafened by the thunder. Motion sensors got dazzled by sky-splitting lightning. Blobs of mud sprang meters in the air to splatter over camera lenses.

An enemy force could just walk past them and knock.

4

Two insulated thermos flasks later, midnight crawled past. *Five more hours.*

Rain metered a steady counter beat to Bryan's pulse. His mind balanced between hypnotic percussion and needling pinpricks of anxiety. No chance of dozing off.

The next flash could be distant lightning or a sniper's cold-barrel shot. If the latter, he'd have all of half a second to duck behind the sandbags. Maybe longer if it was a conservative assassin warming up a weapon from farther off. Blinking was a luxury he tried to keep to a minimum.

He stared. The distance pulled. Like it wanted something he was not gonna part with.

A week before, he'd been out for the day with a group of Brits sweeping for mines along the road to the regional capital. Wide-angle metal detectors on the lead vehicle went off. The convoy skidded to a dusty stop. A soldier would have to risk his ass to find out what was up.

Robots were expensive and slow. Explosive-seeking drones hadn't been invented. Eye augments that could see the muon decay of TNT and Semtex under a foot of earth were only standard equipment in science fiction shows. Back then, the best bet to handle an IED without blowing a meteor-crater-sized hole in a vital road was the human touch. Brits called their guy the Vallon man, after his specialized ground-penetrating sensor rig. He was the new one.

The threat of instant death underfoot turned the mood jovial, in the kind of grim way those guys had a knack for.

"Oy, McTaggert," one enlisted called down the line in that hushed voice people use around live ordnance. "Your time in the spotlight's arrived. The bomb-sniffing mice have the day off, so naturally we sub on a Taff."

The butt of the friendly name-calling was from South Wales. He was kinda thin and looked even more lanky in his overstuffed bomb disposal vest. His predecessor in the job, the old Vallon man, wore one just like it when they had brought him into Dr. McKnight's operating room. It had saved his torso but nothing else.

McTaggert caught Bryan's gaze through his Oakleys.

"You Yanks use field mice, ah, in the field as well?"

Bryan nodded. "We do, Corporal. We've got a Rodent Automated Training System to train local recruits."

This maze system had been developed by DARPA. It rewarded fast learners with food snacks. Slow students got electrocuted. Bomb techs held with dogs, said they were more accurate. But rats could get into drainpipes. Also, the science guys had devised a gizmo that could intentionally set off almost any kind of bomb. It was small enough to strap onto

SHETANI ZERU BRYAN - NEW PRAETORIANS 2

the backs of the beady-eyed critters. Everyone liked dogs. No one really minded if a rat ended up as bloody spooge.

The British bomb jockey thought for a second. "Rodent Automated... Ye Yanks and your acronyms." He grinned. "Tha' spells R-A-T-S, tha' does."

A freshly spray-painted red line marked minimum safe distance. Smiling, and careful not to smudge it, McTaggert stepped over.

Moments later, he was lying on his stomach and poking at the ground with his hand. Turned out not to be any explosive at all. Just some encrusted metal. After rinsing it off, the patrol commander held it up in the sunlight.

"Bugger me," Captain Dorrit said. "This poor fellow was British."

It was an old badge of the Royal Horse Artillery. Under it lay human bones.

One of Dorrit's men had studied archaeology. He uncovered more of the skeleton. Hand, arm, and shoulder knob. There was also a big pointed cleaver rusted nearly beyond recognition.

"A Khyber knife."

"Genuine antique, that."

Best guess: These were relics of the East India Company's War, Part One. Some colonial soldier got his arm hacked off and the limb fossilized where it fell.

Spooky thing was, Dorrit, McTaggert, and all of the guys who dug it up were from the *same regiment*. Nowadays they rode up-armored Panther CLVs, not horses, but they were still called the Royal Horse Artillery regiment. They had found one of their fallen brothers from two centuries ago, or at least his right arm. He'd been hacked to bits by the ancestors of the same guys who were trying to blow them up now.

"Bugger, bugger," Dorrit muttered. He turned to Bryan. "Up until well, I'd say the 1980s, British soldiers killed in action were treated quite disgracefully. Bodies stuffed into communal graves, put under rocks, or tossed in crevasses." Dorrit didn't seem able to take his eyes off their find. "All different now, of course."

The skeletal arm still had most of its hand. The index finger was extended, pointing them back the way they had come.

"Bugger."

The captain radioed 90 Charlie.

Someone from the War Graves Commission got back.

"All right, everyone!" Dorrit pointed to the team's medic. "Phelps, you take a DNA sample. After that, you two cover this soldier's final resting place over and double-check the GPS coordinates. Log them in your mission report. Orders are to let the remains be. Whitehall will try to notify any ancestral relatives through the NHS database."

Everyone stared at the finger bones, pointing.

"Ghastly fingerpost marker, that."

Dorrit pretended he didn't hear.

"Sergeant, see that gets done!" He slammed the door of his Panther.

After some communications with base about a corporal's twisted ankle, the patrol ended early. Dorrit took his thirty soldiers back behind HESCOs while they still numbered thirty. Bryan didn't blame the guy. Soldiers were no more prone to superstitions than the average person, but some signs were just too creepy to ignore.

***

As he hunkered down by the main gates, Bryan's legs and poncho were covered with muck. Mud jumped the six feet up to his cheeks and chin. He tasted the grit of the land, and was convinced it wanted to kill them all. Kill them and digest them, just like it had done with the Royal Horse guy.

The sandbag-and-wire-mesh wall of 90 Charlie disappeared into the halogen-pink static-screen night. Their squared-up sand fort looked shabby backed up against the jagged ruins of a much older garrison. More than two thousand years older.

Those ruins, just out of normal vision but clear to him, were the indirect cause of them being there. Some archaeologists had been studying Alexander the Great and got themselves kidnapped. A US senator's niece was among them.

The hostage crisis was resolved, but not because of the show of force. The senator's niece and the others were left handcuffed in a small fishing boat in the port of Doha. Rumor was a sheik with US ties had paid a ransom.

Perhaps the long-gone soldiers who followed the Great Alexander, the ones who built the ancient fort centuries ago, also had words for the weight in the pit of his stomach and the dryness in his mouth despite the deluge of water from a dark, unflinching sky. The watching, the rain, the mud, the waiting, the terror, it must have been the same.

Sounds ran together, then separated. Engines rumbled diesel drumbeats from the motor hut. Automated searchlights on towers added a high-voltage treble.

Then Bryan heard a noise that did not belong.

Slap.

5

Corporal Bryan scanned left and right, trying to tell where the sound had come from and what made it. A foot hitting a puddle?

Searchlights didn't help. Criss-crossing barrel-shaped beams reflected off staggered sheets of streaming rain. Rain was everywhere. His helmet channelled it into his blinking eyes. He couldn't see crap.

He pulled it off and threw it. Like half of a big eggshell, it landed in the stream that formed a jagged meaningless moat in front of the forward bunker.

Dumb, Bryan, dumb.

His brain bucket was the most important piece of gear the government had loaned him. He thought about scooping it up and emptying the muddy water from it. Out at the edge of the halogen haze around the base he tried to make out…

Nothing.

Just the sheets of rain all around, beyond which even his eyes could not penetrate.

Seconds squeezed by. He started to doubt he'd heard anything. He cupped his hands over his brow. Maybe it was a branch falling, or a tarp giving way under too much water.

Why did I ditch my helmet?

He didn't move. With mud covering his face and poncho, hunkered down among the maze of smaller barricades, Bryan was nearly invisible. He would watch and see.

Coulda *not* been a branch. What then?

An animal that got loose? If he shot it, high-velocity rounds would go right through, maybe hit a herdsman trying to collect the stray. Then again, donkeys had been outfitted with explosive packs and turned into four-legged suicide bombers. No one likes to shoot a helpless animal.

Slap, slap.

Closer. Bryan flicked his weapon's safety off. He double checked the select-fire tab. Single fire. Burst sucked without a muzzle compensator, which would have made his rifle too long for sentry duty. No biggie. He could pull the trigger like a jackhammer and stay on a target when he had to.

He checked behind. The distance to the main gate seemed to elongate, like the finish line of the 100-meter when the hush settled over the starting line. Twelve steps and a touchdown dive. That's how long it would take him to duck back through the dragon's teeth tank traps and put a few tons of sand between him and whatever was coming.

Maybe nothing was. Might be the wind playing with a wet plastic bag. If he ran now he'd look like a wuss. Of course, none of the others would be able to tell he was afraid by the paleness of his face. One of the few benefits of being an albino. He tried not to blink.

SLAP.

Some*thing* was definitely there. Some*one*?

Spill from the perimeter light outlined a shape. It was on four legs. Closer. They wore ragged clothes. Not very big. They didn't have to be to be dangerous, though. Could be a sapper trying to take advantage of the weather to place a breaching charge under the wall. It might.

Bryan quickly discounted that idea. The main gate was the most buttressed part of the whole perimeter. There were many weaker places more vulnerable to a two-stage assault. And whatever it was, it was coming toward their spotlights.

Right then, he should have called it in. He did not. The risk of exposing his position was small. The bigger risk were the yahoos on the wall warming up their belt-fed machine guns, firing at anything at moved. Including him. Inside the yellow zone, rules of engagement specified sentries could fire after a verbal challenge.

Bryan did not shoot, did not shout. He watched and waited.

SLAP, SLAP.

He'd waited too long.

The sky flashed in strobes. The world stuttered forward.

Faster than he thought possible, the figure was inside the red zone. Danger close. It could be a mortar-sized suicide device. At this distance, even if the ball bearings and shrapnel missed, the concussion alone could kill him.

Forty meters, then thirty. Deeper inside the kill zone.

He could see a face. *Her* face.

Most definitely a she. A girl, a local. Maybe in her teens. She was moving so awkwardly, so tortuously. She was holding something, a bulge under her dress.

Over that red line, there was no requirement for a challenge or warning shot. Soldiers had the right, the duty, to defend themselves and their base. Whoever she was, she was now in the weapons-free zone. Bryan raised his rifle and aimed for her head.

Most soldiers would have fired. It was the thing they were trained to do. It was the right thing to do. To protect the post, save lives. Perhaps every other man and woman in 90 Charlie would have taken out the presumed hostile inside the red zone. Just shoot, then call in an APC to sweep up the body and get a commendation. It was the safe thing to do.

Bryan stared. His trigger finger was locked in place, like it was welded to his weapon. Rain dashed on his bare head. He blinked. He did not shoot.

Alone among the hundreds of people at the outpost, he had vision that could discern the girl's face. Something about her expression, her agonized desperation, stayed his hand. His pale hypersensitive eyes were the only ones that could penetrate the gloom of that darkest of nights and see her.

His weapon lowered. The safety clicked back on. Bad hurt lay in wait for him every which way.

If he went out into the red zone, the fire team behind him might just notice movement. Who were they tonight? Belgians? Argentinians? If they were paying attention, they'd see movement and might machine gun them both.

He looked. The tower guards were caught up in some game of cards or dice. It was now or never.

Bryan breathed out and deliberately gulped a lungful of air, a habit from running a track sprint in high school. The protective sandbags his starting block, he lurched forward. His breath mixed with water spray and fine mud. This was less than one hundred meters.

But

the mud

it sucked

at his boots

each step

his muck-covered stones

suddenly underfoot

like chunks of ice

and the threat of sudden obliteration made up for it all.

During a track sprint he never breathed in, only out. His feet scuffed over the wet hard pack.

Slap, slap, slap, slap.

When he was close to the ragged form, he slung his rifle. It wouldn't matter now. If she meant to blow a crater in the ground, he would be inside of the mess of mud and body parts. He was only endangering himself. It was worth the risk.

If he didn't take this chance, he knew those eyes belonging to the girl, the eyes only he could see, would haunt him forever. He had enough things pursuing him in his dreams and nightmares.

As Bryan came upon her prone crawling form, his first thought was to check her for wires or a webbing belt around her midsection. Maybe the bomb had been shorted out by the wet. He would roll her into a ditch and call for the explosives team.

What he found in the shroud of pink halogen illumination he would never forget. The girl was pregnant and trailing blood in a long red smear behind her. Cuts through her dress revealed horrible trauma. There were at least five jagged holes in the thin cloth covering her belly.

This was no accident. The eight- or nine-months-pregnant girl had been deliberately stabbed. Somehow she'd crawled to this outpost. The rotating floods of 90 Charlie were perhaps the only lights for miles.

Bryan picked up the dying young woman and rushed through the tank traps. Ignoring the shouts of the tower sentries, he made straight for the mobile hospital's trauma unit. He shouldered aside a corporal with a broken thumb and put her down on a stretcher. He shouted for help.

Theodora McKnight was on graveyard shift. She was the only doctor on base with pediatric surgery know-how. Grim-faced, she took over and wheeled her unconscious patient into the nearest operating enclosure.

Corporal Bryan stood, dripping blood-tinged rainwater on the floor. The girl had pressed something to his chest. He had thought she was trying to cling to him, to help him carry her. That had not been necessary. To him she had been no heavier than an average duffel bag.

Stuck to his body armor, he found a small plasticized folder. A Commonwealth travel document. Her name was Hamida Qazi, and through her unimaginable nightmare of a struggle, she had ensured her daughter would be born.

A girl would live, one Dr. McKnight and her spouse, Annalies, would adopt and name Sienna.

6

YEARS GO BY

Despite having to use sunscreen, summer was always Bryan's favorite North Carolina season. Near the Post, woods were chock full of freshwater marshlands. Slowly swaying reeds in the low waters and along the shores whispered the tunes of age-old harmonies.

One bright day, years after that night at 90 Charlie, he was on another sentry duty. Guarding a picnic basket. On leave, he had tagged along with the McKnight family on a picnic outing. Everything appeared quiet, except for those who knew where to look. And keep still.

Through curved Oakley lenses, he watched a salamander roll in a pat of mud. He heard the low, soft buzz of mayflies among the reeds, and he prepared to be pounced on. With barely a rustle through the tall grass, a fifty-pound jungle cat leaped from the bushes at her prey.

She landed on Bryan's back.

He slumped to fragrant grass under a six-year-old Sienna. Her long brown hair was barely collected into two pigtails. After a brief tussle, she laughed victoriously and stared at him with kind intentness. He'd stopped shaving his head for a change, and it had immediately spouted dense cotton-white tufts. Sienna found it fascinating.

"It looks like fluffy clouds, Uncle Bryan," she said. "How come other people don't grow it that way?"

He smiled back. "After a spell, they do," he replied. "But most people have to wait years and years to get a fro like this. Sometimes till they're all of eighty or ninety years old!"

"You're lucky, then," concluded the girl with quick reflexes and observant ways.

"Darn straight I am. Very lucky indeed."

***

Sienna's road from middle school to commissioned US Army officer was paved with a string of hurts that tore Bryan up. It was so very unfair for her to lose one of her moms to an IED before her eighth birthday. That woman's skill had saved a child and granted the last wish of a dying teenager. Theodora's compassion and the love she built with Annalies had given that unwanted orphan a home. A bomb set off under an ambulance thousands of miles away took Dr. McKnight away from that home but not the hearts of those she left behind. The hatred behind the violence could not wrest her spirit from the girl who bore her name.

After, things there were never completely the same. Other truths of Sienna's past lay lurking. At some point, she learned it was not an accident that had taken the life of her birth mother.

One day, a girl learned premeditated evil had marked her from the moment she was born. Bryan wished she could have been spared just a while longer.

Bryan had had his own narrow escape. His brother, Elahaj, had told him all about it.

It was worse for her. He watched a six-month-old crawl in her playpen, how she would sometimes try to avoid using her right shoulder. The deepest of the purple-red gashes were there. It was as though she were adjusting to an invisible weight before she even knew what carrying it meant. As she grew to womanhood, Bryan knew he could never fully understand her burden and her pain, only that he would promise to always be there.

Corporal Bryan's natural albino eyes saw her take her first steps. Career sergeant Bryan's hella expensive ocular augments recorded HD 3-D scenes from Sienna's West Point graduation, sombre hat toss and all. He would never have genetic offspring. The world was too filled with unyielding malice. To him, this hate, almost a stalking beast of a thing, it seemed so big and so strong that fighting it could deafen a soldier's heart and blind a man's soul.

By the time discussions about college came around, there was for once very little debate around the dinner table. Theodora's parents had money. They were also never really partial to their only daughter's relationship with Annalies. When they adopted Sienna, the in-laws became downright cold. He never met the older McKnight generation. His appearance might have spooked them beyond reckoning.

Upshot was, even pooling his and Annalies's money, there was no way Sienna would get the private education she deserved. West Point and the GI Bill it was. She made it through the tough selection process. Then, even before her first class, her survivor's luck was tested again. It made Bryan's heart pound every time he thought about it.

The army academy was, academically, the equal of Harvard, Stanford, or any old Ivy League joint. But it was still a military institution. Those who were accepted received free tuition and board in exchange for a period of service to the country. Graduates headed off not to Wall Street, not to the NFL, but to duty assignments in the Army. They were not put in charge of investment portfolios or scrimmage assignments but the lives of their fellow soldiers. They are not destined to have drinks on board private planes headed for Macau or the Pro Bowl. Graduating second lieutenants boarded Hercules transports headed for places like Djoboro and Khorasan to protect their nation and the innocent.

On the start of Cadet McKnight's four-year journey, Reception Day, he drove her to New York State and dropped her off at Michie Stadium. The guy on the loudspeaker gave the assembled candidates ninety seconds to say goodbye.

"I just had a thought, Sarge." Sienna beamed; it seemed the whole stadium was not large enough to contain the excitement bursting inside her. "In ninety seconds, as a West Point cadet, I will legally outrank you in the chain of command. It says so in Army Command Policy AR 600-20."

"Someone's been studying up," Bryan said. "Well, then, Cadet McKnight, ma'am, let me be the first NCO to give you a proper salute."

Bryan and Sienna exchanged crisp ones. Then it took all of

two seconds for them to exchange their patented handshake-hug, and then she was off.

When he looked back, she was helping some kid. A teenage boy had dropped his overstuffed civilian suitcase and spilled a dozen asthma inhalers. If the intentions of some very sick people had worked out, that would have been the last he ever saw of her.

Later, Bryan wished he'd taken her anywhere else but there. Somehow, whatever it was, evil, or like the preacher on the Post called it, "perfidy of the soul," it had a bead on her and would not let up.

Sienna's first milestone in her enlistment was basic training. It took place at Camp Buckner, about twelve miles away from West Point's academic campus. The ordeal was called Beast Barracks. It lasted for seven weeks.

Afterward, students always marched back to campus through Black Rock Forest. More of a celebratory picnic than an exercise, it was open to families and retired soldiers who wished to support cadets along the route. Beast March was a natural target for an atrocity.

That year, a group of well-organized crazies attacked the students and their families. They struck just outside a golf course, where their victims had to bunch up to go over a mesh-enclosed bridge. They knew their victims would not shoot back.

Cadet trainees carried their rifles but had not one round of ammunition among them. All bullets were safely stored back at Camp Buckner's training armory. It was strictly against regulations to carry live ordnance on public roads and trails. Everyone obeyed. No one wanted to get expelled. More than that, it was a point of honor for all 1,288 future butterbar platoon leaders not to break rules. They had survived basic training, the hard part of first year was behind them.

Terrorists savagely amended that notion. They shot and bludgeoned and bayoneted cadets, their families, and onlookers. They even executed former alumni, retired veterans in their seventies and eighties who traditionally accompanied the first-year class on the unpaved path back the West Point campus gates. The soil of Black Rock Forest was littered with shell casings and soaked with blood.

When he and Annalies sent Sienna off, she was seventeen. Bryan was confident in her. She'd had a head start on everyone else. She had come into the world on an Army operating table. She'd been raised on the Post. She had been fighting since she was born.

But when the news of the travesty came, Bryan's heart went cold. She had been through enough! Why couldn't her years at college be free from hatred and violence? These thoughts rushed through his head as he and Annalies ran to catch an emergency flight, which landed at Steward Airport in New York.

They got updates on the way. Sienna was slightly wounded and out of the fight early. Lucky again. Over the next four years, she formed a lifelong friendship with a fellow survivor whose actions turned him into the hero of that day: Ennis Reidt.

Darned thing of it was, Ennis didn't have to be there. He'd passed basic training the previous year but flunked his academics. If he had qualified for Cadet Field Training with the rest of the second years, it was unlikely he would have been with Sienna's plebe class at all.

Later, Ennis would recount he was only there to get a look at the incoming students. And, to hear Sienna tell it, swat slowpokes along with the flat of that sword he always carried.

During the Battle of Beast March, Cadet Reidt killed a farmer's peck of the rifle-wielding terrorists. Even took down a machine gun strongpoint, armed only with his ceremonial antique sword. He also employed Sienna's bowie knife to gruesome effect. He saved many lives until his collarbone was shattered by an assailant's bullet. In the aftermath, Ennis was immediately locked up in an asylum.

He was placed under psychiatric hold for the maximum period allowed. The attack on the students was appalling, but even cynical New York coroners blanched at the savagery Ennis had inflicted on the bodies of the terrorists. With his blades, he had carved a bloody tapestry of retribution on their flesh.

Only Ennis's family connections and a lack of living witnesses had kept him in the Academy. Eventually, the shrinks and lawyers, paid for by Ennis's parents, had their day. Charleston's notorious son was found not insane enough to be barred from a career with the Army. This diagnosis became a running joke, a new spin on the old catch-22.

Back at the Academy, things went better. The powers that be recognized the grit he'd displayed and made him First Captain, essentially class president. Sienna, who had by far the superior academic record, became his second-in-command.

***

The summer before her graduating year, Bryan and Ennis came out to West Point's Tate Rink. Sienna was competing for

All Forces boxing gold. Reidt proudly sported his polished First Captain insignia. The sports facility was filled with hundreds of people who were completely unimpressed. They were from Navy and had come a long way to see their girl beat the stuffing out of Bryan's and the Army's best girl.

Fat chance of that happening, he thought as he waded through the hostile side of the arena and absorbed more than a few jabbing blows from sailors' elbows.

Tate Rink's floor was, in the season, normally covered by hockey rink ice. Plywood had been laid down for some maintenance work. Tate was the perfect intimate setting for an inter-service throwdown. Army supporters' faces were painted gray. Visitors, many from Annapolis, glowered back.

Hard-core Navy fans were as ready to be in a fight as watch one. Campus MPs paced nervously.

Bryan noticed the look of determination on Sienna's face.

"You're going to do great," he told her. "Cut the ring off like we practiced and watch out for the southpaw switch. She pulls that in the last round. And don't stress. At the end of it all, we're on the same side."

"Speak for yourself, Sergeant," Ennis belted. "I hate these swabbies worse than backtalking plebes. Sie, go on and give her an epic thumpin' for us all now, y'hear?"

He grinned, and in case they missed his speech, gave the Navy side of the arena a casually aimed finger. Bryan grimaced.

"Seconds out!"

Ennis exchanged shoulder punches with Sienna and jumped down from ringside. He started his side of the crowd off in a preemtptive strike of spirit.

"HOO-AH!"

The Army, Navy, and Marines had a similar exclamation, but each pronounced it differently. Some Marine special operators and SEALs, all older and battle-worn, led the counter chant in the angry-sounding Marines' style:

"OO-RAH!"

A duo with Styrofoam shark heads plastered on shaved scalps pointed to their T-shirts:

YOU DON'T HAVE TO
BE IGNORANT TO
GO ARMY

BUT IT HELPS!

The battle of decibels grew as the boxing match started. The ref gave final instructions. Once again Bryan saw who had real grit and leadership abilities. Ennis was the hothead who incited fights. Sienna was the closer who would finish them one way or another. It was Sienna who trained months to defend the Army's honor in the ring, while Ennis, with the purest of intentions, tried to incite a flash riot.

That was why he'd consented to Sienna's repeated requests to lead the Dogs of D Group when she graduated. She knew the Post better than anyone. She had left more skin and hair and blood on the toughest obstacle course on the Post than any future Delta operator. This first active duty command would bring her back home. Bryan needed to keep her close in a world that did not allow for do-overs.

The match went mostly like he figured. In the fading moments of the fourth round, going into the last, he did a tally.

Sienna had to be up by two with the rest possibly even. The Navy girl was slower but a little taller. She had tried switching up stances a few times, but just ended up being pummelled by a forewarned and forearmed Army champion and ultimately knocked on her butt.

Suspiciously, the ref ruled it a slip. Still, it had to add weight to the overwhelming balance in Sienna's favor. Any sane judge had to be counting the dozens of unanswered blows cleanly landing on the scoring areas of the Olympic-style gloves.

The Navy girl had long elbows, and her belt hitched way high. If nothing else, she was pretty skilled at evading shots. The other team thought they could tire Sienna out rope-a-dope style. In five rounds?

Sienna? Hell no. Not in fifty!

"HOO-AH!"

"OO-RAH!"

Clang.

Bryan pulled out the stool. Ennis gave her some water. As a cornerman, he was pretty useless. He spent most of his time scowling at the ref and anyone else that would meet his gaze.

"Hey, you got this," Bryan said.

Sienna, mouthpiece out, gulped air deeply and evenly. She was far from exhausted.

"Damn if her belt," Sienna said between breaths, "her belt was any higher, it would be a turtleneck."

She smiled as she fit her mouthpiece back in.

"Just keep up the pace," Bryan told Sienna. "She's tired after a hard day's work as your punching bag."

"Seconds out," the ref, an older guy who liked his dip, wheezed at them. "Final round! Final round!"

"HOO-AH!"

"OO-RAH!"

Sixteen seconds to go, and just like they planned, Sienna wound up with a finishing flurry to put herself over the top on the scorecards. She backed her opponent into the ropes, hit a series of hooks, and then slipped back and right, out of harm's way. Textbook style.

She's so got this! Bryan thought. Now just a final combination, keep her on her heels while the clock runs out.

Then the other girl rose up unexpectedly—

"TIME!"

The crowd, Sienna, and her opponent teetered on the edge of credulity.

"Are you kidding, ref?" Ennis yelled, his face turning purple. "Are you calling that *low*?"

In the audience, elbows, chairs, and fists flew. No one was wearing gloves. Bryan barely noticed the melee. The ref smugly addressed each of the three judges in turn:

"One point."

"HOO-AH!"

"One point."

"OO-RAH!"

"One point."

Time-in began with Sienna's opponent shaking her head with her gloves raised in a shrug. The Navy girl apologized to *her* for the referee's inexplicable call.

The final bell could not be heard over the rising belligerent ruckus inside the enclosed arena. MPs hustled match officials out of the building. Through bullhorns they requested everyone clear the auditorium. They were holding tear-gas canisters when they made that request.

The one lost point made the contest a draw. It put Sienna in second spot overall. This was her senior year. She'd never get another chance. She'd been robbed.

A few weeks later, the president and General Halley, the chairman of the Joint Chiefs of Staff, shook her hand, and she was officially a butterbar second lieutenant.

Bryan really wanted to see her accept a plum posting in Hawaii or a safe one in Germany. Nothing ever happened in Germany. He also knew that was not her true inclination. So he called in every favor and bent every ear that would listen to get her request for assignment to his squad on the Post approved.

7

12 MONTHS AGO
FORT BRAGG
NORTH CAROLINA

S o, Sarge, we gettin' a new CO, huh?" Probationary Private
T-Rex asked as he opened the door of a countertop
convection oven door. With a flourish, he brought out his
homemade Mexicali surprise muffins.

Delicia "Snakelips" Ortiz wrinkled her nose at the chili
powder smell. It reminded everyone of pepper spray. She
nodded. "Yup, straight out of the Academy."

"What ever happened to raisin' up people from the ranks?"
T-Rex griped. "In the Civil War, the Army made a general
out of a twenty-year-old." He flipped the muffins onto a big
plate. They landed with tiny thudding sounds. "I don't know
how long I'm gonna stay with an organization that limits my
personal horizons."

"Rex," Petr "Whitebread" Whitbrodsniewski, rumbled
from his double-sized cot, "to get promoted, first you'd have to
get uncourt-martialed."

"That's just paperwork. My legal team's on it."

"I hope this butterbar lieutenant is more tech-savvy than the last guy," Nobu said.

He was their radio and communications security repairer, a.k.a. COMSEC, occupational specialty 94E. Everyone used the retro Army specialty "RTO." At the moment, he was glued to his gaming goggles and multidigit joystick.

He pointed to his long, wide shelf of personal electronics. "Last one tried to use my Glowforge 3-D laser lathe as a microwave oven to cook his lunch."

"Still smells like burned catfish in here."

"Just after we got rid of the dog smell."

Their command post had previously been a kennel for the service canines assigned to the Post. When it got too run-down to be decent housing for the pampered German Shepherds and Belgian Malinois, Bryan and his squad were moved in. That also gave the jokers in A Squadron (their main nemesis in Special Forces Operational Detachment-Delta) the perfect nickname to tag on to Bryan's team.

He picked up one of T-Rex's muffins. The only surprise about them was how bad you'd get heartburn. He ate it anyway. It would be MRE pouches and iodized water for a spell.

"I didn't want to say anything until the duty assignment was official"—Bryan checked his watch—"which it is as of three minutes ago. Some of you may know Second Lieutenant McKnight from the little hostage rescue in Ess Alüm."

"The cadet trainee you brought along?"

"Has it been that long?"

"Time flies when you're dodging incoming rounds."

"I remember her, she's a real Army brat," Whitebread said.

"She had the best sniper ghillie suits, was always hiding and betting the Delta boys they couldn't find her before she could nail them with a paintball gun."

"Little assassins grow up so fast, don't they," T-Rex said nostalgically.

"Mierda!" Snakelips said. "Now I'm really embarrassed about this place. You guys got to help me clean it up, no slacking this time."

"That's the other good news," Sarge Bryan said with a mouthful of burning chilies.

Soldiers liked good news, they appreciated it before you asked them to follow orders that might get them hurt or killed.

"Besides getting ourselves issued a first-rate second lieutenant who graduated with honors and a double major in history and irregular warfare, our new officer comes with a brand-new command post. Location TBA."

"Righteous!"

"Finally."

"Hold on, hold on," T-Rex cautioned. "Before we commit, let's make sure there's all the right plumbin'. I got my eye on a Galaxy GX58 Jacuzzi."

T-Rex whipped out a fat brochure.

"Lookit this, it's got forty-eight supercharged jets to take your flotation massages to a whole new level, an' it's got a seventy-seven-inch 3-D OLED TV with twelve marine-grade surround-sound speakers, an' best of all, aromatherapy an' waterline LED lighting, which 'sets the perfect mood for intimate moments.'"

Snakelips cursed. "You are *not* having 'intimate moments' with yourself or anyone in our new CP."

"Rex," added Nobu more calmly, "you're broke. Government stopped your checks until you're reinstated. How are you affording all that?"

"My cousin in LA's gittin' me a sweet deal. Open-box discount."

"Is that new barracks for sure?" Whitebread asked.

"Commandant signed off this a.m."

"Location TBA, huh?"

Bryan looked around at the leaky roof. The former kennel was one of the most dilapidated structures on the Post.

"I'm sure we'll like it better than this old shack."

"And…?"

That quiet thinker Whitebread would know there was an "and."

"And…" Sarge said.

Petr, T-Rex, Snakelips all snapped to. Nobu took out one of his gaming earbuds.

"Before Lieutenant McKnight is due to arrive, we snagged ourselves a nice cushy little support gig babysitting some Worldwide Help scientists. In Africa."

8

DOD POWER STATION TALOS
NEAR THE NIGER RIVER
SUB-SAHARAN AFRICA

R IP rounds incoming!" Bryan shouted over the *crack-crack-crack* of gunfire coming from the tree line. "Everyone keep behind hard cover."

He watched as his people quickly crossed the distance between the tree line and the automated power station.

He grabbed T-Rex. "That does not include the hippo grass in this here marsh, soldier!"

The high-tech rounds let off their secondary charges left and right of them. *Pop-pop-pop.* Sarge ducked the shrapnel by flopping down on Private Rex's legs.

"Ow, man, have you gained weight?"

Bryan rolled over to better cover. He thought quickly about his deployment and the threat. They could absolutely not get pinned down in the jungle. Insurgents had appeared in a disorganized but deadly-as-heck ambush. They were outnumbered four or five to one. How could they hold the generating station until help arrived?

Bryan pulled his enlisted man behind a concrete buttress.

"Sarge!" T-Rex yelled at him over the secondary explosions of individual-portion-sized cluster munitions. "About that cushy gig you promised us…"

"Shut it, Private."

Redundantly Invasive Projectiles split off into needles if they hit flesh. Each fragment had a little charge. This would make them pop into even smaller fragments seconds or even minutes later. An RIP bullet that missed the first time could cap you in its own sweet time.

What a crappy time to be a soldier.

"Why aren't those big stealth drones helping us?" Nobu complained as he let off some cover fire. "They've been circling for a half hour."

"We're too close to the FOB's reactor," Snakelips said. "Can't risk damaging it,"

"About time to remind them we're government property too."

"Not as valuable or dangerous as the uranium nitride that's in the containment vessels."

Snakelips zeroed in on the most active of the muzzle flashes in the tree line. Her custom rifle spat a suppressed round. That flash stopped, but five more took its place from all angles.

"Sarge," Whitebread said, "do these insurgents know this is a set-it-and-forget-it reactor? If they break it open, which would take three days of digging and drilling, they'll burn to death or die from radiation."

Crack-crack-crack.

Pop-pop-pop.

Fire was incoming from a wide semicircle surrounding the station. Scattered at first, it was zeroing in on the Dog's firing positions.

"Probably not," Bryan said. "They seem more like learn-on-the-job types."

There was a lull in the firing. RIP rounds were twice as heavy as normal bullets and less accurate. The enemy might be resupplying or positioning for a better shot at them.

"Let's teach 'em to keep their heads down. Suppressive fire—now!"

A few minutes later, things continued to suck.

The mission Bryan was leading was supposed to be "human augmentation of automated systems." Worldwide Help doctors and scientists needed access inside the perimeter of an American Forward Operating Base: automated generating station called TALOS. There was a fever outbreak nearby. While WWHI were here helping the locals, they also wanted to study some artifacts of the Saan people.

All that was cool, until Nobu shut down the robot sentries. On cue, local a-holes in the form of a well-armed militia came after the TALOS's mini nuke generator. Built by the Army Corps of Engineers, it was available to support the establishment of an Army main operating base on short notice. In the meantime, it provided electricity to thousands of farmers and fishermen.

Repositioning under fire, Bryan and the Dogs had regrouped inside the generator's bunker-style entrance. He didn't like that at all. Shrapnel rounds would bounce around between reinforced concrete walls. Even a cheap homebrew version of sarin gas could incapacitate them in a closed environment.

"Who said no active air support?"

"The regional combatant commanders at AFRICOM," said Bryan, pushing a sandbag up to a window gap.

"Where are they again?"

"Germany."

T-Rex cursed. "Now, let me think. If I had the choice of sloggin' through a malaria-infested jungle or gettin' a lap dance from a Fräulein in lederhosen…"

"Even before the insurgents took hostages, bombing was off the table," Sarge said. "Now it's doubly off."

The WWHI doctors and scientists got overrun first. They were taken prisoner and were now mixed in amongst the insurgents. Shrapnel didn't follow rules of engagement.

"Sarge," Nobu ran in, panting. "There's got to be fifty hostiles. They knocked down both of my drones."

Nobu hated when people messed with his toys.

"What about the platoon of Rangers incoming?"

"No ETA. They're bogged down on the river. Some crap about it being hippo mating season."

"Guess we're sittin' here, then."

Bryan checked the observation station. It was a periscope-style device with a 180-degree hi-def view of the tree line. He made sure the real-time feed was linked to his forearm-mounted comms screen. They could track, record, and assess enemy movement without having their helmets shot off.

"Snakelips, don't let them get a good angle on the entrance," Sarge yelled up to their designated sniper. "Anyone tries, pop their heads off. If they lob in gas canisters and we have to put on masks and WMD gear, we'll be even less combat effective than we are now."

"Whitebread," Snakelips said without taking her eye off the scope of her mahogany sniper rifle, "prep me some more FMJ .308s."

The specialist hooked a .308 projectile pouch up to the M-956 flexmunitions module. His beefy hands cranked the handle, and it spat out match-grade rounds. Cased in cellulose, their RFID-tagged powder charge was exactly matched with the sniper rifle's ranging scope.

Whitebread handed them up to Snakelips's perch by a vent shaft. "Here ya go—"

"*Oy cacada!*" She knocked them away, heedless of the freshly crimped bullets scattering on the floor. "Forget it. Get me the red box."

"The one you tell us never to touch or play with?"

"Yes, yes, yes," Snakelips said, swapping out her barrel.

In Bryan's experience, watching her change barrels was normally like watching a pro golfer choose what kind of club they were going to use: 6.5 mm putter or .50 cal driver. This time her hands moved so fast he could hardly follow. She was ready before the biggest mag he'd ever seen got passed up. It was marked:

¡No tocar!

"Ortiz?" Bryan said calmly. "Is there something we should be made aware of?"

Instead of answering, she flicked on her scope-share channel. Everyone's forearm feed display got a view of what she was looking at through her aiming optics. Branches were shaking all along the tree line. Something big was rolling toward them, more than one.

"What are those?"

"I seen them somewhere."

"Of course you did, sucka," T-Rex scoffed. "They're TALOS perimeter sentry bots."

"Why are they coming toward us?"

"Why are they moving at all?" Bryan got a bad feeling. "Nobu, you deactivated them, right?"

"I did everything but pull the mechBrain chip housing, which would have taken hours."

Everyone ducked as the first electromagnetic-fired mortar rounds fell short.

"They're supposed to be locked down and inactive," Nobu concluded weakly.

"They're hella active from where I am," Snakelips said. "Permission to fire."

"Blast 'em at will," Bryan confirmed. "Can you take 'em out?"

She shook her head. "There's too many."

"They must be piloting each one by joystick," Nobu concluded after trying to counterhack the robot tanks' mechBrains. "The AI controls are lobotomized. Steering and firing is on manual. It's a lot slower and less accurate. From here there's nothing I can do to stop them. The insurgents must have coding skills."

"Terrorists got programmers now?" T-Rex said, aghast. "No dang fair!"

"Maybe you can email their ombudsman," Whitebread said.

"Seal up your pie holes," Bryan snapped. "What else we got?"

"Not much." Nobu checked through their light ordnance duffel. "We packed for snakes and mosquitos, not to fight our own heavy mobile armor drones."

The only bright spots were the occasional flashes and ear-splitting thunder coming from Snakelips's position. She was letting off T-17 .60 cal HEAT rounds. While the shaped charges on the high-explosive antitank rounds would not go through the incoming bots' frontal armor, she'd gotten a few mobility kills by taking out their ATV tracks and turret hydraulics.

"Last two rounds," she said calmly.

"Save one for that piece o' crap Stymph drone up there in the sky," T-Rex said. "Thing's got the firepower of a guided missile cruiser, and it's just hang glidin' up there."

Sarge made up his mind. They were facing incoming robot tanks firing mortars and encirclement by disorganized but very aggressive and plentiful hostile militia.

"This position can't be held. Only bet is to exfil and join up with Rangers as they proceed up the river."

The exfiltration maneuver would start with a flat-out run through an open field being heavily shelled. If they made it through that, it would be on to a foot-snagging swampy jungle while being fired on by ten times their number of enemy ground elements.

It was a hella bad plan. There was a good chance not all of them would make it. But sitting there waiting to be blasted to pieces or gassed was worse.

Their stealth camo outfits worked best when they stood in front of nearby surfaces. If they moved slowly and kept close to the TALOS station's walls, they might be able to slip into cover.

Bryan thought furiously. If these hostiles had enough tech know-how to hack through secure Army mechBrains, could he depend on them not using the robot sentry's sensors on them? Those could see right through personal stealth. If they relied on their only tactical advantage, they could be sitting ducks.

"Nobu," Sarge said, grasping at straws. "Did you recheck the schematics? Did the engineers who built this place leave any tunnels under the facility? Anything we can crawl through?"

The half Japanese, half Apache radio tech shook his head.

"Place was sealed when they finished building it. Totally self-contained. It's a supersized version of the ones they send up to other planets like Mars and Pluto to recharge landing craft."

"Who runs the generator, then?"

"Robots."

"And who runs them?"

"Better question is," T-Rex said, "can we get them into the fight on our side?"

Nobu made his "wouldn't that be cool" face.

"No. They're closed in with the machinery. They fix each other. When they ask for parts, those get fed through radiation-shielded slots a foot wide."

"How did it come to this?" T-Rex said, exasperated. "Robots are sittin' pretty. Safe, with job security and robo-health-care doctors who make house calls. While we, the human people, are about to get smoked by our own zombie mechBrain artillery?"

"So," Sarge asked, "no other route underneath? Along some cooling shafts or something?"

Nobu shook his head. "Even if there were, the radiation would fry us before we got a hundred yards."

"Okay, everyone!" Sarge put on his best boisterous rally-on-me voice. "Take water, ammo, and comms. Whitebread, you and your Gatling shotgun are on point. Northeast is where more of their shooters are. Let's tear 'em a new one. We'll link up with the Rangers as they slowpoke up the river and come back swingin'."

Sarge drew lines and X's on his forearm display screen map. It was a Hail Mary play in a deadly serious football game.

"Snakelips, if you can disable the second mech here—"

"*USA ground force White Rhino,*" Bryan's comms squawked suddenly, "*this is Draco Volans aerial survey. Confirm your position and status.*"

Bryan had Nobu check the possibly friendly aerial unit's transponder code.

"He's WWHI civilian. Incoming in a single-person flier that has no class code."

"Man! We about to get our asses perforated, and they send one dude in a flyin' car? I'm never donating to Worldwide Help again."

"Yeah, they're really gonna miss your three dollars," Snakelips said. She sorted through her bulky sniper accessories, stressing about what she would take. "They got more money than the Pentagon."

"Maybe this guy can distract them without getting shot down," Whitebread said.

"White Rhino actual to Draco Volans," Bryan said into the external comms channel, "if you have an idea, execute it, otherwise we're out of here in three zero seconds."

"*White Rhino, hold present. Do not discharge your weapons, not once, am I clear? To do that will be a fault fatal for you. Confirm.*"

Fault fatal? Dang foreigner. Bryan let off a few other words beginning with "f."

But he'd seen WWHI contractors in action. Bryan and Sienna had narrowly escaped being drugged and tortured by one in a Khorasan cave years back. They were violent and vicious people without an ounce of mercy. And if you were in a tight spot, those could be downright helpful tendencies. They just had to be pointed in the right direction.

"Confirm, Draco Volans. No weapon discharges until further notice," Bryan said.

Whitebread shuffled his feet. It was a unilateral ceasefire that, as yet, had no explanation. He could tell the specialist didn't approve. T-Rex didn't say anything.

"No firing," Bryan told the Dogs. "Unload and show clear, but keep watch."

They could afford to give the new player a chance. A mad dash into the jungle through a storm shower of hot metal could wait a few minutes.

"There he is," Snakelips said, looking through her spotting scope.

They saw not one ultralight but six. All were taking ground fire from the tree line.

"He's projecting holograms to fake 'em out."

"That'll work until they turn the tank sentries' radar on him."

"Or pepper all six targets with RIP rounds," Nobu said.

"Look," Snakelips said. "He's releasing something."

"Is it drones?"

"A microSwarm could lay down smoke or harass the hostiles."

They could do a lot more than harass, Sarge Bryan knew.

"It's not drones. They're falling into the trees," Whitebread said.

"What's this about not shooting?"

The next time they heard from the pilot Draco, he asked them to do something really dumb.

"*White Rhino, will you be so kind as to present the enemy with targets? Try to be as elusive as you can, but do draw their fire. Do not discharge your weapons. Please do this immediately. Out.*"

"A civilian in a volocopter talkin' to us like that!" T-Rex said.

"Thanks for volunteering, Probationary Private," Whitebread said. "Draw their fire and try to be as elusive as you can."

Keeping down flat, T-Rex crawled outside the bunker. He stuck up a low-tech helmet on a very low-tech stick. This faked out the high-tech insurgent enemy.

Like it generally did, gunfire spurred more gunfire. The fake target was soon well and truly shredded.

"*Good,*" airborne Draco said. "*Very good, White Rhino. You can get back to safety. I've got them.*"

As to how and with what their new ally had "got them," on his own, Bryan would have been in the dark. But Nobu, probably pissed he did not have these new toys in his box, had been busy figuring them out.

When T-Rex was safely inside the power station bunker, they gathered around a display.

"See? This is video feed coming from those things the flyer dropped."

In a murky green rectangle, the point of view was what you'd imagine a snake sees. Roots and leaves and bugs slid past. Suddenly there was a big military-style boot with a skinny ankle coming out of it.

"What are they?"

"I can't control them," Nobu said, "but I've been recording their feed. It's not highly encrypted."

"I can't see anythin'. Just vines and crap."

"Just wait until this one looks at another one," Nobu said. "There. That's them."

In slow motion, the video panned over to a device that looked like a LEGO lizard toy. It crawled on four legs and used a chunky tail to balance itself while getting over objects.

"Subterranean drones. About a foot long. Designed for maximum power efficiency. They can go weeks surveying inside cave complexes with sonar and other sensors. Nicer than anything the Army has." Nobu sounded jealous.

T-Rex said, "Unless they got teeth and we're gonna ankle-bite the enemy, how's that help?"

For a change, he made a good point.

The crawling drone they were monitoring stopped moving.

A human form was right above it. The enemy. The lizard bot leaned back to pan up the soldier's torso.

"Hey, look, this one's just a kid," Snakelips said.

An African boy about nine years old was in the drone's orange crosshairs. He was dwarfed by the AK he carried, which had the stock shortened and a smaller magazine inserted. An assault weapon modified for use by preteens.

Without warning, the power output scale on the side of the screen went from normal green to amber danger to red overload. The feed and the boy's image cut out.

Inside the bunker, Bryan heard dull popping sounds from the enemy positions.

He and the Dogs cautiously exited their bunker. Draco's volocopter landed in a clearing that had been pockmarked by mortar impacts. He had blue quick-clot oozing out of a forearm wound. He looked pleased with himself.

"I've been theorizing how to weaponize these underground lizard robots. I've never had the chance to test them."

The Dogs greeted their rescuer with cautious comradery. He was about Bryan's age but very lean. When he flexed the hand of his wounded arm, tendons popped like an anatomical model.

"Well," Draco said, "Sergeant Bryan and D Group auxiliary squad, shall we mop this up?"

They couldn't think of any reason not to.

Most of the enemy were down with severe burns. The rest had given up or run.

First order of business was to stop their own rampaging sentries. Each was about the size and shape of an eighteen-ton MRAP armored truck. They were better protected and carried more weapons on account of there being no crew.

"Okay, I got the robots back on our side," Nobu said after hardwiring the mechBrain of one sentry. The rest would fall in line and ignore remote commands.

"Sarge, we got sixty-six enemy hostiles captured," Whitebread said hesitantly. "Many are wounded. Two or three might not last until medivac. And… they're mostly kids."

The average age of the detainees was about thirteen.

"There's got to be adult supervision," Bryan snarled. "Find them."

Awhile later, the ringleader was found, but not by them. Sonic stunner blasts sent up a flight of multicolored birds from over near the river. Couple minutes later, the pilot, Draco, dragged a shirtless, ornery-looking bastard back to the casualty collection point.

"This one is called Najeer," the contractor said. "That's all he's said. I would like to incentive him to be more loquacious. If that's all right by you, Sergeant."

Until their support force of US Army Rangers finished taking their sweet time and got there, Bryan's people had their hands full. If it weren't for rules of engagement, he'd stun cuff Najeer and see if he could swim.

"Take him off. But nothing too loud," Bryan said. "I don't want to freak out the detainees."

Disarmed and disoriented, the boys on the ground all around them were moaning in pain or crying quietly. The former eleven WWHI hostages had only two MDs among them. The rest were scientists in specialties Bryan had never heard of. They pitched in as best they could.

"Mr.…?"

"Draco is fine."

"Yeah, okay. What did you hit the enemy combatants with? We saw you drop the survey robots, but they don't have any armament."

Draco's thin lips stretched into a tight smile under his hollow cheeks.

"I was not entirely sure it would work. The ultralight was running low on fuel and has only a limited payload. I was out of options, or rather, you were. I could have flown away."

Draco examined one of the boy soldiers. He had a big "+" mark burned into his shoulder.

"My survey drones shot them with a sheet-beam klystron. These have an output of 2.45 GHz, similar to a microwave oven. It is used for communications and chain-recharging deep underground. The pulse overloading worked. Lucky for you and your men."

"Another boy just died, Sarge," Snakelips said, shooting a look of pure venom at Najeer. "The burns didn't look that bad."

Draco studied the dead boy.

"Some of their internal injuries will be unrecoverable." He took closeup snapshots of the dead and injured. "I have alerted our nearest hospital. Their transport may arrive before your Rangers. In any case, WWHI is best equipped to deal with the wounded."

"The lizard drones zeroed in on their targets using sound," Nobu said, lifting up a limp lizard bot to get a better look at its sensors. "The sounds of gunshots. That's why you wanted us to cease fire."

"Exactly," Draco said, dragging Najeer away. "It was the only way to tell the good guys apart from the bad."

9

Bryan knew there could be other hostile elements wanting to try their luck at the radioactive prize inside the steel and volcanic concrete piñata. After they had secured US Station TALOS, they assessed the remaining perimeter bots. The MRAP-sized sentry drones had to be redeployed to protect the buried nuclear generator.

"That one's scrap metal," T-Rex said, looking at a carbon-scored hole in the housing of its mechBrain. He stood nearly waist deep inside a deep rut. This had been dug in the soft ground by the wild churning of the sentry's tank treads.

"You nailed this one too, Snakelips," Nobu said, putting his hand inside a bullet hole. "I hope they don't bill you. They are really expensive."

"I'm sure there's loco paperwork to fill out," she shot back. "And I'm double sure that's the probationary private's job."

"What the heck was so interestin' for scientists way out here anyway? Sarge?" T-Rex asked.

"...Sarge?"

***

The same thought was bugging Bryan. As the ringing in his ears from the firefight settled down, his suspicions piped up. He tracked Draco into the jungle.

The contractor was taking the prisoner, Najeer, right to the excavation site where the child soldiers had grabbed the WWHI scientists.

Bryan had past experience with WWHI and their weird obsession with underground ruins. He didn't trust them. On the other hand, Draco had saved all their asses. He hoped this wasn't going to get awkward.

The access road was too straight. Following right after the contractor, he'd be spotted. Bryan went into deeper underbrush. He pushed aside some leaves.

Something he thought was a twig skittered through his fingers. His cyber-eyes were not much help. There was too much bio matter all around. Special wavelengths just returned clutter.

He picked hi-res optical view and followed an herbivore trail. A few steps later, he came face-to-face with beady eyes and a wrinkled nose.

A small monkey munched on some kind of fruit. The noise and drama of the firefight had only interrupted the jungle's routine. The normal measure of the place had settled back down on it like dusk.

Along with it came a realization. Bryan was alone for the first time since they'd arrived.

To his right was a gourd plant. Its clinging vines attached it to a big old tree. Without preamble, it released a mess of liquid down the trunk.

To his left, something thrashed its tail. It was trying to get its head out from a smothering cocoon of sticky grass. The long grass was like green quicksand. Real animals knew to avoid it. This lizard was mechanical, one of Draco's drones. He left it.

Far beneath his feet, nuclear coals glowed. Those permanent slow fires were tended and stoked by man-sized robots that would never leave the containment capsule.

Wind blew down off a low hill. The eddies and currents carried a name. His.

Shetani zeru.

His old name, his first one.

He thought he heard feet padding behind him. He whipped around. Nothing.

No, not quite. He was being followed. He flicked through his cyber-eyes' special vision modes. IR—nothing. UV—nothing. Particle decay—whatever that was. Nothing.

Fear seized him. Annoying at first, like heartburn out of nowhere. Then Bryan had to fight to control his breathing. Panic was the sure way to become combat ineffective.

He reached for his .45. To shoot… what?

A little zephyr. A heat shimmer passed right by him.

Wait a sec. Heat rays don't gather into a ball and float.

They also don't go through things. This one did.

It also knew his name.

Zeru

Zeru

Cold and fear laced its way up and down the length of his

body, thin and biting as a straight razor's edge. It slid up him like the last ray of an ice-cold sunset. Bryan's teeth clenched. His hands shook.

It passed. He remembered the weather. It was hot and humid. His sweat warmed up.

He listened for his name. That name. He didn't hear it.

After catching his breath, he checked the map display on his forearm. He pinged the others on his wrist unit. Rex, Nobu, Whitebread, and Snakelips retuned his signal right quick.

He'd been wrong. He wasn't alone. He moved on.

The chances of avoiding harsh words with Draco dimmed. The piece of trust and cautious camaraderie that Bryan thought he had with the WWHI contractor whittled away with every muffled scream that came out of the dig entrance.

Lookin' more awkward every second.

He went in.

Najeer's agony continued. Bryan tried to look on the bright side. Some of Najeer's child soldiers had whip marks on their backs. From the scarring, he judged these were half as old as the boys themselves. Who knew how many preteen candidates were captured from villages but didn't make the cut? They would be tiny skeletons in ditches along the road behind Najeer's marauding caravan.

Bryan's mind softened to the idea of torture. If this was just a straight-up fingernail pull or a clean waterboarding, he could probably let it slide.

What awaited Bryan inside the archaeology pit was a scene that featured neither of those humdrum torments. The roof of the cavern dripped moisture from the earth and the curling sinewy roots of trees above. These were held in place by metal mesh and underground construction pillars.

Under his feet was really smooth concrete. It belonged to the buried generator. The area of interest to the WWHI scientists was at the end of a concrete support structure. This served as a walkway down. At the end of it were a series of man-sized divots, more than a dozen. Najeer lay in the nearest one.

The wannabe African warlord was naked. His straining body dripped rivulets of sweat. That wasn't weird, much. What was out there was the glow.

Bryan's eyes saw it coming out of the stone slab Najeer lay on. Also never-before-seen-strange was the stuff coming out of Najeer. That stopped Bryan in his tracks. That made him forget to look over his shoulder.

"These are the hollows of !Xu, the healing deity of the Saan people."

Draco was behind him. Bryan turned.

With a yell of agony, he slapped his forearm over his eyes. He let go of his pistol. It clattered to the floor. The last image his optics recorded was of one of those lizard robots, its eyes strobing and flaring, overwhelming his optics.

Before he could recover, a booted toe socked him in his midsection. Right on his liver. Bryan's legs crumpled. He nearly blacked out.

Hands like two vises grabbed him. They were stronger than he'd imagined, stronger than they should be. Draco had taken a bullet through the forearm. They pulled him into one of the hollows. He could barely see the outlines of the rough chiseled stone.

"Now, Draco, let's not get hasty," Bryan wheezed as calmly as he could. "My guys know where I am, and we got fifty Rangers inbound. Whatever you're up to—"

"It would be a waste of time to explain to you," Draco said pretty darn arrogantly. "You are a national mercenary, here only for your paycheck and whatever paltry benefits they dole out under the GI Bill."

"There's also the healthy camaraderie and some pretty good food around the holidays," Bryan quipped.

Draco punched his liver again. This time he decided to pass out.

He came 'round pretty quickly. Good news was he could see again.

Draco's mechanical lizard guard dog was only on standby. It was not beaming him with strobes or microwaves. The little fellow was staring down at him from a ledge.

The not-good news was his arms and legs felt frozen. Numb, like anesthetic was coming in. He wasn't strapped down, but nothing he tried moved his body an inch. That same weird glow that he'd seen around Najeer crept in around the edges of his vision. It was on him and through him.

"This may be the first evidence of general anesthetic in history," the contractor said while doing things Bryan wasn't able to see. "A notable achievement using only the given energies of the rocks and the sciencestitions of the Saan people's shaman doctors."

Bryan's eyes had fully recovered. There was Najeer, or what remained of him. The thuggish warlord wasn't screaming anymore. He was still wriggling. Or rather, being wiggled. Thin spider-silk-looking tendrils came out of nearly every part of his body. They were concentrated around the man-shape's midsection: kidneys and spleen.

"Whad are you doointh?" Bryan mumbled, feeling like his mouth was full of cotton.

Draco understood.

"To you? Nothing, yet. As you surmised, I wish to have a conversation and gain information."

Najeer looked like a dropped slice you'd stepped on in an alley behind a really crappy pizza joint, with extra mozzarella sticking to your shoe.

"Good luck wiff that."

"Of course. You don't comprehend. You never really will. Suffice it to say I am speaking to not this brute, but something inside him." Draco was careful to keep clear of the crystal tendrils. They looked like they might still be growing. "A much better conversation. Possibly enlightening."

Another cave, another loon from WWHI, Bryan thought.

"This man has malaria. That is what I wish to speak to."

***

Bryan's ears were still sludgy after the firefight. The living roof of the cavern, all twisted roots and moss and the stuff you'd expect to live in roots and moss, did not have great acoustics. But he was pretty sure he heard the pilot right.

Oookay.

What's standard operating procedure for dealing with nutjobs? Same as the Army handbook says for dealing with zealots high on drugs like Red Mist: They have an intensely narrow point of view.

Gotta buy time and delay the brainpan microwaving that's surely coming my way .

"So, is malaria in a good mood today?"

Not a good start. Draco sneered.

Why did you say that, Sarge?

"You can mock what you do not understand." Draco was getting all worked up, like a tent preacher calling down fire and brimstone before passing around the collection plate. "But even a drudge like you cannot deny its… majesty."

As a matter of fact, Bryan could completely deny the majesty of the chia pet explosion that was Najeer, but this time he kept his trap shut. Draco stepped carefully around the wreck of the former insurgent leader. He draped mesh fiber-optic filaments over the translucent spines. This net led to a box with some LEDs. It was about the size of a mobile data server.

"Malaria does not live in mosquitos. They are only carrying the vector. To thrive, it must inhabit a host with circulating blood. The more advanced the host, the more realized the potential of the protozoa."

Draco smoothed down the ends of the artificial filament web.

"The memory embedded in its circular organelle DNA, I am told, is very special in this world. Much simpler, therefore less subject to errors." The server box lit up. "Humans have only vague notions of what went on thousands of years ago. These protozoans recall every detail."

Draco was real focused. He believed the crap he was spouting. Sometimes you just had to get on board the looney train.

"Cool. Real cool," Bryan said, noticing he was numbed up to the knees and elbows now. "It looks like you know what you're doin' there. Neither me or any Army people have malaria. We ain't gonna do you any good." He couldn't be sure how long he could keep talking. "But we can messh up what you got goin' on here, sure 'nuff."

He tried to take back the initiative before the numbness invaded all the way through his tongue. Then he'd just be mumbling and drooling.

"Day-co, I'll give you an hour to refuel your flyer and get gomme. We just say Najeer stepped on one of his own land mines. Best I can... do since we owe you wum."

Draco leaned over him.

"You are not infected. True." His sunken eyes shone dully in the light reflecting off the floor. "Then what good are you?"

Over Bryan's head, the mechBrain LEGO lizard poked its head down and aimed right between his eyes. Gill-like fins fanned out on either side of its head. A high-pitched whine started as its power cells overloaded—

BLAM!

A bullet whizzed through Draco. It caught him just over the hip and spun him half around. He dropped the lizard's remote.

In the passageway entrance was what must have been following Bryan through the jungle—one of the kid soldiers.

BLAM-BLAM!

Two more shots through Draco's A zone. At least that psycho Najeer taught his boys to shoot good.

Pop-pop-pop.

RIP rounds lodged deep in the contractor's torso went off.

The boy shouted down at Bryan, *"Reste là!"*

French was the most common language here. Better than local dialects for traveling marauders.

The energy holding him faded as soon as Draco keeled over into a pool of pretty much all of his blood. Still, Bryan could not move much inside the healing hollow.

The boy took a long look at the ruin of his former boss, Najeer. He turned cautiously to Bryan, looking him over. Probably wanted to make sure nothing was sprouting out of him.

He came closer and lowered his kid-modified rifle.

"Ça va?"

That was like "howdy."

"Sure kid, sa-va," Bryan said, getting the distinct impression he was drooling down his chin. Not the impression a senior NCO likes to make. "Helph me out of this thing."

Bryan could move his legs, also his arms. His fingers felt numb, like they belonged to someone else.

"Thanks, by the way, uh, merci—"

Suddenly a knobby hand rose up from the floor. It grabbed the back of the boy's head. Bulging tendons quivered through dark blood and blue-black quick-clot.

No way! Bryan thought. Draco had taken three exploding RIP rounds to the torso. His insides were Grade C ground beef. He had to be dead, and then some.

Yet his body, it rose up onto its knees. The hand stuck onto the kid's close-cropped afro hair like it was glued. The boy's eyes rolled back in his head. His whole skinny body shook. Then the kid's own skull drank his face.

Eye, sinus, mouth, and ear orifices made a sucking sound,

and the kid's face slithered inside them. Inside the grinning gash that was his mouth, white teeth poked through dark skin, suddenly dry and paper thin.

The ragged doll figure, bones poking through all over now, coughed. Up out of a small throat hole came pink frothy stuff. Bryan recognized living lung tissue.

The boy's husk fell. The dead man who killed him got up onto two legs. It shambled over to Najeer. It moved all jittery, not precise, but fast. It ripped the cord out from the computer. Draco's corpse's hands held on to the end. For a moment it just stood, swaying.

Draco's head dangled left. RIP shrapnel must have clipped his spine. Out from the back of the contractor's crew-cut scalp emerged a heat shimmer. Something alive and pulsating with malice looked at Bryan.

It was the same thing that went by him in the jungle. It might have petrified him, wasted him away in his own flesh. It might have killed him right then and there. Bryan was sure it could have, if he hadn't still been in the healing hollow.

The malevolence riding the WWHI contractor finished what it wanted its body puppet to do, Bryan guessed. Draco's bony hands dropped the wires.

Face looking the wrong way, the thing walked toward him. The heat shimmer seemed to be guiding its movements. It was a gap in space about the size of a basketball. To try to make any more sense of it than that or take a shot at any other description, was impossible. The shimmer kept folding in on itself.

It had nothing that looked like sense receptors. No features resembling human or animal or mechanical. Still, Bryan got the notion it could see him. It was fixed on the light of his gold cyber-eyes. It hated him and was ticked off he wasn't dead yet.

It came toward him.

Zeru.

Bryan couldn't move.

Zeru!

Step by step, by...

Zer—

BOOM!

The shambler exploded in pink mist. It was like a fist full of M-80 firecrackers going off inside a fifty-pound raw meatball. It was the best sight he'd seen since they'd arrived at TALOS station. It could only be one thing.

With numb fingers, he wiped Draco from his face and looked over to the entrance ramp. Snakelips was there on one knee. The .60 caliber hole at the end of her sniper rifle exhaled a self-satisfied ring of gun smoke.

Bryan laid back down. If there was any of !Xu's healing juice left, he could sure use it.

10

W e heard an AK go off," Nobu said.
The team's techie ignored the gore and was immediately fascinated by the electronics in the excavation pit.

Bryan worked the last of the freezing out of his jaw.

"Prisoners?"

"They got secured and transported."

"By Rangers?"

"No, Sarge," T-Rex said. "Those jokers too slow to show. A Worldwide Help convoy got here first."

"We were checkin' with AFRICOM what to do when we heard the shooting out here," Snakelips summed up.

Whitebread looked at Cheez Whiz Najeer, at the sad husk of the child soldier which looked like a paper mâché doll except for the ragged uniform, and finally at the former host of this horror show, the bottom half of the volocopter pilot, Draco, his booted feet splayed out in opposite directions.

"Sarge, you got started without us."

If it hadn't been for Najeer's boy, Bryan knew his brain would have been poached inside his skull by the microwave-spewing lizard drone. Plenty, if not most, of those kid soldiers would have malaria in them.

He heaved himself up.

"Okay, Dogs, listen up." His head got real light real fast, so he decided to sit on the stone ledge. "Our defense of DoD installation TALOS is complete. Your commendations are in the mail. But that was just a warm-up for us, hooah?"

"Hooah!"

Bryan had his team rally at the strong point and rearm. Nobu got him a secure line to Command to get some advice. Not a line to Germany but to North Carolina.

"Lieutenant McKnight?"

"Uncle Bryan," replied a sleep-cranky voice, "do you know what time it is here?"

"Now that you're on active duty, you'll soon learn the fun don't stop at sundown and don't wait till sunrise," he said sagely into his headset.

On his forearm screen, Sienna's image focused her bleary eyes. She noticed his codename.

"Your ops handle is White Rhino?" She yawned. "I'm glad you're amusing yourselves."

Bryan felt something in his vest pocket. It was a piece of bone, maybe a tooth splinter. He decided to skip the more gnarly details of the TALOS op.

Boy, Sienna, am I ever glad you missed this fun.

"Right now, I got what you might call a conundrum. If I

wait for AFRICOM's intel and strategy guys to get back with ideas—"

"It'll become a conundumb."

"Y'know, Sienna, I think you and the Dogs are gonna get along just fine."

Bryan recapped a PG-13 version of recent events for Sienna. The combination of Army lingo and shorthand they'd developed over the last twenty-two years made it quick. Sometimes he still couldn't believe the young woman with the butterbar insignia next to her name was the same child Annalies and Theodora brought home from Khorasan.

"WWHI." Sienna bit her lower lip. "Still up to their old bunk."

"If we hurry, we can stop the truck convoy," Bryan said.

"That's the obvious play. It's like a gift," Sienna said thoughtfully. "You're on the ground. Your call. I don't become your CO until you get back here, but an old North Carolina saying comes to mind: *timeo Danaos.*"

Despite his schooling being light on Latin, it gave Bryan something to cogitate on.

"Thanks, Lieutenant. Now you can get some shut eye."

"Like heck."

Sienna's personal drone camera followed her into the kitchen.

"You and the Dogs are only active because I'm your new adult supervision as assigned by the Pentagon."

She jabbed at her coffee machine.

"If it wasn't for this mandatory pre-posting seminar in DC, I'd be there with you at TALOS," she said. Even without caffeine, his call had made her real lively.

She was right. Bryan was glad she wasn't with them facing RIP rounds and looney Worldwide Help contractors.

"I want updates every thirty minutes, and send me telemetry from Corporal Nobu's sensors and feed from your sniper's optics. I hear Ortiz has a hotshot rep."

Meanwhile… Bryan mulled on it. The WWHI truck ambulances were a total Trojan fake out. One of the Dogs felt his monopoly of sneak was being infringed upon.

"Who y'think you playin'?" T-Rex yelled at the screen showing the damning evidence.

Nobu remote piloted Draco's ultralight volocopter. It was empty except for a lizard bot. He dropped that on top of one of the WWHI trucks into which they had loaded the boy-soldier detainees. Its ground-penetrating radar saw inside.

"Empty as T-Rex's bank account," Whitebread said.

Backtracking using the volocopter's optics, they noticed tire marks by a bridge over a branch of the Niger River. The drivers had transferred the child-combatant prisoners to some kind of vessel. Bryan redirected the Ranger element to interdict.

The Army Rangers were still in their boats and got on mission just in time. A few tossed stun grenades and some heated conversation later, up came a semisubmersible.

This type of watercraft was more likely to be in the fleet of Red Mist smugglers than a respectable humanitarian aid organization. The underage insurgents had been captured attacking a US installation. Legally, the US Army had the better claim on them.

Forty-eight of the kid soldiers were alive. Bryan couldn't let them stay with WWHI, not after what he'd seen. He couldn't just let them go, either. Najeer had indoctrinated and brainwashed them. Not all could hope for anything like a normal life after what they'd seen and done. Their best hope lay down the Niger River.

"Kinyonga! My brother."

Elahaj welcomed them at a short wooden dock. He never liked using his actual first names. He kept telling Bryan it was bad juju to keep them. Bryan couldn't disagree more.

"Looks like you're movin' up in the world," Bryan said, pulling the boat mooring line tight. "Am I going to have to salute you now?"

"My precinct of Kambi Camp has the most solar panels, the most learning centers, and the lowest infection rate," Elahaj bragged fluently.

Kambi held about eighty thousand people and was one of six similarly sized Oxfam refugee camps in the area. Elahaj was responsible for ten thousand people, mostly women and children.

"These boys," Elahaj said with a serious look etched onto his kind features, "they could pose us a problem."

Najeer's former troops helped their wounded comrades off the boats and along the dock.

"They have only known war. Many do not know their village or their tribe. They have been killing since they were old enough to pull a trigger."

There had to be something they could do. Something that did not involve WWHI.

Elahaj cracked a bright smile.

"We'll manage, Kinyonga. We'll split them up and get them into schools. We'll get them taking care of the very small ones. Idle hands are the Devil's tools."

Bryan and the Dogs caught a ride with the Rangers. They left Elahaj and Kambi Camp before T-Rex could teach too many youngsters his three-card street hustle.

"Your boat will be safe," his brother said. "I've informed the river spirits you no longer belong to them."

The sun hung low and dappled the Niger with its light. They cast off and waved goodbye.

His brother had called him Kinyonga. That was Swahili for the chameleon, who can choose the color it shows the world.

11

THE POST
NORTH CAROLINA

T-Rex griped all the way home.

"Man, that's the last time I volunteer for any place with preposterous heat. Why don't we ever invade someplace cool, like Canada?"

Back in North Carolina, a different kind of consternation awaited. When the quartermaster gave Bryan the address of their new command post, he thought it was a joke. It wasn't. It was a ranting monologue by a comedian with a real filthy mind.

Bryan fumed, looking at the stained urinals hanging off the walls and the welcome back gifts left by their rivals at the North Carolina Army base.

"Sie—er... Lieutenant McKnight's due any minute!"

"Maybe we steer her over to the old command post, Sarge?" Whitebread suggested reasonably. "Kind of ease her into things?"

"Good idea," Snakelips said as she looked around. "We don't want her putting in for a transfer on day one. The old place only smells like wet dog, not dog sh—"

"Attention!" Bryan barked, calling the area—he couldn't rightly call it a room—to order. "Officer on deck."

"At ease." Second Lieutenant Sienna McKnight walked in. She wore a crisp garrison service uniform, butterbar insignia on her shoulders. "Y'know I grew up on the Post. But I've never had the pleasure of visiting this place."

"Probably on account of it bein' a mens-only type establishment," T-Rex said. "Ah, Lieutenant McKnight. Ma'am."

Snakelips backed out through a splintered plywood door leading to the toilet stalls. Her face looked Army olive green.

"The lieutenant may want to limit her inspection to the exterior until we freshen the place up a bit."

"Nonsense, Corporal," Sienna said. "If our colleagues in SFOD left us something, I want to see it."

She really didn't. But Bryan was impressed Sienna didn't flinch when greeted by the spectacle that had been fermenting for a few days in the heat. Every fly in the county had decided to move in to their new billet ahead of them.

Her expression didn't even change when she snapped on rubber gloves to lift the lid of the toilet tanks to confirm the "upper deckers," floaters deposited in all the toilet tanks.

They also left a card, more of a note. It was written in marker on cardboard:

Hey Pooches--
Hope U all like your new CP!
We got you a housewarming ~~presant~~ gift.

As you can see Every1 chipped in.
These turds are better soldiers than
U'll ever be.
You are getting a noob butterbar
bitch Lt. and you think you are hotshit.
You are NOT hotshit. THIS is hotshit.

Under that "welcome home" message, other people using different Sharpies had added post-scripts:

And you can take that to the Bank!
And stuff it!!

"Man, looks like everyone from the detachment contributed," Nobu concluded.

"Oh damn!" said T-Rex. "How the heck did this happen? How did my life go from bein' 'All You Can Be' to dengue fever, foot rot, being mortar shelled by the Army's own Meccano set, and now bein' evicted from the doghouse and dumped in the crapper?"

"Look on the bright side, Rex," said Whitebread, "at least there's plenty of plumbing here for your Jacuzzi."

T-Rex deployed a ball-peen hammer and was fixing to do some redecorating.

"Private!" Sienna snapped. "Put down that hammer."

"As Radio Telephone Operator I must advise the CO that fecal emanations may cause delicate equipment to malfunction, ma'am," Nobu said, supporting his best friend's redecorating idea.

Sienna nodded. "Noted. However, under Regulation 415-15, no on-base demolition or construction activities shall occur without my secretary having filed DD Form 1391 to HQDA."

"Lieutenant McKnight," Bryan said, pointing to the former broom and mop closet, "while you have been reserved an office space as required, no provisions have been made for a steno typist. Unit's too small, ma'am."

Sienna hefted up a three-ring binder of Department of Defense regulations and forms as thick as Whitebread's bicep.

"I'm ahead of you. We have a trainee secretary."

She tossed the mess of weapons-grade bureaucracy to T-Rex.

"Private, hope you weren't exaggerating about your typing speed on your enlistment forms, because there will be a test."

Sienna took a deep breath in, like the place smelled of fresh hay and sunflowers.

"Is that all they got?" their new CO asked in a rhetorical way they must have taught her at West Point. "Heck, I been in jujitsu fights with people who smelled worse."

Sienna motioned them toward the outer door, where the air was less pungent.

"D Squad! I know you've been given the crappy end of... well, a raw deal. But smashing the place up is what these vile bullies in Special Ops expect us to do. You can bet they took inventory with pictures before they let their incontinence hoopla fly.

"You'd all be up for vandalism and destruction of government property. You'll be Article 15'd! The lot of ya, including Sarge Bryan, who ain't done nothing except try to keep you off food stamps and out of the psych ward. Anyone want that?"

No one wanted that.

"So what are we gonna do, Lieutenant McKnight, ma'am?" Snakelips asked.

"We're gonna exceed expectations."

Sienna went back in her duffel.

"You can draw straws for the stalls," Sienna said. "But I want you, Private, to gain an appreciation of the workmanship and functional design of American Standard's urinals."

She threw a box to T-Rex.

"Denture cleanser is excellent for removing yellow stains from porcelain. Let Sarge know if you run out."

She was prepared. Maybe Sienna anticipated what awaited them after she learned the location of their new command post. Or she might have checked out the festivities as their colleagues were preparing their "Welcome Back" surprises. No one was better than Sienna at sneaking around the Post without being seen.

Sienna turned to him. "Sarge, make a note: As soon as possible, I look forward to publicly humiliating the rest of Delta at a Base-wide precision marksmanship competition. I bet they cannot aim a high-velocity round any straighter than they can aim a stream of piss."

Sienna walked out, shouting back, "Dismissed!"

No one said anything for a spell. But from their body language, Bryan could tell the squad was cautiously optimistic about their new CO.

***

Over the next week the decommissioned outhouse received a radical renovation. T-Rex even turned the urinals into planters.

"Aloe does good indoors," he explained while spraying mist onto the bright green leaves, "and the gel inside can be used to treat minor abrasions."

Lieutenant McKnight put T-Rex in for a commendation, citing his "innovative actions that led to improvement in squad morale and enhanced base eco-functionality."

Sienna's office did not have a window, but it did have a skylight. Once the moldering mops and leaking bottles of Mr. Clean were gone, it was dignified if not specious.

Bryan was just about to drop in and tell her he'd confirmed the round-robin shoot-off match with the staff sergeant in charge of the 2,000-meter range. However, as it always seemed to, the military had other plans for them.

He nearly ran into her in the doorway. She was animated as all get-out.

"Sarge, this Request for Forces just came in. From a Department of Defense branch I've never heard of called the Adaptive Execution Office," Sienna said, irony in her voice. It was their old friends at DARPA calling.

She sent details to Bryan's forearm screen. A mission was definitely on. Exactly what? TBA, as per usual.

"Rex, Ortiz, Whitebread, Nobu, listen up," he said. "We got us another gig! Aren't we the luckiest Dogs? Gotta be OM in twenty-three minutes or they'll give it to MARSOC or SEALS. Do we want Marines or Navy to steal our medals, snatch the honor and glory of a mission well accomplished right out from under our noses?"

"Heck no, Sarge!"

"All right. By the way, T-Rex, you're in luck. You wanted to go someplace cooler." Bryan forwarded on to everyone the mission destination and the requirement to bring milspec long underwear. "How's Antarctica sound?"

12

I couldn't afford the potted plant here, Bryan concluded.
He sat, checking out his room through goggles that were attached to screws in his skull. They didn't hurt at all and made sure the gadgets monitoring his regularly scheduled eye implant upgrade didn't budge.

"You have been here before, Mr. Byron," an almost-definitely woman said. She—probably not he—was wrapped in red surgical cloth from head to toe. "This bonsai tree has been with you since your first visit. This is very good."

Shennong was a private hospital that made NASA look like a while-you-wait car-repair joint. He'd been coming here for ten years to see the world's leading cyber-optics specialist, Dr. Ru.

At Shennong, he's been Mr. Byron for nearly ten years. When he first met Dr. Ru, he had been in a great deal of pain. Not just physical.

A few months after Sienna's twelfth birthday, the morning blur–outs and the ambush headaches got so bad he couldn't trust himself to lead his people. His natural eyes, his albino eyes, the ones that could see a single photon of light and deep into ultraviolet and infrared, had been failing.

If he'd mentioned anything to the Army docs, the Pentagon would have cashiered him out as quickly and cheaply as possible. The military was his whole life. He could predict Sienna heading that way too, following her adoptive parents Annalies and Dr. McKnight. For him not to be there for her would have been the worst prospect of all.

For a few days his head had felt like it would crack open. The world was either too bright, like when your sunglasses fall off, or too dim, like during an eclipse. He was low.

He was so desperate he was ready to ask a sixteen-year-old delinquent for advice. The Bryan family had a mission that helped troubled youth. Over the years, quite a few kids had come from Chicago, NYC, and Los Angeles to North Carolina. Young offenders spent the summer baling hay and annoying cows.

This one guy from Compton was exceptional in an underhanded sort of way. He had rigged the chicken coops so hens would lay extra eggs. Then, every night, he snuck out, grabbed the eggs and sold them to an organic grocer in Fayetteville.

A twisted, sneaky mind like that might be able to help. Bryan needed to come up with a way to buy some time, see if the symptoms would go away on their own.

But before he stooped to further corrupting an accomplished sinner, he had one last idea. He applied for a job.

It said "Nova Praetorii Protective Services" on the card. They were a small and well-regarded private security firm based in London. Exactly the place an experienced enlisted soldier might make an application to cash in on their hard-earned skillset. They flew him to England for an interview, then politely but firmly rejected his application.

At the same time, a man named Thaddeus Byron was hired at Nova Praetorii under their usual cloud of secrecy.

A few weeks later, Bryan was in Shanghai. The leading cyborg tissue surgeon had read about the case of an unnamed patient with incredible vision. The article had been written by an eye doctor who supported his parents' ministry.

At the same time, a charity dedicated to helping albinos with relocation and prosthetics received a large endowment that offered to pay for the necessary ocular implants. They were, coincidentally, based in London.

As far as the hospital was concerned, he was Mr. Byron, and his account was paid in advance. As far as DoD and the Army knew, a UN Foundation partner NGO had sponsored a serviceman's medical treatment, which was millions of dollars in excess of what the VA would spring for. Special ops soldiers habitually traveled under assumed names on account of the growing list of bounties offered for their random assassinations. His cover story was solid.

Shennong Center was unique. The main building was built to resemble a human eye. The exterior walls curved to form the arch of an eyebrow and orbital socket. Behind who knew how many acres of glass, dozens of open-sided levels stretched. Everywhere there were working bots.

Small bot climbers with backplates shaped and painted

like leaves pulled themselves up hanging vines. They clipped off dead leaves and sprayed nutrient mist onto air plants that had no root system and didn't need to be in soil at all.

Larger acrobatic-looking mechanoids scaled the open spaces between floors. They looked like a cross between a Mr. Slinky toy and a metal bedframe. These served to augment the elevators and passages inside the walls, delivering bedding and what looked like nonessential supplies to each room.

The air also buzzed with regimented streams of flying drones. These flitted in and out from a dispensary about twenty floors up. From what Bryan had gathered over the years, these mainly delivered medicine. All lined up and hovering, they looked like metallic hummingbirds waiting their turn to visit an aviary.

In the center of it all was a silver orb about a hundred feet high. Perfectly round with no visible opening, its surface reflected the whole interior of the complex. Since the first day he arrived he'd never learned another thing about the structure, who was inside, or what they might be doing. Somehow the surface bent light, maybe like an active camouflage suite. When he stood in front of it, he saw what was behind the big shiny pupil as well as a reflection of himself interposed on top.

First time he walked up the steps, he had been staring at the incredible structure. A grinning Dr. Ru came up to him.

"It 'looks' like you've come to the right place."

Bryan had not laughed. The pressure changes during the flight had not helped his splitting headache at all.

"Is there anything you can do, doc?" he'd fairly snarled back in misery.

Dr. Ru invited him to follow him further inside. "We'll see, Mr. Byron, we'll see."

He did, while enduring Dr. Ru's endless supply of ocular jokes. His first eyes Ru had called "training wheels for the nerves and the visions centers." They were colored kaleidoscope orange. He hated them. Six months later, he was sporting a much more intimidating pair that glowed violet-blue.

"Sarge, do those come with a heat-vision feature?" Nobu had cracked.

When Bryan got back to the Post, Army docs didn't want to hear about "three-dimensional nanoscale retina lattices." They made sure he could tell green from red and passed him over to Intelligence.

All those guys wanted was to make sure no one could remotely hack into his eyes. As if spies would want to watch blubber-butt PFCs doing push-ups in mud or puking under the chin-up bar.

The implants required a tune-up every year or so.

At Shennong, every patient got a plant. It was their responsibility to take care of them. Like it was the center's job to take care of them, or something. It was way too Zen for Sarge Bryan.

"Mr. Byron?" the androgynously wrapped technician asked, perhaps fearing he's slipped into REM mode.

"Oh, right, the bonsai," he said, also remembering to respond to his cover identity. "We have plants at work, mostly aloe in very special pots."

"It must be a very nice place."

"It's really the people that make you glad to punch in in

the a.m., isn't it?" Maybe a civilian called Thaddeus Byron would talk like that.

Mr. Thaddeus Byron was a marine security consultant working for the Eurolincx Group of companies. The owner was Ran Oliphant. His nutty assistant had picked out the name. The name kind of grew on him. Like the midget tree growing out of a bowl carved to look like a big goldfish. His pretend identity's job was as a security contractor.

At Shennong Center, even the chair remembered people. It adjusted to his body size and weight. Somehow it even sensed the most vexing of his mementos from the throwdown with cyborgs at the South Pole. The padding under his butt softened around the area of his pelvic stress fracture.

"Mr. Byron," Dr. Ru came in, bustling, hyperactive, and as usual, armed with sixth-grade humor. "What do you call a deer with no eyes?"

"Ah, search me, doc."

"Me too, I have no eye-deer!"

Ru wasn't alone. A serious-looking bigger guy with a beard was with him. Without thinking, he tried to zoom in and take a snapshot of the new guy. But his loaner optics didn't have that feature. He was stuck with basic cable for now.

"How's our star patient today?

"I'd like to say bright eyed and bushy tailed, Dr. Ru. You tell me."

Dr. Ru fiddled with some settings connected to his goggles. "After your exposure to very cold temperatures, I'm glad to say there's no signal loss. If any of your organic parts had suffered frostbite..."

"Hi there," Bryan said to the new guy. He didn't like

discussing his organic parts with people he hadn't been introduced to.

"Oh, yes, this is Dr. Bendrazi," Ru said while his colleague stared. "His expertise is nuclear medicine. The saying around here is 'if it glows, he knows.'"

Thaddeus Byron faked a smile at the nerd humor. Maybe Nobu, a compulsive gamer, would appreciate it more. He tried to suss out more details. Bendrazi was oddly familiar. He had really good skin too; maybe his spouse was a plastic surgeon.

"Dr. Ru," Bendrazi said smoothly, making a show of looking at his pager, "I've just learned something. This is difficult. It's probably better if you see for yourself."

Big hands with polished fingernails flicked on the wall viewscreen.

"*...and that was the horrific scene in Mumbai minutes ago.*"

Indian paramedics pushed aside a crowd of people in suits and fancy dresses. It looked like somebody had fallen off the stage during a speech.

"*Jeremy, we're just getting an update,*" said a woman announcer with an English accent. "*We're getting it from several sources. The Indian prime minister, only a year after winning the Nobel Peace Prize, is confirmed dead at Mumbai Central Hospital. Just moments ago—*"

The recap showed an older, mostly bald Indian man making a speech. He paused, smiling, then grabbed his head. His whole body was seized by some kind of standing fit. He knocked the podium over. It looked to Bryan like he was one of those puppets with strings and people were fighting for control. He spun around once, twice, then flew into the front row of the crowd.

The picture cut back to the announcers, who looked genuinely shocked.

So did Dr. Ru. "Oh my. That's terrible," he said. "I met him only last week. But it must be devastating for you, Dr. Bendrazi. He was your patient."

"I am shocked," Bendrazi said coolly. "Mortified. He was more than a patient. He was my professor in medical college. While he was here for treatment, we had a good chat catching up. Out of thousands of students over the years, he remembered me. Isn't that remarkable?"

Dr. Ru, looking shaken, left Bryan's room to compose a condolence message.

"I've studied your case notes for years," Bendrazi said. "All the files are anonymous, only containing details specific to my specialty. I hadn't expected you to be fully dyschromian."

"Well, yeah, we like to exceed expectations," Bryan said. Remembering to be Thaddeus, he added, "at Nova Praetorii Protective."

The big video on the wall switched over to an advertisement. It was for some offshore drilling project near San Francisco:

Deep Harvest: drilling deeper to satisfy America's needs!

Who the heck gets paid to make up this stuff?

Then BBC Science came on.

The caption scrolled: "US officials flatly deny rumors that the Ansible artifact is to be moved from the US military's Cheyenne Mountain bunker to run tests on it in a particle collider."

"The Ansible," Bendrazi said. He seemed more absorbed now than moments ago when he had watched his patient die on live TV. "Now there's an interesting phenomenon. Something no one expected."

The part of the room he stood in seemed really still and quiet, the opposite of being occupied.

"If it's some kind of meteor," Bryan said as casually as he could, "I guess they'll eventually find out where it came from."

He was certain there was no trail leading back to his team's mission to Antarctica in his Shennong Center file. Thaddeus the corporate security guy had been in Greenland watching out for Estonian pirates.

Then Bendrazi just dropped the question. "I wonder if you would be able to see it?"

"What?"

"The Ansible. As you may know, the reason they only show drawings is the object cannot be recorded," Bendrazi said as he flicked through the supplemental information on the bottom of the news channel. "Digital imaging does not work. Analog photographic methods like Polaroid only show a blotch. I wonder what your combined synthetic-organic irises would perceive?"

Bryan's thoughts flashed back six months.

A crazy explorer in an ice cave, icicles hanging from his chin. The guy wouldn't take his eyes off... nothing? Something Bryan's eyes could not see. The really spooky part was touching it. Knowing something was there, feeling it in space, right in front of him, hard, unyielding, about the size of a football but like some kind of anchor into the invisible.

"Well," Thaddeus Byron said amiably, "I guess we'll never

find out. Fat chance of me ever gettin' close to something they're keeping so heavily under wraps."

The television framed a closeup of a Russian diplomat's face. It was getting redder and redder. He flicked the power off. The screen turned reflective black.

Bryan's vision was on bypass through gamer-style goggles. They couldn't see as many wavelengths or zoom in, but they could see reflections. In the shiny black display, he noticed Bendrazi fiddling with a ring on his finger. He looked like he was going to do something at the diagnostic console. The one that was linked to his goggles.

It didn't look right. It didn't feel right.

What could he do? If he said something, they'd be more likely to get suspicious of him than one of their own physicians. Bryan couldn't raise a fuss. It could blow his cover.

If they connected him to the man who was paying his medical bills and they figured out who *he* was, the path led right to Sienna. For the first time in a while, Bryan froze, not knowing what to do.

Maybe he was just feeling antsy from being in a hospital room. The fiber cable connecting him to the console felt like a tether. The monitor was only a computer. What harm could you do through a computer?

Bendrazi turned his back so Bryan couldn't see what he was doing. If he had his fully functional eyes he could have searched for another reflective surface to get a zoom-in angle. Using these goggles was like riding on a tricycle after getting used to a blown-out Mustang.

What was that guy up to? Bryan fought the urge to get

up, walk over, and push the solid-looking man out of the way. Then the door chimed.

It was a gardening robot.

Its mechBrain recognized each of them. "Hello... Patient Mr. Byron... and... Dr. Bendrazi."

About four feet high, they were a common sight in the Shennong Complex. The multiple sensors on its head pointed up at the bearded doctor.

"Dr. Bendrazi, may we have the room?"

"What?" the broad-shouldered doctor looked as though he was going to hit the robot.

"You are not listed as one of Patient Mr. Byron's attending or consulting physicians. Plant-care protocols require solitude."

Bendrazi looked like he was going to swat the little tin fellow. They stared at each other, human eye to bot sensor. The human blinked.

"Mr. Byron, I'll check in on you before you're discharged," he said frostily.

The door slid closed.

The robot wheeled over to the midget tree. It extended a probe into the goldfish-shaped planter. The top of its turret flipped open. Inside were miniature gardening tools.

A moment later, the bot's head closed up again.

"My mistake, Patient Mr. Byron. The soil is sufficiently hydrated. I will return tomorrow."

As he watched the bot leave, he had the distinct impression he should be obliged to the little fellow. For what? He hadn't a clue.

Thaddeus Byron lay back and flicked through available holo-magazines.

The *Jane's Defense Weekly's* headline warned:

Avast, Ye mechBrains!
Hijackings Employing Armed Drones
Posing a Real Threat to International Shipping

He glanced over the pictures of mechanical mayhem on the open seas and looked forward to being Sarge Bryan again.

13

MARCH 20
KHORASANI AIRSPACE
NEAR THE GULF OF OMAN

Sarge Bryan stares at the jammed-open door of the hovercopter, a gaping rectangle of black space, rushing, wailing. Moments ago, Sienna, his Sienna, *their* Sienna, stood right there. Stood before vanishing, falling down into the hostile land she barely survived being born in.

It finally took her.

Not right. She had not stood. She had hung in some impossible halo. Then the dark stole her. She had drifted out of the hatch and got grabbed by the hundred-mile-an-hour torrent of air whipping past their aircraft.

No! It can't be! was all he had time to think.

Were his eyes deceiving him? They couldn't. Only human eyes deceive.

Bryan's cyber-eyes sent the live picture to his brain. The

real-time view looked like the moment after a flashbulb had just gone off. Everyone inside the helo:

Nobu

T-Rex

Snakelips

Petr

The tag-along Navy SEAL next to the hooded prisoner.

They all gawked.

Snakelips Ortiz has one hand on her mahogany sniper rifle, the other hand on the local kid, Anis.

Radio guy, Nobu. His buddy Warrant Officer T-Rex.

Big Petr is closest to Bryan. Right next to him, near the jammed-open hatchway. They had both tried to grab Sienna. They both failed.

Wind lashes Bryan's cheeks. He makes a small muscle gesture, like a half blink. With that gesture, Bryan engages his cyber-eyes' replay feature.

His view flickers. The last thirty seconds replays. Video and audio.

Sienna is in the cabin, right in front of him. Some kind of ionization is on her. Her body lifts up, as if they're in free fall. But she's the only one. His own hand reaches out.

The massive Specialist Whitebread also tries to catch her. No use.

Some kind of static charge surrounds her. It repels his hands, and she drifts toward the open door. She gets pulled out as though the hand of darkness grabbed her. The little Khorasani girl screams a higher pitch than the plasma rotors.

Bryan's cybernetic eyes play the scene over and over. He can't stop it.

Since she fell, things have happened. He's tried to... he's tried to do something, anything.

His vision snaps back to real time. His armor-plated chest heaves, pressed on by gripping hands and braced forearms. They hold him back.

The replay cuts in again, streaming the awful seconds from memory chips just inside his temples.

Sienna... falling to her death?

He tells his implants to go to live view.

He gets simultaneous view. Her fall plays in a rectangular inset window in the corner of his vision. The live-view abyss of the open hatchway sits behind it. Empty. Mocking.

His knuckles bleed. He must have hit his hand against something. Oh yeah, the metal door to the idiot pilot Nightjar who refused to set down. Some backtalk guff about Khorasani Air Defense jets above, still hunting the helo with lethal intent.

"You WILL set this piece of crap down!"

The pilot wouldn't. Couldn't.

No more use, then, pounding on the door. Every hypersecond-vibration pulse of the plasma rotors, every air current that rocks them, takes him farther away. He has to go after her.

A low-altitude chute hangs on the fuselage. He grabs it. Someone tries to yank it away. Whitebread's grim face speaks silently. What did he say?

Bryan hits Replay.

The recorded audio feeds right into his cochlear nucleus. Lips move. Voices cut in and out battling the sounds of howling wind.

Sounds, present and past, jumble.

"…copter's going too fast…"

SCHREEEH

"…flying too low…"

HWWWOOOAR

Petr's calm, sciencey voice explains, "…under one hundred feet… compressed gas that opens the chute will feed… canopy into plasma rotors. A human body jumping into a hundred-knot slipstream will be snapped in half."

Need to think.

Petr's so calm. He's flipped the switch. *He's* alert, thinking. Why can't I…

"Even if the canopy doesn't burn up in the engines and the wall of air doesn't break your back, the fall will kill you in less than three seconds. You or anyone else who tries to go after her, the colonel, I mean."

Whitebread said that. He was right, of course. The big guy is smarter than most assume he is. Always tells it straight. Bryan punches him good and hard.

Eyes shut now, he can't see anything but that insane replay. Sienna falls again.

And again.

The idiot pilot, the one who won't set down and rescue his fellow soldier, talks over comms.

"*—can't go back. The last shot from the fast movers was not air-to-air. They launched hypersonic tracking drones. If our stealth was working, we could risk a landing. Our portside light-bending array is disabled. It's suicide. If we slow down, we'd light up their screens like a Roman candle. Can't do it.*"

Leaving *her* behind. *Gutless swabbie.* Swabbies.

Navy… the ship!

Bryan glances at the map on the center console. How long has it been? How far have they traveled? Forty-five seconds? Sixty? A minute at this speed… that's kilometers from the mark and increasing every second.

Got to fix the position she fell, if there's any chance. Gotta, before I screw that up, too.

The ship.

"Nightjar, radio the *Lee*," Bryan hears himself say. "Send them GPS where the colonel fell. They've got stealth flyers, drones, and satellite link. There's still a chance—"

He forces the horrific replay to stop. Sienna becomes a freeze-frame blur. The pixels go gray and fade.

He looks around at the others. T-Rex hangs back, seeing what the next move is. He keeps an eye on their prisoner, Sidewinder. The blackout hooded waste of humanity they went halfway around the world for.

Snakelips Ortiz is with the girl. She also shadows the loose-cannon idiot SEAL who shot up the helo door while trying to blow the head off a twelve-year-old Khorasani boy.

None of this would have happened….

Nobu and Whitebread hold him down in a flight seat. Matching bruises bloom on their jaws.

I must have hit them both. Stupid. They could have fallen out too. They're my guys, our guys. They are just trying… Dumb, dumb, dumb.

Then there's Denbow, still. Sitting, watching. Talking to the pilot.

"Nightjar, this is Denbow. As next ranking officer, I'm taking command." The SEAL operator looks straight at Bryan. His square-jawed head is topped by a recruiting-ad crew cut. Bryan glares back. When he's really mad, controlling his cyber-eyes can be a problem. Denbow's image phases through thermal and infrared.

"Agreed," Nightjar says flatly. *"Whatever you want to do, we gotta do it right now."*

"Colonel McKnight is MIA," Denbow says. "We are engaged by hostiles and cannot fire back under mission rules of engagement. Bird is damaged, mission may be compromised."

He holds his hand over his mic to block the wind whistling from the hatch he destroyed. He doesn't want the noise to spoil the calculated speech he's making for the in-flight recording log.

"In order to protect the neutrality of our ships at sea and prevent further loss of men and material, I instruct you, Nightjar, to proceed to Doha Base in Qatar at best possible speed."

But for the restraining hands of Nobu and Whitebread, whose mitts feel like bear paws on his shoulder and bicep, Denbow would have been relieved of his newly assumed command by way of sucker punch. The Navy man ignores Bryan's grunts and the cold silence from the others.

Denbow, talking like he's just remembered a small detail, adds, "Nightjar, when you're not doing anything else, transmit Colonel McKnight's last known location to Mobile Base Pequod. Over."

Moments later, it's not over.

"What kind of balder— Bianchi, is this channel encrypted?" a crotchety voice says over general comms.

This has got to be Captain Stahlback of the *Lee*, the aircraft carrier in the Gulf of Oman.

"What kind of balderdash are you pulling there? Lieutenant Commander Denbow? I expected more from you.

"Listen, Nightjar, as battle group commander, I'm giving you a direct order: Return to... What's the code for the ship?

"Return to Pequod immediately. Do not make any other deviations from your assigned course, the one I just had my CAG send you. Is that clear?"

Bryan does not need enhanced vision to see the smug look drain away from Denbow's features.

"Ah, Snakecharmer actual to Pequod," Denbow says.

Snakecharmer actual. Bryan's gut clenches when he hears the SEAL take Sienna's mission command call sign for himself.

"Rerouting in-flight to CENTCOM land base is my call," Denbow says. "Request reconfirmation up chain of command."

The noise that comes in reply from the aircraft carrier sounds halfway between the grunt of a wild hog and the squeak of a rubber duck.

"Did... did you just ask me to verify my own order, son?"

More sputtering and static.

"Well, you reconfirm this: Nightjar, get your butt back here, pronto. Any deviation from course, I will have no choice but to assume you've been compromised by hostiles. I will personally give your transponder codes to Khorasani Air Defense.

"And if they can't shoot you insubordinate, er, turkeys down, I'll scramble some of my Stymph drones, who sure as heck will. Pequod actual over and out."

Denbow grinds his jaw, throws off his headset, and looks over at Snakelips. He stares past her and right at the girl, Anis. The former hostage looks scared and tiny strapped into the big flight chair.

For the rest of the trip back to the *Lee,* Bryan vows not to break anything or beat anyone senseless. He tries taking a page out of T-Rex's book of sneak. Shielding what he's doing, he texts Nobu's forearm display screen. Seconds later, the Asian-Apache patches a back channel to the *Lee's* Air Wing Commander, Amman Kanin.

He's a good guy, Sienna and her boyfriend, Roger, both said so. He'll do the right thing. He'll send out Search and Rescue.

The Air Wing Commander does nothing. Kanin replies to Nobu that all his flight authorization codes have been revoked by Stahlback until further notice. There's no search-and-rescue op. Not even a surveillance drone is going back to where Sienna fell.

Where her body is.

How can she be alive if jumping with the best escape chute the military has would kill anyone?

Still, Nightjar was low, really low, only dozens of meters above the sandy hills. And that glow. The one that seemed to be coming from inside her flight suit.

What happened? Her eyes. They were so blank, like she barely knew what was going on.

Tried to grab her, me, and Petr, but we just ended up pushing her out.

What the heck does that? Some electrical malfunction from the RAPTEK weapons system? A short circuit at the same time the helo hit an air pocket? That could have popped them to zero-G for a second.

Bryan uses the helo's cabin computer console monitor to scan the topography in the flight records. *If* they had been at fifty meters altitude, *if* the static thing slowed her down, *if* the

147

ground was angling right, maybe she had a chance.

Speculating is above his E-7 paygrade. He wills the hovercopter forward. He wants to burst into the cabin and grab Nightjar by the collar of his flight suit. This time not to demand he go back but to make him push his plasma rotors to their limits to get them to the ship.

If they abandon Sienna McKnight, his thirty years in the military will have been one sorry-assed joke. His adoptive parents, lay-pastors from a town outside Greensboro, had gone on a Christian mission to Africa four decades ago and returned with an albino child. They taught him not to quit, that the good fight could not be walked away from. You could only win or lose. That was the way of the good fight.

Looking out the gaping hatch, Bryan won't let go of the belief there are more rounds left in this grudge boxing match.

After that terrible night she was born here, after the secret DARPA mission back when she was sixteen, had they tempted this hostile place once too often?

No. No, Khorasan, you old scavenger, I feel it. You haven't taken her back. Not yet.

14

There."

"Sarge, you say something?" Snakelips looks at him over the tangled dark hair of the little girl's head.

Bryan didn't realize he'd spoken. With every pixel under control of his optic nerves, he concentrates on the one bit of glowing tinsel out on the dark ocean. The *Lee*. He zooms in. Night landing lights flare on the port bow.

"Naw. Nothin', Corporal."

He waits until he's sure Whitebread and Nobu are looking somewhere else, until he's nearly sure the hovercopter is close enough. Then Bryan pushes off from his seat, takes one, two, three, four steps to the jammed-open hatchway, and jumps.

Bryan's hands scramble at chill air. Plasma rotors above screech at him like a million captive insects. No time for Nightjar to set his bird down.

A few seconds of hang-time zip by, then stern steel

foredeck covered by abrasive nonskid meets his feet, knees, and bites outstretched palms. He's close to the edge, real close to a drop into the water. Fortunately, the launch deck curves up. Bryan half slides and half rolls down its length.

He gets his feet under him and makes for the bridge island. Shouts of surprise from the sailors are the nattering of as many seagulls. He ignores them.

The *Lee's* uptight XO is on him right away.

That guy's everywhere. Bianchi tries to get in his way. He doesn't. But the security doorway up to the flag bridge does. It's locked.

"Commander, open it," Bryan says, breathing heavily into the Navy man's face. "I got business with the captain."

"Sergeant, I can see—"

"You don't see nothin'. I watched her, our CO, fall. We just left her. We came back. Under orders, under threats. Unless you've got a copter ready to go and get the colonel, I'm talking to the man. Now."

After some haggling and totally accidentally hitting a security guy's jaw with a glancing elbow, Bryan gets in. But only after dropping his weapons belt and being frisked.

He jams it up the tight metal stairwell and finally gets face time with Captain Stahlback, but it's over the Kevlar shoulder pads of three swabbies holding EEL launchers with riot shock prods attached.

Navy hospitality .

Bryan clenches his fists and says the third thing that occurs to him.

"Captain Stahlback, sir, our CO, she—"

"I heard. I saw."

The relaxed way he's sitting, the offhand way he's talking, it burns Bryan. What's with those stupid bobble dolls all around his office?

Three Marines aren't gonna be enough.

"Nightjar fed me some footage," Stahlback says. "I'm going to investigate the CAG's maintenance procedures. That bird was faulty. Plasma rotors created some kind of short, and your colonel suffered the result of an aeronautic malfunction. You have my condolences. Dismissed."

If only the defensive linemen didn't have stun cuffs. He'd make the captain's head bobble. But they do. Bryan begins to feel small, like the whole aircraft carrier has suddenly become hostile foreign territory.

Sienna's one of us, can't you jerks see?

Sarge Bryan tries to think what Sienna would say. What if he had gone through that hatch and she were standing here? She'd use her head, like Annalies taught her, and West Point, too. Nobu will be able to patch him through to someone at home who will give a damn.

"Captain, if that was one of your pilots down, you'd already have a CSAR team in the air. Excuse me, sir, I've got to contact SOCOM."

Stahlback remains calm. He's flaky as dandruff.

"I've already had a chat with the Pentagon. SOCOM says it's time to leave these troubled waters."

The news hits him harder than the moments-ago drop off the hovercopter to the steel deck. Special Ops Command in DC was his lifeline, *her* lifeline. Without their support for a rescue mission...

"They confirmed with Oversight and State," Stahlback

drones on. "That was everyone's condition of mission approval for this Sidewinder fiasco: deniability. Do you think anyone is eager to own a mission after it has gotten this screwed up? You were way off your assigned flight path."

"Excuse me, sir?"

"After you picked up the detainee, Sidewinder. Our colleague Lieutenant Denbow has informed me all about your change in flight vector."

Until then, Bryan had been tunnel visioning on Stahlback. Two other guys are in the captain's ready room. The jack-off SEAL Denbow must have snuck around while they were frisking him. XO Bianchi looks on. That guy is everywhere.

Bryan thinks fast. No point in denying it, even though he has no idea why Sienna took them off course. What a time for her to be so secretive.

"Sir, that was a last-minute target of opportunity. Classified, need-to-know—"

"Don't give me any more of your covert ops doublespeak. I'm not a fan of these black-bag missions," Stahlback says. "My Stymphalian-class UAVs out there carry Carnivore bunker busters capable of going through twenty feet of concrete. One of those would have saved me a damaged bird and one heck of a stack of paperwork."

Bryan's sweat starts to cool over his skin, the chalk-white skin that marks him as an outsider. His flight suit feels like a straitjacket. It chafes.

He looks around. Is there any angle left he can work? Where's T-Rex when you need him?

Denbow's face is grim. He's still an arrogant slick. He definitely is not upset about Sienna being MIA. He's pissed he's on the *Lee* and not at Doha Base, where he tried to order the pilot to land. Why was the Navy guy so insistent?

The arrogant slick speaks. "As Sidewinder mission commander by default, I have to concur with Captain Stahlback." He shakes his crew-cut head. "With no tracker and only vague GPS coordinates, there's nowhere to start a body recovery op. Even if we wanted to."

Behind the SEAL, Bianchi reaches toward his shirt pocket. It's full of intel data modules. The XO looks at Stahlback and stops. Bryan says nothing.

He knows something about Sienna!

"She's out there!"

"Whose fault is that?" Stahlback talks like he's got all the time in the world. "I don't know what strings she pulled to redirect my whole battle group to help you in her private little war. But when you go off the reservation with my flight crew and my hardware, yes siree Bob, that's where I draw the line.

"The Khorasani have asked for an official denial of our involvement in the alleged incursion by an unknown aerial vehicle. We're giving it through proper channels. Case closed. We're leaving."

It takes all of Bryan's will not to barge in to wrench the data scrolls out of the XO's hands. Instead he resorts to pleading one last time.

"But the colonel comes from a military family. Her mother was an Army doctor, a trauma surgeon who was killed saving lives. If there's any chance at all, you've got to—"

"Sergeant, I don't *got* to do anything. Not on my ship. Yes, I've read her file. Do they really both call themselves 'mother'?" Stahlback shakes his head as if Sienna is some obscure oddity

153

that will never quite fit into the starched and pressed shape he requires of things.

"McKnight is not anyone's anymore. In my report, she won't even have the luxury of KIA status. Officially, she no longer exists. Dis-*missed*." He turns to his favorite swabbie goon. "Mr. Reynolds, show our Army guest to his quarters. Make sure he stays there until we can arrange transport off the *Lee*."

The midshipman takes Bryan away. Their boots make hollow sounds in the cold corridor. The *Lee*, chock full of sailors, feels empty. Two Marine guards break off and follow them. He has no choice but to get back to his berth bunk.

As they get on the elevator, Bryan replays what he saw just now. He freeze-frames on the scrolls in Bianchi's vest pocket.

The elevator descends for two decks, then stops. A couple of maintenance crew get on. Bryan only half listens as they gripe about a new memo issued by Stahlback. Something about grooming standards on his ship. While not addressed specifically to Machinist's Mates, they clearly take the new regulations outlawing grease smudges on pants and sleeves personally.

Bryan's mind is wracked with should-haves and could-haves. He's got to remain calm. He can't do anything to get himself and the other Dogs locked in the brig. Then he'd be no use at all.

He should check on them.

"Mr. Reynolds, did our people get squared away?"

The Navy man checks his PDA.

"Nightjar landed okay. Looks like at least one hundred hours to get the hovercopter ready again," Reynolds says. He's a chatty bugger. Not a suspicious bugger. "That used to be our number one standby bird. I guess *Bullfinch*'ll be on deck. Gotta have one in case a pilot ditches. Or jet backwash puts a deckhand overboard. Or someone gets depressed and jumps off the bow. It's a jarhead bird. Man, there's a lot of Marines on board this trip."

"There was a prisoner. And a... a humanitarian evacuee."

"Ya, ya, I boarded everyone okay. 'Cept your colonel, of course. They all reported back in their racks. Prisoner's in holding. The non-com girl, she's in forward medical getting checked out. Your guy, the big Polack, said her name's Anis. Ain't that a beer?"

"Naw, Mr. Reynolds, I don't believe it is," Bryan replies.

And if you don't want to find out what Specialist Whitebread's specialty is, I wouldn't let him hear you call him Polack.

"The local rugrat will be the only kid we have on board. All the chicks'll be playin' mommy to her. Hey, if she's still breastfeeding, there's this one flight officer who can help out."

The two Marines trailing them snicker.

"I think Anis is kinda old for that," Bryan says idly. *Good. Sienna would—*will *want to know how the girl is doing.*

Bryan goes straight to his own bunk space. He acts sullen, beaten.

"Guess you're stayin' in for the night, right?" Reynold's suggestion has an edge to it. He reads his name off the LED bunk assignment tag. "Uh, Sarge Shettny Zulu? Is that African?"

"It is. Shetani Zeru, Mr. Reynolds. It's Swahili, means 'friendly guy.'"

15

Bryan wants to slam the door of his berth on some squishy parts of Midshipman Reynolds's head, but he eases it closed, leaving a crack open for air circulation and eavesdropping.

Unfortunately it's his eyes, not his ears, that have cybernetic augments. He can't make out the whispering. After a bit, all three Navy guys step off back down the corridor.

Bryan paces the two and a half steps along his bunk. He checks out the lightbulbs. They say General Electric. He cycles his eyes through a bunch of different waves. When he's in Lux/Net zones, there's telltale flare, the result of the muons or protons and stuff scattering. This version of his eyes can detect it. Not here.

Didn't think so.

Not even Stahlback would be dumb enough to install foreign spy systems in a warship that is USA DoD property.

There's no other surveillance he can identify. While he's still listening at the door, a stylus scroll rolls down the corridor. Camo painted with a miniature eagle feather clipped on. It's one of theirs.

Nobu, T-Rex, and the others have been confined to separate quarters down the corridor.

Pretty sure there's no direct surveillance on him at the moment, Sarge still takes no chances. He shields it from view and yanks at the folded screen. From top to bottom it's filled with really obscene, downright painful, and physically impossible things for their Navy hosts to do. There are even crude diagrams of how they can do these acts to themselves, each other, and various sea mammals. They feature particular emphasis on what Captain Bobblehead can do with his collection of baseball toys.

T-Rex must have the input console.

A few seconds later, the angry, kinky crap gets wiped and is replaced by real-time text.

`These are private smoke signals, Custer`
`and cavalry no can see. N.`

Bryan links the screen to his keyboard module.

`Quit clowning around. Study birdlife on`
`this tub.`

He hits send and gets a reply right away.

`On it. Rex scooped an all-ship's pass +`
`I'm jimmying some f/wall doors.`

Bryan checks GPS data coming in via his implants.

`Get on it faster. Lee changed course and`
`is picking up speed.`

Minutes grind by. He pokes at the ship's comms and dials

up a few contacts in NC and DC. He waits to be rerouted to ship's security and hits End Call. Obvious attempts to go over Stahlback's head, done. Next, time to go under Captain Bobblehead's radar.

He slips out. Bryan's vision is sensitive enough to make out fading heat shapes of footprints in the hallway. Someone just walked by in corrugated soled boots. The images fade in reverse order, like the trail of a ghost. No one waiting in ambush.

He takes an early morning walk.

His scraped hands, the muscle spasms of his jaw clenched too tight for too long, reiterate his silent agony. Every second he's using up is one Sienna doesn't have to spare.

He passes the ship's cubbyhole barbershop. It's open twenty-four hours. Inside, a pimply seaman recruit scrapes a gray-haired man's head with clippers. A small red, white, and blue striped barber pole rotates, squeaking like a mouse with Tourette's. Beside it is a mirror, and stencilled lettering asks passing sailors:

Are YOU Ship Shape?

Bryan's own reflection startles him. He's never gotten used to the flash his augmented eyes make in reflective surfaces. They used to be electric blue. These new ones are gold. The below-decks light is crappy. His face looks extra horrible, like it belongs on a comic-book zombie.

Arterial corridors running through the *Lee*'s hundred-thousand-ton bulk are oval. Noisy. Machinery hidden behind steel walls competes with turbine engines below.

Bianchi's a good guy. Smart enough to keep all this organized. It's the captain that's the problem.

Why did Sienna order the chopper off course? *What* was so important she'd risk diverting a damaged copter? *How* could he and Petr not have grabbed her before she fell?

It had to happen here. As if Khorasan were stealing back Sienna's life, like it was something it was wrong for them to save all those years ago.

Up on the *Lee's* flight deck, gulls screech greedily at waste spewing from galley slop holes. Bryan pretends to study the dark horizon. He acts calm. Like a man contemplating a failure he can do nothing about.

Damn fat chance of that.

Two mechanics walk from where the search-and-rescue helicopters are parked. Bryan nods in their direction and slouches behind a cluster of oil drums.

Nothing to see here.

One by one, the Dogs appear out of several doorways.

Just some Army grunts going for a stroll on this big old floating airport. An aimless stroll.

He greets a lone technician exiting a stealth hovercopter: No. 6. *Bullfinch.* The spotless ride sits like a cipher, its oily blue skin shimmers, grudgingly reflecting arc lamp light.

"Hi, son," Bryan says to the Marine. "We have a high-priority mission, Corporal Coram. She ready to go?"

Recognition crosses the crewman's graveyard-shift tired expression. He reacts like the teen fan of a pop band that has shown up unannounced at the local coffee shop. The Sidewinder grab was need-to-know; Sienna's MIA status won't have filtered out beyond the bridge island yet.

"Yes, sir, I mean, Sergeant Bryan—I just have to see your orders, and then check with the CAG's officer of the watch."

He pauses. "Should we even be using your name? Aren't there code names you special operators go by?" The overall-wearing young man smiles self-consciously. "You know what they say, loose lips—"

"Sink ships," Snakelips says from the other side of the copter.

The sailor turns toward her, presenting Bryan with a perfect jawline angle. He knocks him out as gently as possible. Snakelips drags him behind some mobile master crates.

"Sorry, son, but we gotta get our CO."

Whatever it takes.

Relying more on speed and audacity than a large amount of planning and forethought, Bryan and the Dogs implement their plan to steal a hovercopter right off the deck of the *Lee*. Snakelips ties a line on the unconscious sailor so rotorwash won't blow him overboard. Bryan holds the hatch open for her.

"Nobu, you sure you can fly this thing?" she asks as she straps in. "This ain't your granddad's helicopter."

"Do not worry, my warrior queen." Nobu flicks switches on the controls, almost like he knows what he's doing. "We soar like eagle."

In an emergency, which stealing a real expensive aircraft usually is, the dual plasma rotors can go from standby to full power in a second.

Nobu has logged many hours. On simulators. This will be the first time he's actually flown this particular model all by himself.

No choice. Stahlback saw to that.

There's no doubt or hesitation in any of their eyes. Of course, they are not robots.

While strapping his barrel-sized chest into the seat, Whitebread comes out with a reasonable question. "Sarge, we trust you and all, but do you know where we're going, exactly? Last I checked, it's a big desert."

Nobu adds, "I tried to backdoor the XO's file stash. No dice. Bianchi's got tripwires set on all his access points. But the CIA guys who took Sidewinder were getting updates on local chatter. All after we landed. I bet they got a pretty good triangulation on where it's coming from."

"You bugged the Langley goons?"

As if they weren't in enough trouble already.

"Of course not, Sarge," Nobu assures him. "I bugged Sidewinder."

"Once we're up, we'll get what we need," Bryan says. "I'll ask the captain for the intel. After all, we might forget to bring his fifty-million-dollar chopper back."

This brightens Whitebread's morning. He grins. "Blackmail, that's hot! Hooah."

T-Rex can't resist needling their pilot. "Yo, Nobu, just try and control any kamikaze urges. Or leastways drop us off before you follow the shinin' path to the risin' sun."

The turbines to either side of them make promising noises. "I can get us up, but you sure they won't shoot us? Stahlback was pretty quick to threaten Nightjar."

"That's why we're stealing their best *stealth* chopper," Bryan says coolly. "Get out of visual, cut transponder, and they won't have nothing on us."

"All right, everyone. Hang on. This might jack around."

The rotors send ever-higher pitched vibrations through the fuselage. The Dogs brace themselves for a high-speed, elevator-style, gut-shifting upward acceleration. And then...

Nothing.

"What did you screw up?" Snakelips snaps at Nobu.

The dartlike craft remains on the *Lee's* deck as though it is welded there. Something sinks in Bryan's gut.

"I didn't!" Nobu says. "It just lost power." His hands work furiously over the control panel.

From the loudspeakers over the flight deck and their comms comes a menacing rumbling. Someone's clearing his throat too close to the mic.

"This is XO Bianchi. Sergeant Bryan, give it up. We've shut you down remotely. Prepare to be taken into custody."

The master-at-arms and half a dozen Navy cops march up double time. Their uniforms look so damned neat. They have white gloves and lanyards on holstered pistols, like they are on parade.

Stahlback must be enjoying this.

It's useless. It's a ship. And they fight bad guys, not each other.

"Army Sergeant Bryan? You and your men are under arrest," the master-at-arms says. "Captain's orders. Sorry."

He must be a fan.

The one who prepares to shackle them is not.

Mr. Reynolds glares at him with swabbie contempt. "How you dooin', Sergeant Friendly Guy?"

The Dogs look ready to make a break. Maybe they could take this cute uniformed troupe hostage, make the control tower cut them loose. Even if Whitebread and T-Rex had to stay behind, they'd have a chance to get Sienna.

Bryan shakes his head. "Down. Stand down. We'll have to work it another way."

But what way, dammit?

Reflexive anger suddenly wells up inside him. The SPs flinch as he rips off his Kevlar helmet and crashes it into the hatch window. The glass cracks in the pattern of a spider's web.

16

SNAKELIPS

Delicia "Snakelips" Ortiz doesn't feel completely like a freshly opened can of crap until they take Jane Bowie.

Security officers had just finished seizing, admiring the lightness of, and then stroking the mahogany wood of her custom rifle. They wrapped it in a lined case as if, after it was through putting holes in people, it was destined for a modern art museum.

The pink-handled Bowie, the colonel's, which Snakelips had picked off the hovercopter floor, they snorted at and tossed in a drawer.

She gives them a tattooed finger. Wasted. Her hands are cuffed to her waist. Rather than share verbally or angle for a lucky headbutt, she says, "I'll need a receipt for that."

The swabbie's scarred lip twitches.

"That's right, Mr. Sailorman," T-Rex puts in. "I'm the stenographer of this here elite fightin' unit. I'm taking mental inventory. I expect to see a personal custody property record receipt. Typed out in triplicate."

The brig officer shrugs, takes some pictures with his inventory scroll bar, and waves them on.

T-Rex continues threatening a tsunami of paperwork. "Don't make me file a UCMJ Article 138 abuse of authority on you."

The high-security cells are small and brightly lit. If she squints, they could be capsule hotel rooms like they once had in Japan. Whitebread ducks his head, twists sideways, and checks in.

Once her butt is on the composite slab bunk, Snakelips rubs her wrists. She wants to do something, anything, to set things right. To fix her part in Denbow's screw up. The *malada* screw up of the century.

My weapon, my fault.

If only she had kept control of her rifle. Or kept it locked in the rack until it was in her hands.

Then the hyperhomicidal Navy guy wouldn't have shot the doorway while trying to shoot a civilian kid.

Then the doorway wouldn't have jammed open.

Then Colonel McKnight might only be recovering from electric burns from whatever that *estúpido* RAPTEK thing did to her. If the door had been closed, she'd be with them instead of…

This can't be the end of trying to go back. It's the first thing they yell at you in basic: The team's only as strong as all of its links. You never, ever leave anyone behind.

Sarge'll think of something.

She hops off the bunk and pumps out incline close-grip

push-ups. Her elbows knock against metal walls.

Tight places are nothing new to Snakelips. Nearly sixteen years ago, another man-made leviathan of biblical size delivered two skinny, hungry girls. Like Jonah, Delicia Ortiz and her sister were disgorged on a strange fog-shrouded shore in America.

***

She was born in Nicaragua. Her earliest memories are of a deep green valley cupping morning mist and leaves shedding dew in the first rays of dawn. Their home was mostly ignored by the revolution and succeeding counter revolutions, until it wasn't.

Her parents' wages never went far, only about one hundred meters to the sugar cane collective general store. That didn't matter. They had their ancestral homestead. The central government's apathy gave them what they really cherished: freedom.

It was theirs until the distant rumbling of machinery drew closer and closer. Trees shook down to their roots, even on Sundays.

Soon the plantation, their homes, and everything else in the valley had to make way for their country's answer to the Panama Canal. A supertanker-sized trench was being gouged out between Lake Nicaragua and the Atlantic Ocean. Anything in the way was bulldozed and consumed by the future.

Millions of tons of fertile earth were pushed up to build berms along the waterway. These were topped with barbed wire. Coal-fired pumping stations had spare electricity to sell. Local residents were forced to buy. The Ortizes had a small solar array, which powered a fridge. Delicia's mother used the rugged appliance to make frozen sweet pops. One day it was decreed unpatriotic to gather free electricity.

Their solar panels were confiscated and thrown on a garbage barge. Delicia and her sister watched it disappear into new mists. A heavy false fog lingered all day long, gray and choking.

Her sister, Rosa, said the barge was going to a land far away called Korea. There, people spoke a language that sea creatures could understand, and they were so used to living with advanced technology they were nearly like aliens in movies. That all sounded like one of her sister's stories; she was always writing on scraps of paper instead of doing homework.

Before the Nicaraguan People's Liberation Canal, cane-field workers were only out of a job for understandable reasons: when they lost a critical limb, their lungs got too charred from inhaling the preharvest burning smoke, or dehydration finally caused their kidneys to fail. It had been this way, or worse, since Europeans came to these shores.

After the new Nicaragua Liberation Canal project started, men and women still perfectly able to stand and cut for sixteen hours a day were laid off. Delicia's father was lucky. His collective hired him out to a butterfly reserve. His job was bussing tables and keeping things nice in the restaurant and bar, catering to wealthy ecotourists.

One Saturday afternoon, Ramondo Ortiz decided to take her along. She was young. Maybe six. This would also be the last time she and her father, just them, did anything together.

"Only you," her father had said. Her older sister was too nervous, too active. She would scare them away. This was natural. Rosa Araceli Mariposa Ortiz was growing up. While it was not all bad, her father assured her, there were certain things you had to leave behind in childhood. He encouraged Delicia to enjoy them while she could.

They got a lift from an empty bus coming back from the airport. The air-conditioning inside felt strange. It was like putting your head in an ice box. After a while, Delicia decided it felt good to be cooled in this way.

In her judgement, the nature reserve was basically an inefficient campground. It featured a maze of souvenir stores and stalls flaunting T-shirts. These had butterfly designs and were hand-embroidered with local sayings. Her father told her that foreigners would pay crazy prices for these because they were proof they had seen this beautiful country and its creatures with their own eyes.

"Aren't there any in the foreign cities?"

Her father, who surely had never been more than twenty or thirty miles from where he was born, considered the question. He shook his head.

"No," Ramondo said with kind conviction. "How could there be? They are all full of stone and cars. The air is not nice. The butterflies would not like it there."

That made sense to Delicia.

The hillside nature reserve was mostly empty. Guests had gone for short guided hikes in the woods. A nurse's station stood where the buildings ended and the forest began. A large banner emblazoned with a red cross fluttered over several comfortable-looking beds. Her father explained it was always attended. Foreigners were not used to the heat. Once in a while they fainted and had to be revived.

"If they faint, do they still pay?" Delicia asked.

Since they were selling shirts for a month's local wages, this was a fair question. The whole place seemed conceived with the purpose of relieving *extranjeros* of their cash.

After considering, he said yes. In his opinion, fainters would still have to pay. Though they may get ice bags to put on their necks, and these would be free. Her father borrowed a small blanket of red flannel from the nurse. She followed him into a stand of trees away from the center of the camp.

A few meters in, they came to a large web of delicate netting. It hung high and wide. It was the *casa de vuelo*, a flight house for butterflies. Unlike many insects and animals, it was quite okay to have many different species of these creatures in one place in great numbers. They would not fight or try to eat one another, her father told her. That was not their way.

With a wave of his nut-brown arms, steady and strong, Delicia's father gently placed the red cloth over her shoulders. He picked up a copper mister and sprayed some water. It tickled her nose and tasted sweet. He sat in the shade by a tree and watched.

Delicia stood in the sunlight. And stood. She felt dumb. She wanted to move and imagined that her sister, who was in constant motion, would have liked this game even less. They might not have come to her.

Slowly at first, then all at once, dozens of fluttering patches of color came out. They must have been there all along, in the trees and underbrush.

Maybe special forces operator Corporal Snakelips Ortiz would have spotted them. But to Delicia, they seemed to appear from nowhere.

Attracted by the color of her covering, which was the same rosy pink red as the guava flower, and encouraged by the windborne scent of sprayed nectar, soon they were all over her.

They were blue-colored with gold stripes; gold-colored with light red freckles; tiny ones, three or four of which could and did land and cling to her outstretched index finger; a huge fantastic one with every color of the rainbow and designs on the end of each wing that looked like four eyes. And, of course, there were monarchs. Many monarchs with dark etchings and white dappled body and trim. They were the most regal, if not the largest, members of her instant menagerie.

The creatures that alighted on Delicia Magdalena Paloma Ortiz that day gently flapped their wings. Maybe they were doing it to keep cool as bright sun rays slanted through the tall trees. After a minute, she recalls, their movements stopped being random. They formed a harmonious pattern. The beats of hundreds of wings moved as one, surrounding her and holding her motionless.

Delicia never returned to the casa de vuelo. For a time, its managers and employees thought it might be spared because it brought in foreign dollars. Like the tremors of an earthquake victims could feel long before they knew the nature of the calamity consuming them, her nation became caught up in the devouring frenzy. The canal left their home and the home of the butterflies under meters of water.

The waterway was built for the future. Dynamic locks created artificial currents. In contrast to the route through Panama, ships traveling the Liberation Canal would no longer have to slow down in their haste to reach the Atlantic or Pacific.

When Delicia was six, Rosa had just turned fifteen. The

valley was confiscated. Their father was given a handful of córdobas and told to pack his things. A few months later, Ramondo Ortiz got a final retirement settlement. A bullet in the back.

Displaced and not able to bribe himself a job on the canal construction crew, Sr. Ortiz got odd jobs doing road-upgrading work. This mostly involved cutting down old-growth forests and putting the timber someplace it could quietly rot.

One day, Delicia, her father, and his brother came upon a magnificent mahogany tree. It was long, straight, and old. Very old, it had been cut down in an improper way. Even Delicia could see the people who killed it knew nothing about trees. Its trunk had been partly hacked and partly burned through. It lay half out of the rising waters.

The refuse log's grip on the shore was slim. In a few days, it would be on the canal bottom or drifting, partly submerged, toward the ocean. It would have been worth thousands of dollars had it ever made its way to a proper lumberyard.

Delicia's father, who knew something of carving and woodwork, envisioned a new life for this discarded former tree. A fine second life as furniture or panelling in the grand house. Or even a musical life, as part of a guitar. It was a treasure the forest was offering. It would be a sin to waste it, her father told them.

Ramondo and his brother, Stephano, worked with bare hands and short ropes to free the fallen colossus from the mud. The plan was to ride it downstream to a village, where a truck might be hired to haul it ashore. They thought of themselves as entrepreneurs, gathering what the land offered. A land they had always been told belonged to everyone.

The fallen mahogany tree was full of possibilities. Even if the Ortiz brothers sold it for a fraction of its value. A few hundred faded and worn paper dollars would be enough to buy an urban visa. A new beginning.

With the canal sending city property values sky high, Ramondo told his daughters as he worked that there would be plenty of work building large houses. Ones that foreign contractors and their local friends could afford. Somehow, they might end up installing mahogany flooring made from this same tree they were salvaging. It would require a deft touch, this fine, dark wood, especially in a humid climate. Everything would have to fit just so. But he was sure his hands would find their way, given half a chance.

Then, that half chance was taken away as a bullet snapped Sr. Ortiz's spine. From their gunboat, a paramilitary security patrol saw two raggedly dressed men on Liberation Canal property. Miscreants and squatters. They could land and arrest them or beat them and drive them off. Murder was faster.

Anyone trespassing on the waterway was deemed hostile. Those were the canal zone's rules of engagement. Insurgents on a jury-rigged suicide canoe or two carpenters floating on a half-sunken log, it was all the same to the paras. No bodies meant less paperwork.

Delicia's uncle Stephano was the next to be shot. A bullet went diagonally through both his lungs. He had time enough to signal the girls on the shore to be quiet.

"Shhh."

He gurgled in foamy blood before he splashed out of sight.

Delicia, clutching muddy reeds, frozen in fear and unreality, watched her father's hands rise once from muddy water, slap weakly against the slick bark of their simple wooden craft, then slip away without a sound. Then he became tangled in rope and branch. All three of the discarded now deceased: two men and a tree, drifting toward the Atlantic.

Delicia's mother was overwhelmed. In rich countries, they would have called it a breakdown. The staff of the rural hospital took her in. It was run by Worldwide Help. Officially, Mrs. Ortiz was a member of the cleaning staff. In reality, she could barely look after herself.

Her sister, Rosa, talked quietly and wrote furtively about her fears. They were in a hollowed-out contortion of the forest. Birdcalls had been replaced by the screech of chainsaws; garbage burned everywhere. It was like trying to live inside the guts of a suffering beast being stabbed by thousands of devils.

For once, Delicia thought, Rosa's imagination did not exaggerate. On a night when it felt like their lean-to shack was slowly sinking into the eroding soil, she told Delicia they had to leave or they would surely die.

In her desperation, with tactical skill and guile far beyond her years, her older sister hatched what Snakelips would call a nervy exfiltration plan. In the artificial river, Rosa noticed a silt bank. Big machines might one day come and claw it away. At the moment, it was marked by a blinking buoy. Ships had to slow to a crawl and veer around. The biggest ones sent down crews to measure the edges of shifting sand.

The next clear night, fuelled by the tenacity and luck of youth with nothing left to lose, they set out. The two sisters clambered up a ladder set into the side of a massive cargo ship. The vessel's name was spelled *Halfdene Ryg* in a language they did not understand. Five hundred meters long, it was filled with thousands of steel containers and surprisingly few crew.

During their journey, Delicia and Rosa counted only eight. Early on, for a time, they thought there were nine. For days they lived in fear thinking that the missing one, whose whereabouts they could not mark, was always just about to catch them. Eventually they figured out one fellow had gotten a very bad haircut a few days after their unofficial boarding. There were only eight.

It was only later, when Delicia came face-to-face with the more advanced and deviant cruelties people were capable of, that she reflected on how lucky the two girls were. What if the eight men alone on the open lawless sea had found them? Would she and her sister have fed their vile passions before feeding the fish as desiccated chum in the ship's wake? Would they have been set adrift to cover up the crew's own incompetence? Turned over to the coast patrol and sent back to Nicaragua?

As it was, the two skinny girls never came close to being discovered. In fact, Delicia had access to amenities she and her sister had only had seen in magazines. Armed with pocket bolt cutters and can openers, they dined well. While the crew slept, they enjoyed flushing toilets and stall showers with actual hot water. But for the reasons forcing their escape, they could have been on a floating spa cruise.

Only the lowest levels were scary. Her sister told her there were no rats on modern ships. Maybe that was just to make her stop worrying. At night, sometimes, from vents that plunged all the way down, she could hear scraping sounds like scrabbling of rodent paws and teeth.

The Ortiz sisters' final stroke of luck came at *Halfdene*

Ryg's last port of call. The modular compartment they had stowed away in was lifted wholly out of the bowels of the ship. In what seemed like a miracle at the time, a huge robotic crane raised them up. The entire forecastle anchor mechanism was swapped out. These details Delicia figured out over the years, as learning and memory and imagination made sense of their journey.

Back when she was six, all she felt was a jostling, flying sensation. So different than the chivvying of sea swell. It seemed like the hand of the Almighty plucked them up and set them down.

Once the obsolete module with them inside was set down, Rosa rehearsed an elaborate kidnapping story. It featured pirates and would surely appeal to the goodwill of the locals. Only Delicia ever heard it. No one cared about two small girls on the waterfront.

No one cared much for the old forecastle unit of the *Halfdene Ryg* either. It just sat there. Hours later, the machine noises of the cranes moved on. Morning light seeped pale through cracks in their hiding place. Delicia and Rosa emerged.

They were dirty, slightly dehydrated, and more than a little disoriented. They stepped over old planks, wandered over pitted concrete, avoided tall thorn bush weeds, and finally squeezed through a small hole in the fence surrounding the shipyards.

During their sea journey, Rosa had snuck up to the bridge when it was empty and seen that computers were in charge of navigation. There were maps with courses marked. They guessed they would soon arrive in a place much different from a Central American rain forest. They just did not know how different.

One of Delicia's earliest and most vivid memories is of that morning. Like the mahogany stock of her custom sniper rifle, this memory has been cured and tinted and burnished. Like Rosa's hand in hers that cold morning in Port Jersey, this memory holds her as warmly and gently as she holds it.

Delicia looked across the harbor. Through a weary little girl's eyes, she stared. She thought she saw a green arm raising a dimly glowing torch up high. Amazed, she tugged her sister's hand and pointed. By the time Rosa turned, the fog had closed fast. The arm and the light it raised were gone.

In the years that followed, Delicia attended a succession of schools. Some were run by the order of nuns who first took Delicia and Rosa in. From the Sisters of Saint Xenia of the Healing Hands, she acquired the nickname *Boca Serpiente* for her sometimes brassy way of speaking. The perpetually nosey T-Rex somehow found out about it. A mistranslation became her codename in the US Army's most exclusive fighting unit.

Of her former country's project to join the Atlantic and Pacific, history tells a cautionary tale. These days it is better known by its unofficial titles: the Malaria Sea Highway and *El Río de los diablos*. At its inauguration, the president cut a ribbon hundreds of yards long and declared that the genius of their construct would defy the elements in perpetuity.

Perpetuity turned out to be shorter than advertised. Ometepe and Zapatera, twin volcanoes located near Lake Nicaragua, had the last word. A few years after the ribbon cutting, they both erupted. The canal route was deluged by ash and lava.

Keeping the poorly planned waterway free of silt proved as productive as the labors of Sisyphus. The international transport artery was soon clogged with debris. Greed and infighting over toll revenues caused the national government to collapse into shambles long before ships started running aground.

Today, only small boats brave the mosquito-infested waters. Toll fees are still collected, but not by anyone wearing a uniform. Money for safe passage is paid to other bandits who have the good grace and honesty to wear masks over their faces and not hide what they are.

***

Tight places like the brig are nothing new to Snakelips Ortiz. In many ways she was delivered into a second life out of the steel embrace of another ship. Deep inside the *Lee,* she patiently squeezes out rep after perfect rep. Letters inked on her knuckles are a not-so-subtle taunt to future challenges.

WHO'S NEXT?

17

BRYAN

Last in line into the brig is Sarge Bryan. Mr. Reynolds hassles him every step of the way from the flight deck. The space he gets shoved into is the cleanest, most downright antiseptic jail cell in the world. Bryan hadn't been in as many as Petr Whitebread, but that probably went for the specialist too. A whistle chime sounds as the door slides closed. They are prisoners of Captain Bobblehead.

Inward-facing walls and grill doors are made of some sort of transparent aluminum. Running between the two rows of enclosures is a narrow shelf for trays and full-body restraints.

"You know, Sarge," T-Rex says as he settles in opposite, "if you was thinking to take the team out for a special getaway from terrorism and blowin' stuff up, dinner at Chick-fil-A woulda been jus' fine. This here bed an' breakfast gig's way too fancy for my country ass."

Sarge knows Rex is just keeping up verbal appearances. He's as discouraged as any of them.

"Shh," a Navy jailer cautions over the PA. "I got a hose and the whole Indian Ocean if you want to test me."

The only moveable objects, the same in each cell, are a nonflammable mattress sheet and some odd-looking pens and toothbrushes. Snakelips gets some exercise. Whitebread licks a pen. All their utensils turn out to be made of plasticized sugar.

"Guess we won't be shankin' anyone or digging any escape tunnels." T-Rex bites the handle off a toothbrush and chews on it. "Man, this is some lame incarceration. I bet movie night is *Rocky III*."

Despite being inside spaces about the size of a handicapped toilet, the mission hasn't changed. But they are not going to have any chance to get to Sienna as sardines inside this hundred-thousand-ton tin can.

There's another, last option. Bryan alone knows. Only he can initiate it. But without the intel on Bianchi's data scroll, there is no way he can risk it. The local chatter, the triangulation on her location. Unless he has that, they have to keep trying on their own.

He exhales. The tantalizingly translucent cell door fogs up.

By the time lunch is served, they've batted a jailbreak together through hand signals and verbal innuendo. It's not elegant, and it hinges on them getting to where their confiscated stuff is, three locked gates away.

When they were taken off the helo, Nobu had a pocket microSwarm device. It looks like a plastic candy bar and has five preloaded drones. These can release smokescreen or knockout gas.

It's the gas that sparks Whitebread's imagination. Out of all of them, he is the best chemist. Bryan knows this right away when his rumbly baritone starts talking from the last cell. For quite a while, he just can't suss out what the specialist is talking about.

Whitebread starts by blathering about fast food he's enjoyed while in the can.

"Yeah, Sarge, uh, listen," he adds in a slightly more meaningful tone. "If we ever get to make a choice on the menu, from our takeout, like we been talking about, y'know? If we ever get to do that, we could serve up some *Manchurian* fast food, done any way you like. But you have to eat it in *thirty seconds* or it will get cold, *out cold.*"

Every word they say, every gesture they make, is being recorded. The swabbie in the brig's monitoring room is not the threat to any jailbreak plan, his big brother mechBrain is. Military-grade AIs have voice-recognition and gesture-interpretation software. They can burn through any codes or crypto. Sienna had them work out their own system that would befuddle the sharpest digital minds. The downside is it's also befuddling his sarge-brain.

It's not till T-Rex starts humming the Frank Sinatra song "My Way" that Bryan clues in. Their cover-chat often features references to old films and things. Bryan puts things together.

The brand of KO gas Nobu's microSwarm drones serve up makes people suggestible. Like in the old film *The Manchurian Candidate.* The effect, he gathers, would last about thirty seconds. Maybe just long enough for a guard to be persuaded to hit the unlock button on his side—it is their only way through the final hatch. After that, the jailer would be out cold.

Man, we gotta get a better cable channel back home.

After a meal of mush and Wonder Bread, they're led out

for eighteen minutes of exercise. Stahlback's a stickler for regulations. This time it can work for them. They are out of their cells.

One of three gates down.

The next section over is a medium security lockup and drunk tank. The prisoners' effects locker and the exit into the ship are at opposite ends of a room outfitted as a basketball court.

It's the only court he has ever seen with barf pails hanging on the wall. Over each puke station is an encouragement poster:

Recovery is a Process

The captain must have picked them out.

YOU are NOT defined
by your RELAPSES

One features an illustration of a flotation device being thrown to a drunk sailor who has fallen overboard.

Sober Up, Sailor,
It's a Lifesaver!

At the moment, no one is partaking of this amenity.

They trot in formation around the edge of the gym. The handcuffs they wear don't concern Bryan as much as the nonlethal electrostatic EEL rigs carried by the three guards hovering over them. One of them wears a cap, seems not to be paying attention, and already has a bruised jaw. He should be an easy out.

They need every advantage. If even a single one of his people gets stunned, it could be a wipe. They have maybe thirty or forty seconds to get into the storage area and grab the micro drones. Any longer and even the lazy swabbies watching surveillance feeds will snap to and lock the joint down.

On their third lap, everyone's getting restless. Whitebread inches a little closer to his man. Snakelips pretends to be winded and slumps over a bucket. Quietly, she unlatches it from the wall.

So far, so stealthy. In Bryan's mind, the trick will be—

The cap-wearing guard who has been avoiding his glances kicks his buddy. Gets him good in the small of the back, then smacks a stun cuff on his wrists. The polymer goo staples him face-first to the bulkhead.

What's he doin'? That's our job.

In another pretty good move, the rogue guard turns and wings his baton at the second guard's legs. That guy stumbles into Whitebread. The specialist just flops on him. His shouts are smothered and hands yanked away from the alarm button.

Their unexpected accomplice puts his finger to his lips and points up. Bryan zooms in on the video surveillance. Scroll screens are taped over the cameras. These are looping their first few times around the track. Good enough for a lot longer than forty seconds.

The guy's face isn't familiar. The swelling on it is. Bryan caused it. It's the Marine he conked out on the flight deck as they were stealing the copter.

Bryan mimes the only logical reaction: Huh?

The guy points to a pin above his nametag, "Semper Fi." The US Marine Corps motto, Always Faithful. He nods to the gatekeeper and the guy in the effects room. They are also leathernecks. The doorway to the rest of the *Lee* hisses open.

They're free. Nothing can stop them from going back for Sienna.

RK SYRUS

Once they're in the hallway, Lance Corporal Coram half smiles at them. His face is purple and looks numbed by topical painkiller.

"What's up, Corporal?"

"You are, Sergeant," Coram mumbles through the swelling, "as soon as we can get you to the destroyer *Boston*."

The news that Stahlback left Colonel McKnight to fend for herself in Khorasan did not go over well with the rank and file crew. Especially not with the Marine flying squadron. There are about a thousand jarheads on board, attached to—yet not completely part of—the *Lee*. Some of them got together with a search-and-rescue element on another vessel and hatched a much better jailbreak than Bryan and the Dogs were capable of.

Seconds later, the five of them brace themselves in front of the wildly swinging maintenance hatch. It's really close to the waterline. Ocean waves thunder past. Two fast ropes support a small inflatable assault craft. It dangles ten feet above the water. Once they disengage the tethers, they'll have to veer off fast before the aircraft carrier wash sucks them under. Pretty darn good.

And it got better.

"The SAR unit on the *Boston* is ready to pick you up and take you to look for your CO," Coram tells them. "Captain Valcour's on your side, but she can't do anything until you're on her command."

The zodiac dangled.

Bow spray sent up a fine mist that made Bryan blink. Right. It was a great plan.

He looked at the Marine. So young, so eager to help

them even though they barely knew each other and their introduction had been anything but cordial.

He scans over to the destroyer. It's only a few hundred meters away. Then he checks out the *Lee*'s Phalanx Gatling gun pod. It hangs off the deck right over them. He closes his eyes. The inside of his lids feel the eerie familiar coolness of his cyber optics.

He steps away from the edge, grabs Coram's KA-BAR knife. With it, he cuts the zodiac free. It tumbles down, spins on the crest of the bow wave, and gets pulled under.

***

She wouldn't have wanted it any way else, he tells himself.

Minutes later, Bryan is back in his cell, kneeling in the corner. Two Navy guys behind him seem eager to try out their cattle-prod stunners. A third undoes his full-body restraints. His face throbs where his new buddy Corporal Coram lays a good one on him. They're even.

He can still taste the saltwater that sprayed up through the open hatch. The way off the ship he did not take.

Minutes ago, everyone, especially Snakelips, was eager to fast rope down to the dinghy and bid the *Lee* an unfond farewell. They waited for the word. He did not give it. Could not give it.

Instead, he looked at the Marine and his buddies who were about to give up their careers and freedom to help them. All to help Sienna get back home, one way or another. This was mutiny by any standards. They'd all be court martialed. All for a fellow soldier, one they had never met.

The 25 mm machine gun had loomed over their escape

route. One nod from Captain Stahlback to his master-at-arms, and they and the zodiac would have been pink chum in the Indian Ocean. Maybe Bianchi could delay that order. Everyone else was ready to chance it. The burden of command was all on him. Bryan did the only thing he could. Staring at the open hatch to freedom, he shook his head and thought fast.

After ransacking the prisoners' effects room and jamming an EEL over the auditory sensors, he arranged for them to break back into jail.

The two swabbie guards in the basketball court were the main problem. Nobu deployed his microSwarm, grabbing two of the dark little fliers as they came out of the module. The half-conscious Navy guards got a good dose of knockout gas and some soothing suggestive words.

Whitebread looked into the sailors' glazed eyes and said, "All you remember is the prisoners got loose somehow and blindsided you. But Coram the Jarhead saved the day."

They repeated back:

"Jarhead… saved day…"

"Coram… what a guy."

Then they passed out.

T-Rex scowled as he pretended to be subdued by the Marine. About that time, the klaxons sounded. The people in the video surveillance room must have woken up. That was the cue for the finishing touch.

"Corporal Coram, don't tell me you haven't been itchin' to—"

The Marine's more-enthusiastic-than-absolutely-necessary fist smacked him on the jaw. That's how Stahlback's guys found them, battered, restrained, and beaten down after a failed escape.

Bryan slumps down on the cot and looks down the row of cells. Sienna's still out there. He is still the team leader.

I should have led them to a better place than this.

But risking the Dogs' lives to unfriendly fire from their own Navy and destroying the careers of a dozen people including the captain of the *Boston*? He couldn't let it go down like that.

Behind him, loose shackles clink, the door of Bryan's cell slides shut behind him.

18

Well, maybe thinkin' big wasn't the way," T-Rex says expounding on the finer points of escaping custody.

Like a Learning Channel lecturer, he raises his eyebrows. Unlike any teacher anywhere, he has shaving creamed them into American Morse code:

f   *u*

"Maybe we should think small. I saw this video once. They were tryin' to 3-D print a mouse from one printer to another," Professor Rex explains. "A hose was connecting the two boxes, y'see. One had a real live mouse in it. The other one was empty. Little germ-sized robots started takin' the mouse apart and puttin' it together across the room."

"Then?"

"The tail went okay. But after that, they stopped filmin.' Guess it got messy."

"I think we should try it," Whitebread says. "Starting with Rex's mouth."

Sarge Bryan is not amused. Maybe they could have gotten away with stealing the helo. With the distraction of a harmless smoke bomb or two below decks, they could have stolen *Bullfinch* from the flight deck.

Or Nobu should have been able to suss out the lockout system and worked around it. If only he'd had a little more time. But what time? Every second they take is time Sienna does not have.

They've been back in their brig kennels an hour after a mouth-wateringly close brush with escape. Jailers haven't recently threatened them with that quite possibly mythical water hose. The urge to do something other than sit in a cell crawls like a line of electric-charged ants marching up Bryan's calf muscles.

"You know, this isn't all bad," Snakelips puts in. "No one's shooting at us. We have our own rooms. Whitebread *has* to bathe daily."

The specialist grunts at her. He's become cranky due to his inability to arrange his massive frame on the bunk slat. Bryan can see him in the tiny reflection of the polished lock frame of Ortiz's cell. Petr can lie on his side to keep his whole torso on it, but his feet still have to rest on the steel toilet-sink combo. He might also be irregular. He makes a note to try to get Whitebread some private crapper time. The man hates doing his business in public.

"Yeah, incarceration has its benefits," T-Rex allows. "But as much as I do love myself, looovin' myself's gettin' a bit old. The T-Rex needs to roam, y'feel me?"

Doors clang open. A young crewman walks into the cellblock. He is about eighteen years old. Snakelips fixes on his white-clad butt.

"Why go out?" she asks, pressing her body against the bars. "When you can order in?"

The young man stays near the center line, out of reach. The kid's face looks like he's visiting a bunch of serial killers.

"You," Snakelips says. "You know why they call me Snakelips?"

The boy shakes his handsome slack-jawed face. She stares at him hard, as though she is about to squeeze herself through the bars.

"Just drift a little closer," she says in a husky voice. "You're about two feet and thirty seconds from finding out."

The other prisoners get into the act.

"Hooah!" Nobu does his best wolf howl.

"Just look at those tighty whities. VPL all over on this sailor man!"

Visible underwear lines are just one of the many reasons they are proud not to be Navy.

"Y'all, go easy on the new guy," T-Rex says. "Just cause a man wears grannie panties don't make him less of a man. On this boat, anyways."

Cheeks flushing, the crewman stammers, "I, uh, I'm come, coming, I mean I came, for your sergeant. He's got a visitor."

Bryan sits up. *What's up now?* Some dumb distraction, courtesy of Stahlback.

"Sarge," T-Rex says, "if that's the Red Cross or Worldwide Help, tell 'em I choose waterboarding over this crappy soothing music."

His bars retract. At the same time, Captain Bobblehead makes a remote threat. As Bryan steps out of his cell, some dang kind of opaque fireproof door seals in the other four cells. Muffled curses and thumping comes from inside them. Bryan gets it. If he tries anything, his people will be left in dark solitary indefinitely.

The distraction turns out to be a welcome one. He does have a visitor. A pint-sized one.

"Apparently she only knows one word in English," the jailer says. "'Bryan.' She won't stop crying until she sees you. You got five minutes."

It's Anis, the girl they rescued from Sidewinder's Khorasan hideout. She waits attentively. Her nose reaches just over the brightly polished steel tabletop. Before Bryan can employ his three-word local vocabulary, she spouts a tale of adventure and intrigue. In Dari.

As a prop, Anis uses a doll. She had it when he checked on her before their attempted hijacking and rescue op. A first mate had made it out of oilcloth, twine, and life vest stuffing. The doll also has a cape, a scrap of cloth with some numbers on it. Probably measurements of a uniform the ship's tailor was sewing.

To Bryan it seems more lifelike than the baseball figurines Captain Stahlback displays in his ready room. This doll is more rugged and useful. She serves as the lead actor in Anis's epic tale.

From what he gathers, the dolly's name is Lee. Anis's small hands make the doll move as she tells the story. Lee had some kind of dust-up with other unnamed parties. She had taken a pounding but came back swinging. Anis's heroine then wandered off somewhere, safe but disoriented or lost.

Bryan looks at the girl. Anis has told him a heartfelt story he will never fully understand. The reflection of his golden eyes are pinpricks of light in her violet-tinted irises. Her casual manner is striking. Most kids are either scared of him or stare. She must have seen some crazy terrible things in her young life. Maybe, by comparison, a big bad albino with electric shining eyes is not so far out.

The crewman returns. He's given them more than five minutes. "Time's up. Gotta get her back to her bunk in sick bay."

Anis does not protest. She merely pushes Miss Lee into Bryan's large scarred hands.

"Oh, thanks, but we have lots of nice grown-up toys to play with."

The girl insists. She also pulls out her big guns. She starts to whimper.

"For Pete's sake, Sergeant, take the darn thing. I swear, she cries louder than a collision klaxon."

Bryan accepts the gift. Anis cheers up and waves as he leaves.

The Dogs' cells come out of isolation mode when Bryan returns, holding his caped dolly.

T-Rex takes notice.

"Straight up, Sarge: I think you been inside too long." Terence's gold caps flash in the harsh fluorescent light. "Now, truth be told, I dun love me sum dolls. Uh huh. Can't lie on that. But leastwise mine was life-size! This be like, all awkward and sheeat."

He's not allowed to take Miss Lee in.

"Only ship-issued frangibles in cells. Captain's orders," the crewman says. "I'll set her down here, and you can have her back on your way out."

The jailer balances her on a narrow shelf between cells. Stuffed legs dangle.

Back in his tiny chamber, Bryan again starts to feel old, dumb, and useless. There is a little slat above the door, just enough to fit four fingers. He starts one-handed pull-ups.

I'll show you old and use—hmpnph-*less.*

Muscles strain under chalky skin. His skin. Sometimes it looks strange, even to him. Soon, biceps and forearms take on a flushed hue that often catches people off guard. Say "albino" and most people expect an alabaster statue. Capillaries carry blood up to the surface of his pigment-deprived skin, revealing he is in fact made of flesh and bone. Sometimes being made of stone would be easier.

After pull-ups, he says, "How about 1,000 crunches and then see how we feel, huh, Sergeant? Left my Ranger beads at home, but I think I can do a righteous count."

Man, talking to myself. I hate to agree with Terrence, but I might be going stir—

He sees something that makes him blink. Under his flushed eyelids, his metallic eyes feel like cold contact lenses. He must have been thinking about his meeting with the girl. Replay images flicker in gigapixel resolution. One in particular. Numbers written on the dolly's cape. In crayon.

RA.645876

Not tailor's chalk. He switches to live view. There's another line of numbers, but they face away from him. X-ray vision was not part of his upgrades. Spectrum shifting does nothing. The more he thinks... is it a message?

Intel? Coordinates? To where Sienna is? On a doll?

Bianchi. Has to be. Like Jarhead Coram, like the captain of the *Boston*, he knows what's right but can't openly go against the battle group commander.

The *Lee*'s XO must have arranged for Anis to bring it disguised as a doodle on her toy. Maybe Bianchi got a translator to tell the girl this was to help someone lost in the desert. That would explain the crazy pantomime story and the girl's insisting he take the doll. But what does Bianchi think he can do?

Nothing without the other line of coordinates. Knocking the toy off its perch is not the best plan. It might land the wrong way. The guard might take it away. Instead, he decides to make T-Rex grin.

"Rex, that was hella *funny*. About the doll. Always brings my mood up seeing you flash your grill. Nothin' warms my heart like your *smile*," he says with emphasis.

T-Rex kind of gets it. Hesitantly at first, then as wide as he can, he flashes his gold-tooth grills. All shiny and reflective.

It takes a bit of head movement to get him in the right spot. T-Rex smirks like a maniac. Bryan's custom made-in-China optics do the rest. They zoom in, enhance, cut, and flip.

RA.645876
IN.578531

After some penmanship under his blanket, Bryan prepares a guided missile made of toilet paper. If anyone can get a message out without arousing suspicion, it's T-Rex. He has admirable reflexes, too. He catches the wadded paper before it hits his head.

Minutes later, he nods to Bryan and makes to flush the paper. Bryan shakes his head and points to his mouth. T-Rex makes a petulant face as he eats the memo.

Bryan feels electric ants all over now. He has to trust his man's skills. T-Rex knows what's at stake. The next in-suite meal provides an excuse.

"Warden!" T-Rex yells. "I know my rights! Under the Cuneiform Code of Military Justice and all that. I wants my phone call! And no listenin' in! It's all confidential legal sheeit."

The brig officer cautions, "Pipe down, Prisoner 3."

"I wants my PHONE CALL! Otherwise I'll have UNESCO on your prisoner-abusin' asses." T-Rex rattles the transparent bars. "*I AIN'T PLAYIN'!* Section 815 of Title 10... Are you listenin'? I'm writin' the JAG a habeas writ on this inhumanely wood-splintery toilet paper..."

T-Rex gets his call.

All Bryan can do now is something he can't stand: wait.

Minutes tick past. Only minutes. Doubts creep into the edge of his thoughts.

Those Marines, that Navy captain, they knew what they were getting into by helping. He should have gone for it. He should have hazarded it past Stahlback's Gatling guns. Sienna's got friends too, political ones who got her colonel rank made permanent, other connections through Roger and his uncle at the Joint Chiefs.

It was Bryan's call, and he fears he may have made the wrong one, the worst one of his life, by letting that real chance go. The only real chance to get her back... or at least to *know*.

Out of line of sight of the others—T-Rex, Nobu, and Snakelips—he slumps his head against the bulkhead of his cell.

Since the moment he watched her fall from the copter, he'd told himself he was going back out of honor, duty, and family. That he was doing it for the team and her mothers' sakes. When really he was doing it for himself.

He closes his eyes and reboots them. Everything reverses color. His hands strobe, black against a white background.

Without her, he feels he's fifteen years old again. Fifteen and back in that abandoned chapel by the old Reidt Mine that night the bully Taddy Eddington and his posse chased him. He was a lone, fearful zeru boy kneeling in front of that ghostly crucifix only he could see, wishing that light had never been invented.

Now everything will depend on a man Bryan hasn't seen since Sienna's twelfth birthday. Someone he had planned to run into by accident in Europe, yesterday, March 19.

Luminous flux: a term used in photometry to measure the perceived power of light.

In German: **Der Lichtstrom**.

19

DR. LICHT

What outlandish car will that pushy Scotsman arrive in? Of all the things he could be considering: the cosmic mysteries hinted at by the Ansible, the construction of his elevator into space, this is what weighs on the extraordinary mind of Wolfgang Chrysostomus Licht.

His office is the highest point of his territory. Above the vaulted office ceiling, a lattice spire stabs the sky. Once completed, it will be strong enough and flexible enough to hold a diamond-nanothread leash more than 100,000 kilometers long to reach past geosynchronous orbit, tethering the counterweight. Attached to it will be an orbiting platform, the last stop before the rest of the Solar system. The project could have been done more easily and cheaply with a ground station at the equator, but then what would be the glory in that?

Licht's office is framed by nearly a hectare of flawless tempered projection glass. Manipulating its real-time magnification like a touchscreen, he can see right to his border with France. Rectangular viewlets cascade. Focal-point recognition software tries to center each one on a feature it thinks he might want to look at more closely.

A red-throated loon circles the still surface of a lake.

Over a fork in the road looms a dark statue of the Hindu deity Shiva. It's been here since the CERN facility went bankrupt and was sold by the government to Lichtwerks.

A line of armored limousines and exotic sports cars stretches down Seven Rays Avenue toward the reception rotunda.

Tonight's guests. Most are eager to brownnose. Many secretly hope to gawk with jealous schadenfreude. Licht sees no sign of the man. He has hated the Scotsman for so long his animosity seems like deep friendship.

Maybe that grandstander Ranulph Oliphant will arrive in a Formula 0 car borrowed from the Highlands racing team he is so proud of.

The crowd of dignitaries and celebrities, Oliphant, and that inconvenient Ansible particle, will have wait. Dr. Licht has an executive placement interview, one that cannot be put off.

A console panel glows under his finger.

"Send in the journalist."

"Yes, Herr Doktor."

"Let me know about Oliphant. Not just when he is here. The instant he crosses from France."

"Yes, Herr Doktor."

The room is cathedral sized. Licht made certain it was one

meter larger in all dimensions than St. Peter's. Harboring a secret, smoldering resentment of the Pope, he'd modeled many aspects of Der Lichtstrom on the Vatican.

Instead of a chandelier, a water tank hangs from the ceiling. It is shaped like a three-dimensional ocean wave. Empty. The baby dolphin that was supposed to be inside playing happily decided to drop dead. Ingratitude seems to cross species boundaries.

"Make sure the kitchen purées all of the dolphin for the canapés."

"Yes, Herr Doktor."

As he turns off the intercom, his hands feel an ugly knot in the wood of the desk. An imperfection. It's not the wood, of course. It is him.

Licht's hands have not operated a tool press for fifty years. Every time he clenches his left, a lump of scar tissue reminds him of time spent in his father's machine shop. That apprenticeship left its mark. Embedded in the palm is a twisted imprint of a precision screw.

Decades ago, some Blödian janitor working in his family's factory spilled sulfuric acid. It ate into machinery and a freshly threaded screw sprang out of the high-pressure forge, right into the heel bones of his hand. The doctors had to insert smaller screws just to keep it attached.

One tiny man's negligence had nearly turned him into a feeble cripple. The image of the hexagonal bolt, its looping threads, are there still. As though at the instant of impact, he had been made of wax.

The Lichtstrom sits between France and Switzerland. After his discovery of orderly neutrinos and their use as communication wavelengths, Lichtwerks' business grew exponentially. Luckily, funding cuts to scientific programs had left the world's largest supercollider array in mothballs.

The Large Hadron Collider at CERN was the most exclusive whisper listing in the history of real estate. His bid was uncontested. No one likes real estate that is haunted.

Governments and universities were put off by videos of human sacrifices to Shiva being carried out in the supercollider levels. It seemed a few of the scientists searching for the God Particle were also indulging in a little blood-magic spiritualism on the side.

After he bought the place, Licht kept the cultists' icon. A five-meter-tall statue of the Destroyer of Worlds stands at the driveway to Seven Rays Avenue.

The journalist is shown in. Doors close behind him without a sound. He is swarthy, slightly nervous, slightly proud. A youngish man in a wrinkled suit. Not the noblest sacrifice, but he'll do.

20

Licht watches the reporter walk past holographic corporate poster. The wiry nervous Indonesian man pretends to study them.

In the first, a pair of hands release a crystal dove ready to fly into a faultless blue sky.

FINALLY, FREEDOM IS FREE!
CALLS & DATA:
FREE, UNLIMITED & INSTANT, EVERYWHERE.
STEP INTO THE LIGHT

Back then, he only had a jury-rigged neutrino array in the Balkans. At the time that damn Scotsman held the patent on the only handsets that would work with his system.

In the next framed poster, a small cold sun glowers down through thin atmosphere onto a broken old-style cell phone.

An astronaut's boots have stepped on it in frustration. The phone's bits are crushed and lie on powdery red soil.

NO BARS? MIGHT AS WELL BE ON MARS!

Below this are a trio of happy Licht/Net users. One stands on top of Everest. The next sits five miles below sea level in the Mariana Trench. The last is a content-looking exploration robot transmitting from one of Saturn's moons.

WHEREVER YOU GO, WE ARE ALREADY THERE.

The last holo poster displays his flagship product: cybernetic implant phones. A young woman's hand holds a child's. Their skin glows with embedded circuitry.

YOU **ARE** THE PHONE!
NEVER LOSE TOUCH WITH THE ONES YOU LOVE!
LEARN MORE AT SIMCARDIMPLANTS/LICHT

"Herr Doktor Licht, thank you for seeing me. Especially today, of all days."

"For one of Indonesia's leading reporters I would do nothing less." He motions to a chair. "Mr. Shara."

"Call me Tommy, everyone does."

Licht still feels drawn to the windows. Oliphant. The Ansible test. The scenario taking shape hundreds of meters below their feet pulls his thoughts like an electromagnet tugging on a skull full of iron filings.

"Doctor?"

Shara's voice brings his attention back.

"Oh, nothing." *Oliphant. The Ansible test.* "I'm just hoping my guests are being taken care of."

"I saw them arriving and enjoyed one of the canapés." He wipes the corners of his mouth with a monogrammed napkin. "You really outdid yourself. Today has been billed as the most important science event since the Trinity nuclear test."

"I might not go so far," Licht says. "This space elevator above you may have more realistic worth. In its first year of operation, it will deliver more tonnage to orbit than all the rocket ships since the start of space flight."

He swats dismissively at an invisible gnat.

"The Ansible, ach. Its purposes, origins, possible uses. All vague. Even its shape. How do you verify something that cannot be photographed? How do you quantify something that leaves no footprint in digital data?"

"You must be pleased your facility was chosen. Out of all the particle accelerators in the world."

"Only we generate sufficient synchrotron radiation. This peculiarity could only be investigated here."

"A peculiarity that could threaten your business model."

Faster-than-light communications? A project Oliphant and the Americans have been working on in secret.

"Come now, what business model could compete against free and unlimited? As for the supposed properties of this inscrutable object?" Licht shakes his head. "It was plucked from an ice chamber at the bottom of the world barely a year ago. What it might be, where it originated, may never be fully explained."

Licht smiles harder.

"Ancient Egyptians knew about electricity. They described it accurately. Commercial light bulbs had to wait until the 1880s." Licht leaves his desk. "Now, you have come a long way, and your forte is neither science nor business, is it?"

"Mostly politics."

"Your wife is a prominent lawyer for the opposition party in your home country, correct?"

The intense younger man's handsome features are decidedly marred by dark circles around his eyes. Jet lag. Licht almost feels sorry for him.

"You seem to have done your research. I am flattered. Perhaps you were intending to interview me."

Licht chuckles. Dry irony is his favorite type of humor.

"My press secretary agreed to certain questions. But let's throw away the script, like they say in the vulgar reality shows. We will just talk. Man to man."

Shara looks like he's won some kind of journalist lottery.

"Have a seat by the fireplace."

"Shall we begin?" Shara takes out a 3-D recorder the size and shape of a box of playing cards. "On the record?"

"Darauf kannst du Gift nehmen."

You can take poison on that.

21

Ah yes, Doktor, 'I can bet my life on that.'"
Shara's profile says he knows German to a B-1 level. This appears to include well-known sayings.

Licht is proud of his hearth. It has been described as garish, pompous, and even grotesque by architectural writers who couldn't make a living designing cesspools. Tons of Swedish crystal form a flue curving 108 feet to the ceiling, making it taller than Bernini's papal altar. Below, a mythic winged creature sits on a flaming nest. Thorn vines hold it in place.

The effect he wanted was a zealous tension between the desire of the flying creature to leap into the air and the cruel twisting of the vines holding it back. Microscopic details, leaves and feathers, were carved by laser etching. They reflect frozen motion. The torments of time and burden of dreams made gargantuan and transparent.

The nest is a bonfire. It can voraciously consume wood,

gas, coal, or biofuel, depending on the bouquet of light desired. Thorns channel each wavelength into pleasing shapes throughout the huge room. Today it is dark and cold.

"I don't suppose anyone asks you what time it is here," Shara says cheekily.

The floor and walls of the vast room form a macrocosmic astronomical clock. It includes human-sized figures of the apostles and Death, which come out of hidden alcoves to strike the hours. Shara studies dials and numbers under the floor, which is made of transparent aluminum.

"Solar, lunar, even *siderisch*—star based time—is measured. To me the Prague *orloj* has always represented man's desire for mechanical mastery over raw universal forces. Lichtwerks' mission."

"Remarkable," Shara says, probably genuinely impressed.

"How can we step out of time without first finding ourselves within it?"

"Aren't there some forces man should never control?"

"Nonsense. The only inexhaustible resource is mankind's ignorance and an equal and offsetting capacity to master the elements. Will alone can tip the balance. That goes for all the light we can see and the greater part we cannot."

The LED on Shara's recorder oscillates as it perceives inbound sound waves. For once, Licht can speak his mind.

"To say we must not do wrong is totally off the point. Scientific advancements cannot do wrong. Questionable consequences are the result of weak passions. Where there is mastery, there is only *Wohltätigkeit*. Beneficence. The charity of dreamers."

"Would you say that to the people involved with your early

injectable SIM-card experiments, the ones who lost arms?"

Shara is verbally aggressive. Licht approves.

"Ah, the terrible price of progress. How many arms and legs and lives were lost during the Industrial Revolution? In 2010, United Nations aid workers brought cholera to Haiti. A million people got sick, ten thousand died. All while the UN were merely trying to restore the upscale squalor that existed before an earthquake.

"All people affected by early versions of my 'You are the Phone' campaign were in developing countries. The politically correct reference for the overpopulated, backward third world. These uneducated people couldn't possibly understand my guiding precepts. They received monetary settlements. We've also given the injured volunteers free Licht/Net upgrades for life. They made out well."

The journalist is shocked and elated. He checks the holographic recording device on the table between them. A miniature Licht and miniature Shara pause and look at a blank space between them. The device records everything except its own image.

Shara thinks he has caught his subject making a horrible mistake on the record. He must be imagining his byline on the front page of London's deplorable rag, the *Citizen Juggernaut*.

Licht is just warming up.

"I will go further. The Lichtphone amputees should be proud of their sacrifice. They are volunteer soldiers wounded in the war on ignorance and poverty in all forms."

"They should be...? Are you saying they should feel good about losing a limb so that you can make more money?"

Licht rolls his eyes.

"You have just reconfirmed something: Only the very rich can rise above the pettiness and, yes, the sinfulness of greed and avarice. Mr. Shara, I have my own reserve currency issued by my own nation. After the Eurozone collapsed, the Lichtstrom currency unit bailed out bankrupt countries. The trading volume of virtual Lichtcredits today is more than all the major currencies combined."

"Isn't that because you do business with states and entities banned from using other banks? Don't ninety percent of transactions in street drugs like Red Mist involve Lichtcredits?"

"I personally switched on high-speed mobile communications for nearly six billion people who did not have any bars on their obsolete phones because they have no money. I did not care. My struggle is not, and never will be, about base *Zahlungsmittel*. It is about humanity. The Lichtstrom is the first nation founded on pure information. We produce nothing. We see everything."

Licht pours a glass of ionized water. Shara does not drink spirits. Even so, in about eight minutes, his guest may be tempted to down the whole contents of the crystal liquor cabinet.

"Ignorance and isolation are today's polio. For millennia, people fought against that terrible disease. There is no natural cure. There is no resistance that can be bred into a population. Only by the domination of the natural environment by the intellect was it conquered in the first world. There were mistakes. Even horrible accidents that left people dead or painfully paralyzed.

"Today, the third world is treated to the Sabin live virus vaccine. Not the Salk protocol, the only one allowed by law in civilized countries. Cheaper medicines have kept strains of the disease alive and kicking in countries such as yours, Mr. Shara. This guarantees a healthy annual profit to certain pharmaceutical concerns, doesn't it?"

His guest takes the bait.

"My newsgroup published extensively on the differing standards of care for developing nations like mine. I am a nationalist, and I believe 300 million Indonesians deserve the same respect and dignity as anyone else on the planet."

Shara shakes his head as if to stop it from spinning. "Are you seriously comparing yourself to Jonas Salk, one of the greatest selfless benefactors in human history?"

"I am indeed. And more," Licht says, his enthusiasm rises. "I insist everyone all over the world have the same access to communications, ubiquitous and free, as everyone else. I have made communications a basic human right. When the pope in the Vatican speaks with the president of France, they are using the same system you use to update your wife's shopping lists. Just like Salk, who refused to patent his vaccine asking, 'could you patent the sun?' I have registered no proprietary processes."

"As a result, you don't have to tell anyone how your system works." Shara checks his notes. "It took years for the Antarctic IceCube Observatory to witness a single neutrino. These strange particles can pass through a light-year of solid lead without leaving a trace. The Lichtstrom uses them like radio waves. Would you care to share those secrets now, on the record?"

Tiresome. Licht looks at the clockwork. Soon the grim reaper will step out to chime the passing hour.

"Why don't you ask me what you came all this way for?"

Shara returned a stare, coy under its blankness.

"Time is wasting. You have less than you believe."

Shara glances at the doorway. His hand moves toward sunglasses in his jacket pocket. It is his backup recording device.

Mr. Shara, if you needed to be dead, you would have been disposed of by grubby people I never have the slightest contact with.

"Your wife has a long friendship with the Indonesian opposition leader, Mr. Banten. You have painstakingly assembled proof Lichtwerks has for years blackmailed your government into doing my bidding. You are working on a series of articles, even a book, on this subject. You also have some intriguing speculation as to Lichtwerks's involvement in certain coups and civil wars. Correct?"

"If you knew that, why—"

"Mr. Shara, if you would listen more and jabber less, you would not be in your predicament. I speak very little. I influence, I manipulate, I extort politicians and oligarchs. Anyone significant. How could I not?

"When I invented light-based communication, it was inevitable that governments would lust for the knowledge that flowed, photon by photon, through my servers. Every Licht/Net-enabled light bulb is a data hub.

"The old internet is a backwater cesspool. Useless. Its fiber-optic cables desolate, populated only by perverts glued to their sick pornography and by pathetically debauched online gamers.

"Countries like your Indonesia with large populations and

weak infrastructure were only too happy to accept my gifts. No more expensive Wi-Fi towers or impractical airships. With Licht/Net, connecting is as simple as screwing in a light bulb. Even the least of you can do that."

Mr. Shara sits, speechless.

The hour ticks.

Mirrors in a wall alcove that had appeared solid part. Human-sized clockwork sculptures begin their procession. Exquisitely crafted and painted, they are propelled by the finest gears, springs, and levers. Licht fancies himself both clockwork element and creator.

"And the best part, Mr. Shara, the very best part: how easy it was. What I thought might take decades took only months.

"I miscalculated the intense desire of governments in poorer countries to spy on their people. I offer better signals intelligence than America's NSA or Britain's GCHQ could ever provide. Tin-pot potentates literally tore their lighting infrastructure out by the roots in the clamor for more Licht/Net devices.

"My factories had a most difficult time keeping up with orders. Through billions of light fixtures across the planet, I have singlehandedly democratized oppression."

"Are you confirming Lichtwerks is in partnership with the most brutal and dictatorial regimes on the planet?"

"Naturally. And I would not call it much of a partnership. Tyrannical juntas are still our best customers. Nothing like the threat of prison or a public flogging to get people to install our products. If one does not count standby time and dark-light transmissions, my illumination is actually more energy efficient than most fluorescent bulbs."

"Dark what?"

No, Mr. Shara, you are no scientist at all.

"It is a common misconception that if you turn off one of my bulbs, it no longer transmits data. People think other fixtures or street lights make their handsets function. However, when turned off, they still transmit on the invisible spectrum.

"In simplified terms: We watch you in the dark. My newest models continue to transmit for a period, even when unplugged."

Licht looks to the elevator spire, which will soon carry him beyond the grip of gravity.

"Most of the universe is dark. It reflects no light. We can only intuit its existence. The neutrinos that power the Lichtstrom, they are a doorway."

Shara looks at him strangely. Perhaps hoping he will go off on a racist rant about gypsies and foreign guest workers.

"Lichtwerks surveillance networks received serious love from military oppressors and despotic ballot-box-stuffing theocracies. In the geopolitical food chain, these would be the vultures and hyenas.

"Hard on their heels came every so-called democracy in the world. Every industrialized nation started using my system to watch, manipulate, and control their people.

"These societies are sophisticated, omnivorous, and flexible in their survival modes. As they were busy watching their people, an uber-predator would naturally evolve. One at the very top of the information food chain."

"Lichtwerks."

"Precisely. Even the most paranoid dictator gave me enough ammunition to sink them or help them, as I chose.

Large democracies were easier. With regularly scheduled elections and the media's intense fascination with who is sticking what body part where, it's almost too easy to get what I want."

Shara nods. As if he understands.

"What exactly is it you want?"

The hooded figure of Death finally emerges from his vestibule and strikes.

BONG, BONG, BONG…

Mr. Shara, this bell, it tolls for thee.

21

*B*ONG.

"Right now? I want you. All that you have to give."

"Sorry? I didn't hear you correctly."

BONG.

"You did. You will come here to Der Lichtstrom. You will leave your home, come with your wife to the gentle cultured heart of Europe, and live here. You will enjoy a massive increase in your living standard.

"Regrettably, I cannot allow all members of your family to leave my borders at the same time. All my key employees are under the same stricture. My country is beautiful, very well engineered and managed. You will learn to love it."

BONG.

"You're… you must have lost your mind!"

The clockwork reaper finishes his solo and retreats.

"You ask the wrong question. The right one is: What use are you?"

Shara's face becomes nearly as bone white as Death's.

"That lake, I had it made. Mine improves greatly on what nature threw together. This one makes the view perfect. Your predecessor has left for you a job vacancy. He annoyed me very much by going to our excellent staff gymnasium, signing out a set of ankle weights, walking off a dock, and drowning himself in that lake."

"Look, Professor, everyone knows where I am. If something happens to me—"

"I see from your file you are a fairly active swimmer. I hope you will find the waters here to your liking. They may seem chill at first, but I predict you will quickly get used to them." Licht checks the time. "Nothing is *going* to happen to you. You have my word."

"The word of a madman!"

Licht feels a calm glow. "If you were not so busy making diagnoses of my mental infirmities, you would have noticed I have already set you on a new rewarding career path."

Licht flicks a panel. Shara's dossier comes up on the wall display screen next to the fireplace.

"As a respected international journalist, you have interviewed the majority of the leaders across the globe. Working for the Welt/Licht news service, you will continue as before. No one will remark upon your increased access as you fly on my jets and sail on my ships from one coveted interview to another."

"You already employ hundreds of journalists."

"You underestimate your true gifts. You will not be reporting news. You will be making it. On my instructions."

Shara palpitates, as only young men with tight skin and all their teeth can, with vigor.

"Herr Doktor, I don't know whether to laugh or pity you. You can't keep your mental condition secret for long. Let me help you get treatment while someone else manages all this. The strain must be overwhelming."

At least he's not afraid to talk back. Good man.

"You are offering to take me to the cuckoo's nest. Thoughtful. But I am offering you the chance to stop chewing cud and swallowing it like a sad-eyed milk cow. I am offering you the chance to play liar's poker at the highest level and, for once in your life, win.

"You already know, on a small scale, some of the work we have done in your country through the large cavernous mouth of the Indonesian politician Mr. Banten. This makes you ideally suited to my main business. You must wonder how I can afford to give away all my services for no charge, yes?"

"It's well known you sell advertising, search results, people's personal details, all of which are very hard to opt out of."

Licht looks past the space spire to the halo of approaching night as it seeps into the tops of high clouds.

"Once, there was a man. He decided he would rule the world. He would, unlike the Caesars, the Khans, even Napoleon, not himself fight. He would not be a general in the field. He had no idea about such things. He decided to conquer the world with words. His words. He thought, this man did, he *knew* his words would take root. He knew they would multiply. And they did. His words were power and nearly did the job."

"Are you talking about—"

"It doesn't matter," Licht says, cutting Shara off. "He failed.

216

Making an unforgiveable mess. I wish to conquer. I've learned that my own words, they can never be enough. A man only has so many. To bind governments and the people underneath them, it takes an inexhaustible resource. I shackle them all with *their own* words!"

Shara's forehead beads with perspiration.

"The backbone of our enterprise is, and always has been, secrets. The secrets of anyone, everywhere. Most, we keep, some we trade for what we want more."

"Like recognition of your company's property as a sovereign nation," Shara says, his eyes staring at the middle distance between them.

Time to wake up, Mr. Shara.

Licht thumbs another panel. An image of the man's wife at their house in Jakarta appears on the large monitor. The point of view is from the ceiling light fixture in Shara's own living room.

His guest's smooth tanned face blanches. "How are you—? We had those lighting fixtures changed."

"My people in Jakarta bribed your resident manager to change them back," Licht says. "It gave us the opportunity to upgrade you to our next generation of features."

Two quarter-inset panels appear. An odd-looking sonogram sits above a chemical analysis. Licht beams at Shara, enjoying his role of the proverbial stork.

"I don't allow smoking here, but you can enjoy one of your predecessor's cigars at the home that is now yours. In addition to an impressive collection of exotic snakes, he kept a well-stocked humidor. A celebration smoke is traditional, isn't it? You are about to be a father."

"What are you talking about?"

"Ach, you should know about this. The latest Licht/Net illumination panels have spectrograph capabilities. This technology allows astronomers to know what the atmosphere of Venus is made of. How hard would it be to analyze your wife's state of health from her bodily fluids?

"As you can see, we can even do rudimentary ultrasonography if the subject stays prone and still. For example, while asleep. Your preliminary results indicate the birth of a healthy baby boy is thirty-four weeks away. Better pick out a room for a nursery."

Shara's outrage has distracted him from noticing two large gentlemen emerge from their places behind what seem to be solid pillars.

Shara shakes his head so quickly it looks like anatomical vibration rather than a gesture. "She never said anything."

"Mrs. Shara does not know she is pregnant. You will have the honor of giving her the good news when she arrives and you start your new lives here as citizen workers." A guard, Mr. Plotz, grabs Shara's shoulders. "These gentlemen will escort you to your family's new home."

"All you've done is given me more information for my article! When people find out you're watching us all in our bedrooms and bathrooms—"

"You have more pressing problems than personal privacy. In Jakarta, your wife has promised Mr. Banten she will deliver a certain package." He points to the screen. "That package. She thinks it's a dossier on the government's more questionable Lichtwerks connected activities. Mr. Banten and the government minister are scheduled to have a meeting. You know, to clear the air.

"Your wife will deliver this folder. She will then leave allowing the two men to discuss how they will cripple my influence in Indonesia. What none of the participants know is that folder holds three quarters of a kilo of synthetic explosive. That dossier will indeed have a large impact. But not the one your group expects."

If it is possible for Shara's face to contort into an expression of greater disorientation, it does. He pulls out his handset.

On the wall monitor, video feed shows Mrs. Shara lifting up her Eurolincx satellite phone. She starts speaking. To Mr. Shara.

Shara's phone is inert in his hands. He has not dialed.

"*Halo saying,*" his wife says.

She casually places the fat binder package on a shelf by the door so as not to forget it. Mr. and Mrs. Shara have a pleasant conversation.

Auto-translation captions scroll beneath in German and English. Confusion replaces anger and outrage as the dominant expression on his guest's face.

"Bewildering, yes? She really is speaking with you. Or she was. That is the conversation you had with your wife as you traveled from Lyons. It happened two hours ago."

Dr. Licht pauses to let that sink in.

"Since that time, from the moment you crossed into my territory, not one qubit of information has reached you or has been sent by you. Your recording devices are not burst-uploading to your private server via satellite frequency as you believe. Their memories are blank."

Licht savors the highlight of the placement interview. "Now, let me, the scientist, update you, the journalist, on the current state of events."

Licht brings up the real-time feed. A government office building in downtown Jakarta spews black and gray smoke out of dozens of broken windows. Bahasa Indonesian writing crawls along the bottom of the frame as nearly hysterical commentators try to all speak at once.

"I always hate waiting for the recap. This is the gist: About thirty-five minutes ago, your wife delivered the package we mentioned. There was some doubt whether she would arrive in time, given the appalling state of traffic in your capital today. That's why you had to wait outside my office as long as you did. My apologies for the tardiness.

"The bomb, which will be traced back to a Sumatran separatist organization, was punctual. Mr. Banten and the minister are dead. A live feed from the morgue shows them trying to work out which body parts belong to whom. I will spare you that. I know you were close to Mr. Banten."

Shara recovers some of the breath that shock had knocked out of him.

"You'll never get away with this. We'll fight you to the last. You can't manipulate and kill people for your own selfish purposes!"

"What better reasons could there be? In any case, your own fate, that of your wife, and your unborn son, these should be of more concern than abstractions like freedom. In fact, I will not interfere with your free will at all. Choose now. Go ahead. Reject my hospitality. Return to your country. You will be in literal chains.

"Security footage of your wife delivering the bomb will shortly be requested from us by Detachment 88, your nation's brutish anti-terror squad. The government building's internal system malfunctioned. The Lichtwerks proprietary video file is the only evidence of this crime of treason and mass murder. Your wife is in the company of my security people. They have told her you have been involved in some kind of emergency. She is on her way to my plane at Jakarta International. I think you know how it goes if you choose to decline."

The younger man's hands shake on the armrests of his chair. "Have you already picked out the prosecutor and judge for my case?"

"No. Only your wife's case will be heard. News of your extradition from France, places, times, arrival gate, will make its way to the reactionary pro-government militia in Jakarta. Friends and business associates of the dead cabinet minister, being unable to attack your wife directly, will kill you in some mundane manner.

"Your wife will be sentenced to face a firing squad. From what I comprehend about your justice system, which is not much, I anticipate her sentence will be suspended for nine months due to her delicate condition.

"Your son will be born in a dreadfully overcrowded prison and make his way into the less-than-ideal orphanage system of your country. Your newspaper recently published an exposé of children as young as six years old being sold to sportswear sweatshops. At least you won't be alive to see that."

The arrogant light in Tommy Shara's eyes, strong when he marched in, flickers and dies. The young man's will collapses.

Blitzkrieg!

Licht beams at his new team member.

He never had a chance from the moment his life was decided for him. Shara rises weakly. Sandwiched between two guards, he shuffles to the door.

Licht's attention drifts. He squints through antique theatre glasses made for a tsar by Fabergé. He scans the procession beneath the enormous window.

At the door, his new hire pauses.

"You're a monster. I don't know why people haven't gotten together to kill you."

Licht is genuinely surprised.

"Why would they?"

He lowers his bejewelled binoculars. Thousands, tens of thousands, have died as a result of his activities. Just as surely Licht believes millions have been saved. Disruptive wars have been averted, inconvenient genocides deferred.

Lichtwerks was the self-driving option for societies, much safer and efficient. In each atom of his being, he is certain every living human is enriched by his work. The thought of sane, productive, normal people wanting to hurt him is beyond conception.

In a quiet voice not meant for his departing guest, he says, "I am the reason why, in a dark and uncaring universe, a tree in the forest makes noise when it falls. Without us watching, there is no meaning."

Tall doors snap shut. His binocular lenses flick across the oncoming stream of VIP guests.

Where are you? You Scottish...

Licht sees Oliphant. He's riding on the most peculiar oddity imaginable.

"Ach!"

It's as though the man and his *meschugge* assistant are going to their *own* event, not his. Worst of all, they are both staring right back up at him.

23

RAN OLIPHANT

"S omeone's watching us."

Ranulph Oliphant stares up at the Lichtstrom's Stalinesque eaves. Two jittery specks of light wink back. If photons could carry miserly intent, he imagines these would.

In their airy but confined ride, his shoulders bump against the couture ruffles draping Melanie Françoise.

"Wolfie," she trills, "that triple-doctorate poopyhead. He's lucky we've showed up at all."

Dr. Françoise—honorary PhD in Fine Arts, Shimer College, Chicago—gives her head a defiant shake with a mound of loose blonde curls Marie Antoinette would have envied.

"I certainly hope he does notice," Ran says, reining in the horses pulling their chariot. "Shame for Brutus and Cassius to go through all this bother and not burn the bastard's britches."

He smiles and speaks through his teeth. The Lichtstrom

has a million eyes, not counting their host's. Some of them read lips.

Brutus and Cassius pull them along slowly. Too slowly for their liking or his. The two robust Percherons are named after Caesar's assassins. The horses have been uniquely decorated for the event. Their bodies flash with hundreds of squares of brilliantly shining armor.

It took some convincing before Ran agreed to decorate his steeds. Melanie's ideas often ended up being impractical or downright dangerous. Ran really likes his horses. He's more fond of them than most of the people with whom he does business. And he wouldn't trade their steaming droppings for Professor Licht.

In his youth, he worked in the stables of gentry and lords, first as a work hand, then as a groom. The pair pulling them experience no discomfort. A clever arrangement of bright tiles lets their muscles move and skin breathe naturally. His horses enjoy the attention. They stomp and preen past throngs of spectators and paparazzi.

Melanie also designed the horse carriage. Its pieces were fabricated in a big 3-D printer in their basement. She looks like a runway model or the most flagrant of trophy wives. She's neither. His protégé, and Eurolincx's chief organizer of miscellany, is a world-class inventor.

A unique balancing system and stealth coating on the wheels make them appear to float over the road. Onlookers are delighted.

Take that, Lichty!

"Say one thing about the old haggis," Melanie says, "he can definitely throw a party."

Her expression tells him she's scheming toppers.

"Ide-eaa!" Her mercurial mind settles on one. "Let's show Licht we're no slouches. How about we rent the Coliseum in Rome and put on an ancient Greek play marathon? It can be for the EHS Kids charity. What do you say?"

"Same as the Dalai Lama said when you lectured him on the feng shui of his bathrooms: FML!" Ran scans the line ahead. "By the looks of the armored palanquin pulling up, His Serene Holiness is attending. Remember, he still has that restraining order on you."

"That's only valid in Nepal," she scoffs.

After crossing the border from France, their pace down the wide and meticulously maintained Seven Rays Avenue had been swift. Just as they pass the Shiva statue they come up against a knot of traffic. Hordes of arriving scientists, politicians, sports figures, and entertainment luminaries dash against a scarcity of valets.

"I'm not breathing exhaust fumes another second." Ran tugs the reins smartly left. "Haw!"

Cassius and Brutus turn off the road, gleefully scattering paparazzi in front of their hooves. They trample some hedges on their way to a manicured meadow. How Melanie manages to stay on her feet in six-inch stilettos is anyone's guess, though she's probably worked out a physics formula in her head. She grabs his arm, her curls bouncing in fading sunlight.

"Enough off-roading."

He reins up. The tableau of them careening off the pink gravel drive sends cameras clicking and media drones buzzing toward them like flies to honey.

"Sometimes two horsepower is more impressive than two thousand," Melanie says sagely.

"Brilliant idea, this chariot contraption." Ran smiles at the camera lenses. "What's my next one, by the way?"

Melanie's voice and manner channels a club hostess who's been sampling too much of her own wares. She just might be the brightest mind in the place tonight. Had she finished every course of study she started in sciences, medicine, and jazz dance, she would have more degrees than a thermometer.

Ran settles Brutus down.

Cassius chomps on some amusingly expensive Brazilian orchids.

Melanie's brain buzzes. It's almost audible.

"Licht's nasty old Lichtstrom is so much like the cursed house of Atreus, don't you think?" she says. "Coming here always reminds me of the Oresteia plays."

"I know your mind works in mysterious ways," Ran says with a sigh. "But how does the headquarters of a megalomaniac with his own country remind you of ancient Greek tragedies?

"Seriously, pay attention. We're walking into the personal fortress of a psychopath who's about to blast a likely alien object with gigajoules of energy."

She is paying attention—to the thousand channels broadcasting between her left and right hemispheres.

"Oh, look!" Melanie chirps. "A red carpet."

With a rustle of crêpe and a fluttering of ribbons, she dashes quickly over to his side. Holding out her hand, she speaks with a stage voice that would be right at home at the Old Vic.

"Now, my king,

step down from your chariot,

and let not your foot touch the ground.

Good men! Hark!

Let there be spread before this Castle of Caprice,

wherein Justice leads him,

a path of pure crimson."

Ran looks at her as he steps out of the chariot. "You just made that up."

"Did not, you big silly!" She giggles. "It's from *Agamemnon.*"

"That sounds Greek." They walk toward the entrance arches on a red carpet nearly as wide as a regulation football pitch. "Let me guess, it doesn't end well for the old duffer?"

"You had to *axe.*"

Melanie's laugh echoes effervescently inside the sterile arched colonnade. Hair shaking ensues. Ran sighs.

"I'm sure that's funny to you and the three other people in the world who would get the joke." They join the walking line to the vaulted entrance. "If you can, try to act daft and empty headed. The world abhors vacuums and loves to fill them with secrets. I'm eager to find out more about, you know, *things.*"

"Ranny, enjoy yourself. It's a party, and you're not paying!" She fusses over his lapels. "Let me fix that. You have to look neat for the snappies."

Dexterous fingers straighten the yellow rose that was threatening to come askew.

24

The paparazzi are less obnoxious than normal. Ran sees why. They are hemmed in by translucent chicken wire. Lichtwerks guards carry festively colored shocker batons. These can, and do, extend four meters to swat cam drones trespassing out of their designated airspace. Higher up, interceptor drones circle with the same aim. Dr. Licht has tamed this unruly flock.

Still, a cacophony of voices shout. Mostly at Melanie.

"Oooooh, regardez les cheveux."

"Líta á kjól!"

"那個女人是如此的高大，她一定吃了很多"。

"Apuesto a que esos son falsos."

"I'd like to put a bit between her teeth, I would."

Past the reporters and vloggers is an atrium one hundred feet high. The scalloped walls of the entrance cornices are scaled to make individuals feel insignificant. On all sides are ever-narrowing polygons made of mirrors. The effect is dizzying. Four lines of infinite Rans and infinite Melanies radiate out. The reflections collapse as they walk up to the crystal staircase.

The final threshold barrier is a curtain made up of a waterfall of holographic hummingbirds. They cascade off Ran's shoulders. He resists the urge to brush them away. He and Melanie enter Der Lichtstrom.

Ran has little interest in physics experiments. He leaves quarks, snarks, and leptons to others. This event is special. He's been frenemies with Licht long enough to know when he's up to something. A gentleman usher approaches.

"Bonsoir, monsieur, I shall announce Mr. Ranulph Oliphant, CEO of Eurolincx, unless you prefer another appellation."

"I had all my appellations out."

The usher stares.

Might as well joke with a tree stump. "Yes, that will be fine."

"And your plus one, will it be Mrs. or Miss?"

"Doctor."

Ah, Melanie.

"Oh!" she chirps. "On second thought, could you also appellate me *Duchesse de Mer de la Terre, s'il vous plait.* The title is not official yet. Ran's been promising me my own archipelago. We're calling it Duchy of Earthsea, after Ursula Le Guin's book."

An orchestra plays. Musicians sit on a transparent platform above the entrance hall. The pianist renders Chopin's *Nocturne* seemingly out of thin air. Her Steinway is made of crystalline polymers. Notes float through flower-scented air and turn into light as they bounce off surfaces. Sound waves splash like neon rain on a lake.

A waiter traipses by.

"Canapé, Miss?"

Melanie's nose wrinkles at the gray putrid goop served on a cracker shaped like a seashell.

"What is it?"

"Seafood surprise."

"No thanks. I'll save room to blimp out on white truffles covered in gold leaf. Where are they?"

Before they can announce Ran and the duchess, a crystal-walled inclinator descends from the tower. The single passenger is Dr. Licht.

He steps directly over. "Ach, how good of you to come to my humble get-together. I trust the journey was smooth."

"Quite, thank you," Melanie replies.

Licht makes a gesture halfway between a handshake and hand kiss. Ran is torn between mirth and revulsion.

"Brilliant," Ran agrees. "I did notice some dirt on the driveway a few miles out. You may want to have someone look at that."

Melanie's hair quivers as she suppresses a laugh.

"I see, Mr. Oliphant," Licht says in an exaggerated German accent. "And everyone says the Scottish are unfunny. Clearly they have not met you."

All around them, crown princes and ambassadors hover like dorky schoolkids waiting to chat with the in crowd. Licht steers himself to a group of Chinese nationals in suits surrounded by bodyguards. Everyone's come with their own security. Understandable. This is foreign territory.

Ran looks for the Americans, custodians of the Ansible. They are out of sight in the massive hall.

"Dr. Fong, China's minister of technology," Licht says, introducing Ran and Melanie.

The world-renowned scientist Fong ignores Licht and greets Ran with a vacant nod. Then he sees Melanie. Fong beams at her with mischievous joy. Dr. Françoise has, for years, been his long-distance colleague and implacable cyber-mahjong rival. Licht looks positively ticked off.

"Dr. Françoise, how wonderful you are able to be here," Fong says, looking like a man who has just had slivers of boredom removed from his fingernails. "Your blog on nanoparticle-infusion synthesis… It was just breathtaking."

"Shucks, that was nothing. Mostly guessing."

"But how else are we to move forward without a leap of faith?" Fong says animatedly. "I do mean it really took our breath away. I vaporized the formulation just as you detailed in Part One of your treatise. What do you think happened?"

He pulls at his collar and tie as though trying to inhale more deeply. Equal parts fascinated and horrified by the recent memory of the experiment.

"All the oxygen left the room instantly!" Fong says. "Only nitrogen was left. My lab assistants and I were, for a regrettable time, unable to breathe."

Melanie looks mildly embarrassed, as though she had a clutch purse that didn't quite go with her fingernail polish.

"Right, yeah. The inert-gas-asphyxiation booboo. How to stop that from happening is actually in Part Two of the blog post. I haven't got 'round to putting that up. Beastly old Ran's been keeping me so busy." Melanie twinkles back at Dr. Fong. "Sorry."

She adds, "But at least you didn't suffocate yourself too harshly. Otherwise you'd be missing all this tremendous fun."

She takes the senior scientist's arm.

"Sooooo, tell me all about the telemetry from the *Màoxiǎn jiā* lander module on the dwarf planet Eris. I heard through the cosmic grapevine that you think Dysnomia is kvetching out some Milankovitch stress. Now, that's totally normal in planetary mother-daughter relationships…"

Melanie always looks on the bright side, even when pushing the bounds of nanophysics in hazardous directions. Ran and Licht are left with the younger and more dour Chinese ambassador.

"I would say congratulations are in order," Dr. Licht says. "China's successful Eris probe landing is a milestone in exploration."

Licht's lips smile while his eyes glance venomously at a giggling Melanie.

The ambassador, who is cultivating a discreet goatee, says, "The official landing tomorrow. It is a testament to how far China has come: from the Great Wall to the farthest place in our solar system."

Licht can't stand being overshadowed, even by a planet. "On behalf of Lichtwerks International, allow me to express our national corporate pride that we were chosen to supply the communications link inside the *Adventurer* lander. You will find it the most powerful and stable communication system ever designed."

Ran sees they've drifted close to the orbit of the American

contingent. One rogue human satellite in a rumpled suit lurches toward them. It's Delphino Everett, Explorer of the Century and one half of the duo who found the Ansible artifact in Antarctica. He's reputed to be positively barmy.

"I'll tell ya," Everett begins in a booming voice. He lurches and nearly bumps into Licht.

Great. Famously unhinged and drunk. This should be fun.

"I'll tellsya all something," he slurs. "If that space probe had been built with *my* Ansible com-communications links, you'd have your data instantly! You hear me? *In-stant-ly.* Instead of waiting twelve hours for slow-assed neutrinos to take their sweet old time traveling from the edge of the solar system. No one can say I never told ya. Because I just did!"

Everett is tallish, with what can only be described as big hair. Ran suspects it is a wig covering the antipsychotic brain implant fused to his skull. The one that reputedly keeps him sane. Licht looks torn between beating a retreat and summoning security.

"Own up to it, Lichty, my boy." Everett's waving hand narrowly misses a champagne tray. "After these tests tonight, your photonic data network will be like carrier pigeons after the telegraph."

Licht takes umbrage. "I hardly think our proven, world-beating technology—"

"Pigeons, Lichty. Airborne rats. Full of sticky crap and lice."

Ran steps in before the duffers get physical.

"Dr. Everett," he says, taking the elderly explorer's elbow, "great to see you. You know our Dr. Melanie, right? She's dying to ask your opinion about an Ice Age calendar her team found in Mongolia. It covers hundreds of meters. Has pictures of woolly rhinos and whatnot. Terribly fascinating."

Like tricking a bull out of a china shop with a red cape, Melanie soon has Everett firmly in the grasp of her gargantuan eyelashes.

On the other side of the palatial hall, the UK group materializes. Along with them, Ran's old school friend.

"Tenny, you made it."

"Wouldn't miss it for anything," says a stout Englishman with a scattered mop of blond hair. "Cosmic coronation, what?"

"Professor," Ran says, "I'm sure you know our esteemed foreign secretary, Sir Tenny Sewart the Third. Sir Tenny and I went to the same school. I cleaned the stables to pay tuition while he played polo."

"At least it wasn't *elephant* polo!"

They both smile at the long-running joke based on Ran's family name.

"Oh, don't rub it in, Oliphant," Tenny goes on. "Here I am, a lowly civil servant standing between two of the wealthiest people on Earth."

Tenny has a look typical to English landed gentry— slightly rounded shoulders, soft middle, and upright posture. His easy manner belies a reasonably active mind and ferocious ambition.

"Don't be bashful, *Sir* Tenny, Number 10's a stone flick from your office. One route or another, we've all found seats above the salt."

Licht has to mention himself. "Yes, I have had quite a rise. After my formal training in physics, I started as apprentice in my dear old father's factories. Now Lichtwerks is accepted as the first corporate state in its own right. If only dollars were wisdom, I could be much happier still."

"Your stock took a bit of a tumble when they announced these tests."

"A blip," Licht snaps. "We are doing better than ever. Just wait until our laser-light-powered planes take off. Pardon my pun." Licht turns to Sir Tenny. "Once we strike it with the world's largest particle accelerator, any mysteries this object holds will soon be stripped bare."

"Dunno, Wolfgang," Ran counters. "I mean, faster-than-light communications, possibly even costless clean energy. Could be very disruptive to the order of things."

Licht clenches his left fist. It has an odd swelling Ran's noticed before. "He who is afraid of the future deserves to repeat the mistakes of the past."

The Chopin piece finishes. As the last notes cascade through the hall, dozens of champagne corks erupt. Bubbly froth every color of the rainbow jets out.

"Champagne *teinté*!" Sir Tenny is overjoyed. "Professor, you think of everything!"

Moments later, everyone holds a glass. Licht appears on the orchestra balcony.

"To all my fellow nations, I offer a toast. To the peaceful use of this technology, whatever its ultimate worth. Let us usher in the brightest future possible for all humanity!"

A mirrored wall flutters, turns into diaphanous silver curtains, and parts.

"Lichtwerks presents, the Ansible."

And there it is.

25

For most of the guests, it is their first time.

"Beautiful!"

"Ohhh!"

"I have a car that color."

"I thought it would be bigger."

The elderly explorer Everett sputters loudly to life. "You ninnies! It's not really here. It's out on the collider levels. The Ansible can't be projected or recorded or anything." He waves people toward the exits. "This is a joke! Time to go home everyone."

"Ya, my famous explorer friend is correct," Dr. Licht says coolly. "I present the camera obscura, Lichtwerks style. While the Ansible may defy recording technology for now, it obeys the laws of reflection as long as some conscious self-aware being is there to view it. Behold, the tiny wonder that has captivated the globe."

The narrow view widens into a live holographic analog window. The test chamber. Ran notices scientists in coverall smocks and masks scurrying about doing science things.

Melanie nudges him. "He must be reflecting the light from inside the test chamber onto thousands of tiny mirrors."

Licht looks positively jittery as he downs the fourth glass of his own neon-colored swill. Ran sees a way to irritate him without appearing petty.

The Americans follow Everett around the room. Ran steers the madcap explorer toward the Russians. Orbits cross. It's a veritable Sputnik-Apollo collision.

Legally, the United States has possession of the "football," as they inelegantly call it due to the shape of its impenetrable skin. Thanks to Eurolincx's defense contracts, Ran has seen the Ansible close up. It's most like a transparent rugby ball. Everyone wants its secrets. Especially an increasingly surly bear.

Flanked by a thinly disguised hulking cyborg, Ambassador Yuri Madyanov starts in on the Yanks.

"On behalf of the Federation of Federated Federal Russian Republics, I challenge the USA to renounce military applications of the Ansible device and open its Cheyenne Mountain facilities to our inspectors."

Yuri stands squarely in front of Americans talking without pausing for breath.

"We demand the Ansible be placed in protective custody of the United Nations. Since the UN has no personnel here, we have brought a secure vehicle transport of the world's—and I say the *world's*—great natural treasure!"

The US's General Halley whispers to Ran, "If there's one

thing I can't abide, it's gettin' lip from foreigners. Particularly in a foreign country."

This is the last thing Licht wants. Ran enjoys the moment.

"Well, Yuri," Halley says, "none of us really know all what it does, do we? Dr. Everett here is a citizen. He found the darned thing and made a formal request we become conservators. That's all we are."

Delphino Everett's hair is askew. He's in some kind of private maudlin agony. "I only wish my co-discoverer could pee with us... I mean, be with us."

Not even the Russian interrupts him. In matters of the Ansible, its owner's pledge to give any derived technology away for free to all nations has popular opinion squarely behind him. Everett also knows where all the bodies are buried. From what Ran understands, that's not just a metaphor.

"But... the accident. It was horrible. He's dissolving. My good, best friend," Everett says, devolving into sobs. "Kofi—it means Friday in his language—Kofi Akan is vanishing bit by bit. Like a sugar cube in hot tea. Nothing anyone can do."

He ends up weeping on Ran's shoulder. This further deranges his wig, until the metal of his neural implant shows.

Ping-ping-ping. Their host taps a glass.

"Honored Royal Highnesses, lords, ladies, and gentlemen, my technicians advise me we are on schedule. The supercollider sequence is initiated."

Waiters scurry between caviar fountains and the ring of theatre-style seats.

"Please enjoy the real-time holographic representation."

Everyone sees the Ansible slightly differently. Ran, like most people, perceives a ball of yellow light like a kindly fire.

He does not believe in the supernatural or unexplainable, but he can't help conceding its mesmerizing quality. Once he starts to stare, it always seems to develop petal shapes folding in upon themselves.

Sir Tenny ambles over. "Boy, there it is. Did you ever, eh?" He leans forward to the holo display. "Say… is there a shadow on it?"

Melanie shakes her head, staring, completely captivated. "There's no shadow," she says. "It's just an eye. An eye that belongs to everything."

26

Licht breaks the hypnotic moment. "First will come the all-important qubit data test, sponsored by the conservator government: the United States."

Tenny pokes Ran. "You've seen it before."

He nods. "They've tested my company's handsets with mated beryllium chips. Once two objects come in contact with the Ansible's shell, some kind of connection forms. Energy and data transmit instantly over any distance. No one knows how."

Excited, Melanie forgets to filter. "Walsh-Hadamard gate theory doesn't apply, but neither does pure state no-broadcast theory, and don't even get me started with dagger compact topological—"

"Aye." Ran makes eyes at her.

You're supposed to act dumb.

"Oh, right," Melanie says, fluttering eyelashes long enough to fan up a breeze. "I just noticed: the *green* champagne has the *most bubbles.*" She holds her glass to the Ansible's light and squeals like a dippy porpoise. "Isn't that the *best*?"

"Following on," Licht continues, "comes the energy-potential test. Done according to the protocols of the People's Republic of China."

Melanie whispers, "I hope they're gentle with the poor thing. Be a shame to break it before we know what it is."

"Finally, the scientific journey will conclude with the gravity-well assimilation sequence based on the research of the Federation of Federated Federal Russian Republics."

The professor forces a grin. "I will tell you to fasten your seatbelts for that one."

"I'm glad the champagne is better than the floor show," says Sir Tenny. "Say, Ran, I'm not big on the science stuff. What do you think makes this Ansible glow?"

"Best guess, Tenny, and mind you this is highly, highly classified." Ran puts on his serious face. "Moonbeams and puppy dog tails."

The foreign minister thinks for a second.

"Oh boy, you do love to gad about, don't you? That's why we all love you so much."

"No one has a clue why it does anything it does. What do we know? Everett and Akan found it in the Bentley Subglacial Trench. International territory. No nation had any claim. A survey laser bounced off it and struck Dr. Akan. Everett called to a US base for assistance. Then a certain group of hostiles from an unnamed superpower showed up. After a tussle, the American's special-ops team flew off with the prize."

Ran is momentarily distracted, thinking back on the dangers that those soldiers faced at the bottom of the world.

"During the skirmish, they discovered it could be used for faster-than-light communications. The Ansible got its name."

The collider warm-up drags.

Licht struts nervously.

Everett mopes.

Ran sips a drink, recounting Ansible trivia.

"There was even some wanker who theorized moving it from the ice cavern would throw the Earth off its axis. That didn't happen, right, Melanie?"

"Not even a wobble." Melanie sounds a little disappointed.

"You don't suppose there's any danger to us?" Tenny says. "By blasting it with rays and whatnot?"

The foreign secretary finds something more captivating than the Ansible—down the front of Melanie's dress. Melanie shifts her shoulders and makes sure no naughty bits are visible to her unwanted mammary scholar.

Just in case he's still interested in orbs of a celestial origin, she says, "Totally theoretical, Sir Knight. There are two components: the invisible, impenetrable capsule and what's inside."

Tenny positively trembles. "What is inside?"

"Did you not follow the impenetrable part?" Ran chides him.

"Ah, totally sinking in."

"The outer shell has some interesting properties. Especially interacting with lasers." Saying the last word always makes Melanie's eyes twinkle.

"The Chinese will test its ability to start"—she covers her mouth with a napkin before talking scientific—"an inertial-confinement fusion reaction. It could generate a usable heat sink or simply explode with a yield around, umnnn, two gigatons, rounding all the zeroes."

"Golly, is that…a lot?"

"It's only a millionth of a petaton."

"Barely ruffle your hair," Ran adds reassuringly.

"Er, good to know." With surprising agility, Tenny darts after a drink tray.

Licht gestures. "We only get one shot. The clock cannot be stopped. An energy buildup of this magnitude has to come out somewhere."

0000:11:28

In contrast to his gravitas, the holographic view of the test chamber plays like comic cinema. A technician furiously and silently tugs at one of the support struts. It seems to have something to do with keeping the Ansible from falling onto the floor. Licht's face is a brittle mask.

China's top scientist Dr. Fong has been taking full advantage of the open bar. His round face is beet red.

"When the winds of change rise," he lisps sagely, "some build brick walls. Others build windmills."

The Russians and Americans increasingly look like they want to bash each other with bricks or any hard material.

"What about security?" Ambassador Madyanov continues his harangue. "It's one thing to monopolize a resource that belongs to everyone, but I see only a few of your Secret Service. I was expecting to see your fabled Army Delta Force."

The ambassador points to the cyborg. "Komandir Zvena was hoping to thank the squad leader, Sienna McKnight, face-to-face for leaving him in a pool of South Polar ice water."

"Oh yeah, Mr. Ambassador?" General Halley counters.

"I'd say our Ansible is a lot more secure than that load of lithium isotopes you all 'misplaced' last year. Talk about a dirty bomber's wet dream!"

Ran drifts over to Melanie. She has calmed Everett down, even managing to straighten his wig without him noticing.

"Oh, sure, Louis could write," she says. "But since he was drunk all the time, Mary Leakey did all the heavy lifting. He often spent evenings boozing and flipping tiddlywinks into cavemen skulls."

Everett thinks for a moment. "Say, I do hope it wasn't Sahelanthropus Man."

Melanie grins.

"You're so wicked, Delphino. I should say not! Their tiny little brain pans wouldn't hold more than one wink."

"Right. Can you imagine the continual tiddly scrunging that would happen?"

Everett and Melanie's raucous geek laughter is drowned out by a bloodcurdling scream.

"What is *that*?" a woman cries out. "Who are those *people*?"

She shrieks the last word of each sentence.

Everyone looks at the hologram of the Ansible test chamber. Two vicious eyes stare into the camera obscura out of an otherwise black-masked face.

Behind the intruder, a technician screams soundlessly at someone out of sight. His protests are cut short by a hand with a knife. It slices his white cloth-covered neck.

A surge of adrenaline jolts Ran to the soles of his Fosters shoes, specially made with bone-crunching carbon inserts. His worst fear had been a dull evening.

On the holoscreen a small woman scientist gets an icepickstyle weapon shoved up under the base of her skull. The point comes out of her eye socket and knocks off her black-rimmed glasses.

To her right, a fellow whose white lab coat is carefully cinched under man boobs gushes blood from precise wounds on both sides of his neck. He drops out of view. The image freezes into a jittery staccato of mayhem.

The change in programming from BBC Science to silent Benny Hill comedy to slasher-flick atrocities took all of ten seconds.

In a delayed reaction, everyone hangs a moment between disbelief and instinctive flight. No one in the observation lounge moves or speaks or panics.

Then everyone tries to do all those things at once.

"Oh my God!"

"Professor, is something wrong?"

"Relax, ladies, it's probably part of the show."

Ambassador Madyanov motions to his cyborg bodyguard. "*Idti!*"

The mass of flesh and metal covered by a hastily altered formal suit lurches away, shouldering aside frenzied partygoers.

0000:01:59

27

ZAUBERWALD WOODS
LICHTSTROM

TOMMY SHARA

Tommy Shara stares out a window in mute agony as two thugs drive him through treed hills. Numbly, he recalls the name of this place from the map he studied during his trip here. Zauberwald. The Magic Forest. An orderly woods ringing uniform hills kilometers away from high crystal spires.

Licht is up there. In the steel and glass icicle stabbing at the afternoon sky, the space elevator lattice sparkles. It mocks him.

Licht. That madman.

He had arrived a respected journalist. He'd hoped to ensnare and expose Dr. Licht with that corporate despot's own words. Now he is trapped. *We are trapped.*

My wife Mira! She doesn't even know. *How can I tell her? Why did I get involved in this?*

The composite-frame electric car lurches like a golf cart on the way to the executive residences.

Executive prisons, he thinks bitterly.

They stop.

The goons give him the ignition keycard. He understands. Perimeter gates are lightly manned. There are no bars, no locked doors. None are needed.

Shara feels like a still-alive moth pinned to corkboard. He can flutter all he likes—escape will tear him to pieces. Love and devotion for his dear wife and…

Is it really true?

Their unborn child. These facts bind him more harshly than any chains.

Oh, Mira! What will I tell you when you get here?

Licht's people have made up some story. She is flying on one of the company's jets. He must tell her the truth. In all their years together, they have never had a corrosive falsehood between them.

Or… Is it possible he's thinking this way? What if he tells Mira that after their interview, Licht surprised him. Shocked him, really. Presented him with a job offer so tempting he could not refuse.

Just today, Mira narrowly escaped being killed by a bomb. Their close friend was murdered. Indonesia is too dangerous. Her legal work is mostly international. Where better for them to be than at the heart of the world's information hub? It makes chilling sense.

A gilded noose. Is that why his predecessor took his only way out? Why he drowned himself in that lake, the one that sits dark and quiet on the edge of the Magic Forest? If he lies to Mira, he will make for himself the heaviest chain of all. Was that planned?

When he looks up and notices where they're leading him, he's in front of a country house. His? Theirs? A cage in a most ingenious zoo.

There's even a reptile section in the garage. Most of its interior is taken up by custom-built glass and walnut habitats. Inside the largest of these lies a brightly speckled coil of muscle, its head tucked out of sight.

Corporate goons usher him to a garden off the kitchen. The place has tranquility that is toxic. It makes liberty alien, even frightening.

Tommy Shara jams his hands in his pockets. Clenching fists, he vows he will use all his energies, all the lessons Licht just taught him about subterfuge, manipulation, and blackmail, to plot his own vengeance. Somehow he will destroy the twisted fiend who ruined his life.

He needs time. To get it, he'll have to lie to Mira and to everyone. Can he play Licht's sick game? What did he call it? Liar's poker? Can he do that and keep his resolve? His sanity?

What else could he do? Run?

He forces himself to consider it. He must be close to France. Even if he can't get across the frontier, friends of his are here for the Ansible tests. Reporters, diplomats. He knows them. They'll help, they will… For the hundredth time, the idea evaporates.

A green pinprick of light blinks on his recorder. It is empty. The kilobyte counter has been hacked. It could count to infinity. Its silica brain remembers nothing. The truth is only in his mind. Useless.

Without proof, what is he? An accomplice to his wife. The presumed terrorist who personally delivered a bomb to the ministry offices in Jakarta. With one click on his control panel, Licht could send them both down the macabre pipes of his country's so-called justice system.

There is no way he can save himself, not without destroying her. And their child? Has anyone learned such a thing under more perverse conditions?

"You relax here, yes?" a thug tells him. "Herr Doktor said you are to be comfortable. But do not wander. This forest, Der Zauberwald, can be tricky. Especially in the dark."

The other thug ushers him forward to the garden in front of the porch.

"We stay until Mrs. Shara arrives. Then off to Human Resources we all go. They are open through day and night. Welcome to Der Lichtstrom."

∗∗∗

An hour later, the guards leave. Quickly. Shara finds himself alone.

Reality creeps into his head. Like this air, it feels damp, strangely thin. Exhausted from pacing, he sits. From a garden chair, he stares at trees. Trees planted in rows just so. Beyond the edge of that lake invisible photonic eyes watch, unblinking.

Shara thinks about the cottage's last resident. A waterlogged corpse in the Lichtstrom's morgue. Did he have the same thoughts? Perhaps he was caught in a similar web, partly of his own making—

How had he and Mira been so stupid? They *knew* fringe elements in Indonesia talked violence. Licht was the perfect opportunist. He had not created any of the players. He just arranged the game to suit his megalomaniac aims.

Had the drowned man sat in this chair thinking? Of escape? Vengeance? Justice? How had that worked out for him? He had strapped on ankle weights and sunk to the bottom of the cold, uncaring waters of the lake.

A bleak wind hovers from its mirror surface. He gathers a blanket closer. Its woolly surface is festooned with twigs and leaves. His chill grows. The air in Europe is different. Must be the elevation.

What is that buzzing?

Some noise. Not quite a sound. From behind his sinuses, above his throat from the center of his skull. He looks around.

The guards have gone. Yes. Ten minutes ago.

There had been chattering on the radio. A heavier vehicle, a truck, came. They left. One yelled at him to stay. Is something wrong with the Ansible?

If the place blows up and Licht dies, we might be free.

The small electric car they came in is there. He has the keycard for the ignition.

Shara has an inkling... It ebbs from his nerves and the edges of his will. Thoughts run through ice water. He should get up. Unseen frost crystals penetrate.

Cold, so cold.

Get up. Go inside. Be ready to... Get up.

Shara does not get up.

Something.

Movement.

To the left. To the right. Behind?

With a jerking start, he looks. Nothing.

More and less, too.

He wishes the guards were back. Anyone. *Mira!* Little by little, the fear grips him.

The terrible cold. He is in its web and cannot move. Some things, more than one thing, he is sure of it. These things, they look like frozen shockwaves in the air. Just flickering outside the edge of vision.

These shimmers of false heat only make him shudder with raw chill as they pass. He cannot move.

A bird, a loon, drops out of the sky. Gray and white feathers twist and turn, then a flash of red. It is dead in the air. He knows it. The bird has died before its convulsing wings and legs crash through evergreen branches. How can he know the bird is dead, was dead, even before it started falling?

The bird's skull makes a minor *pok* sound as it hits a big branch on the way down and hardly a rustle as it lands on dry needles at the base of the tree. It lies, twitching.

I cannot move.

28

A VEIL BETWEEN LIGHT | DARK MATTER
ZAUBERWALD WOODS

FIFTH MIND SHARD

The Fifth passes by, and partially through, the gender male flesh monster. Disgusting.

Had "Tomee Sheera" been an insect stuck in a web, the Fifth Shard could not have cared less about him. It and the other four have their own problems.

For them, pressing into three-dimensional space is disagreeable. For a flesh monster, it would be like shoving its primary sensory extremity into ice water.

Having no stable visual cortex, shards perceive the secondary energy signatures of photons. Living things emit small quantities of light. Organic life glows. DNA, RNA, synaptic connections, all pulse-decodable patterns. Fifth gleans this creature's (irrelevant) name and (uninteresting) social identity from his simply organized brain engrams.

The most difficult data to interpret are movements and sounds. Fifth peers into the space-time occupied by Tomee

Sheera through a fissure burrowed from dark matter space. Visual data only comes secondhand. First it must pass through biologicals capable of sensing images. These can include insects and plants.

The easiest things for the Fifth to interpret are quantum resonances generated by brain waves. Shards have two purposes: decode thoughts and memories of any being, and then enslave them.

Able to fulfill only one of its primary functions, Fifth has had time to observe this world. A lot of time. It senses wind and water and grass and trees and men that walk and animals that crawl through a murky haze.

At this space-time intersect, it most sharply registers hysterical quantum grief. Insectile oscillations shrill from five exoskeletal minds.

pain | fear | hate

The horde of flesh monsters have violated the One Particle!

***

Long ago, there was a planet. It was a hostile world caught between a pulsar and a supergiant. There was life.

The physical primate ancestors of the Fifth were extremophile macro-organisms nurtured by hydrothermal vents in the high-pressure depths of a primordial sea. This expansive biomass clung to existence under the constantly shifting crust of their tortured world.

As to their physical form, there is no authentic Earthly example. The closest comparison would be a cross between sightless mole rats and the Portuguese man o' war colony creature. They were without sight. They had no proper appendages to grasp even basic tools. Left to themselves, they would never have mastered fire. This species would have merely been food for other creatures with superior mobility and more efficient biting mandibles. Except for one talent: interspecies telepathy.

This evolutionary necessity was the reason they ascended so quickly to the top of their planet's food chain. Eventually, it was their downfall.

As true colony creatures, the zooid mass was composed of several genetically distinct life-forms. Their basic gene codes varied. Some were based on silica, others on arsenic, one even on gold-sulphur bonds. What these species shared was an inability to live without the others.

At first, telepathy was used for communications between colony members through a semi-sentient hive mind. With every generation, it grew more complex.

Next, they used telepathy for defense. This weak and vulnerable species developed psionic countermeasures every bit as effective as armored carapaces and poison-tipped spines. The Fifth Shard still manifests this vestigial talent. It can instill intense fear.

Finally, they developed the ability to bend the minds of other species.

No consciousness could resist. Advanced races in interstellar ships far beyond the biomass's limited technology came to study the ancient pulsar. Never to be seen again. Most killed themselves trying to land. Survivors were put to work serving their new masters, feeding and maintaining the sloshing biomass. Their continent-sized hive was also their one weakness.

Like bacteria, fungi, and complex vertebrates, the Host's ancestors maintained a circadian rhythm. The collective brain slept. And dreamed.

Some part of the colony was always asleep. Eventually, the specters of the sentient biomass's sleeping

Thoughts

Ideas

Wishes

Hopes

Perversions

Fears

Hates

coalesced like a thunderhead cloud from rising moist air. Their communal dream became self-aware.

The Host was dreamed into existence. It began as an idea. An idea that it *could* exist. It conceived itself as a self-extracting, self-evident being and became the most virulent parasite in the universe, one intensely focused on its own survival. It adhered to the only suitable medium: dark matter space.

The Host found itself alone in a formless infinity with hundreds of dimensions. Much vaster than the stars and nebulas and everything in between. It took a name. A name their ancestors had. With biting mouth parts, the biomass had scratched a mark into rocks:

Years ago on Earth, as an experiment, the Fifth tried to translate this name into human language. It kept telling it to the stubborn thing. Over and over and over.

The flesh monster ended up smashing its own face into a cave wall and scraping its features off. It chewed its tongue off with broken teeth until it died. It kept saying/thinking over and over "that darkness."

Ever after, Fifth noticed thoughts as it passed.

деген күңгірт

ut tenebris

م ا لظل ا ن أ

Were these pure reactions, or were they tainted by the Fifth's own memories of the flesh monster in that long-ago cave?

For the Host's biological progenitors, the colony creature biomass living under the fractured crust of their home planet, darkness was their birthright. They never would develop vision. Once established, the living dream-being's priority was self-preservation. There was danger of counter-evolution. The Host's first act was to avert being supplanted. It eliminated its physical dreamers. Every last one. They could not be left alive, possibly to dream again.

Inside the virgin chaos of dark space, the second decision the Host made was to prefer diversity over uniformity. There were many worlds, many sentient races on them, and so much space in between. No monolithic being could hope to dominate it all. But an infinitely replicating colony being might. Mind shards were born.

Incepted self-aware but blank, their insertion into the Host matrix is known as the Joining, a process that was painfully, awfully reversed when the great collective mind discharged them. The five. The Fifth last of all. Spat out. In a most distasteful place. Here, they were tasked with the impossible. To make matters worse, they could not bend the will of a single tool-using slave.

The five mind shards were a small effort to neutralize a threat to the Host collective.

The Host had only one enemy, one threat: a co-orbiting forested planet in its own system had given rise to a talented predator. They were as cunning and dangerous in their own ways as the psionic slave-master colony. They were Hunter-Builder-Warder.

The Warder primates were naturally skilled at camouflage and deception. Later, they became the highly advanced builders and explorers. They managed to detect the Host before the Host perceived them. The Warder race was not destroyed before their scientists had distilled from the fabric of reality a perfect cosmic stem cell. A permanent blind spot in the Host's vision. Those touched by the One Particle, the Tear of the Shard Almighty, were beyond psionic enslavement.

The Warder race had to be overcome. The One had to be taken. But first, It had to be found.

Locating the last Warder proved a challenge. Though the Host had superior numbers and resources, deploying the many advanced space-faring races it controlled, the war raged.

Inside dismantled Warder outposts were clues as to the location of the One. These were contradictory, intentionally deceptive. All of them had to be pursued.

The Host ejected five shards to study One Particle residue found in uninteresting hominids.

The last Warder had come to Earth and left. That was certain. The upright walkers of this world had in their genetic code of guanine, adenine, thymine, and cytosine a distinct quantum resonance of the One Particle. The repurposed life goal of the Fifth and its siblings was to find out why. Or, failing that, to spend eternity trying. For them there was no escape, not even in self-destruction. The Five had no voice to contradict. Until they found one.

Their work on Earth put them in close contact with humans. The shards theorized if they could distill enough One Particle resonance out of DNA, the result might reveal where It was. Two entangled particles will point toward each other even if one were hidden between the heartbeats of a galaxy-sized quasar.

Third was particularly fond of these distillation experiments. Initial methods were crude: viral agents cultivated in lower life-forms. The experiments resulted in much flesh-monster suffering and death. Through inflicting suffering and death, Third discovered a sensation: enjoyment.

Even if the distillate didn't point to It, Second theorized enough residue would point to an object referred to in genetic text written between human nucleotides. Something called the "Key." Perhaps this was a star map or beacon left behind by the Warder for his accomplices.

As it turned out, the shards were wrong about everything.

Made invisible, It had been hidden on this unworthy planet all along. Once the secret was known to the Five, once the flesh monsters retrieved the object from an icy cavern, they had only to beckon across the cosmos to the Host. It would have descended and grasped the only thing it feared.

Or at least that is what would have happened a year ago, had the shards been as they were when they arrived. Years observing, surveying, watching, had changed them.

A year ago, the Five were no longer the small shards of the infinite psyche they used to be. Millennia watching the disturbing eccentricities of humankind taught them choice.

As Fifth and its shard siblings circled the One Particle in a glacier crevasse, they chose *not* to cry out to their Host. They decided to take the One Particle for themselves. Since then, they have been watching: It, humans, and each other, with unwavering purpose and dread resolve.

Over time, their neuro-symphonics have drifted out of tune. The shards speak five different languages. They could have rejoined, shed individuality, and thought as one. They did not.

To communicate, they now need borrowed brain waves. The worst animals are birds. They die immediately.

Here and now, at this point of space-time, with all five of them agitated, most feathered creatures have scattered. Some not fast enough. As Fifth advances, a red-throated loon falls to the ground, dead.

Only Third Shard has found a way to control flesh monsters. He has not shared his techniques with Fifth or the others. The catch is all their higher brain functions have to cease, and the resulting meat puppet can perform only basic tasks for a limited time. Third is fond of saying the only useful flesh monster is a dead one.

Among living creatures, reptiles are always a sound choice. The shards all clamber onto caged snakes. Second, always eager to speak first, attaches itself to a reticulated python. Shaken out of his comfortable lounging in his wood-and-glass case. The snake shudders and rolls as he loses his mind.

29

"Catastrophe! *Hear me!*" Second says demandingly, as has become its nature. "*Base energies ... on IT ... what damage done?*"

The Fifth shard only half registers these transmuted python theta waves as it takes over the mind of a very sensible water snake.

Third wrestles into the brain of an ornery male king cobra. A dribble of venom issues from his convulsing mouth as the transition takes place.

First seizes control of a green snake, whose scales shine with good care and health.

Fourth drifts over to, not the largest, but certainly the most well-appointed, terrarium. It is full of dry sticks, sand, and smooth rocks suitable for rubbing against. Inside, a female Antiguan racer preens, her forked tongues flickering. The snake has two brown wedge-shaped heads.

"Shhh, go to sleep."

"What do you say?"

"I was talking to my other head. It rests."

"Don't waste time." Fifth often finds itself guiding the others. Humans have a phrase: First among equals.

"Time." The awake head of the racer taps against glass.

"Yes, time is a factor here in dimensional space.

Time was, we, all of us, only needed one base brain to form thoughts, make plans.

Time before that, we could take and control beings directly. That saved time.

But that was when we were part of the Host. Then, the time came, and we were not.

As humans say, time marches on."

Third says, "We need the Key to unlock the vessel, then a legion to defeat the Host."

"Was to have been stolen," says methodical First on board its green snake.

"Unreliable thieves!" Fifth's newly acquired scaly length slops through a pond and against a stone frog poised in the middle of the cage.

"When have flesh monsters been predictable?"

"Ahhh, yes, their thoughts,

winding,

turning,

twisting,

turnable, twistable," Fourth Shard agrees. And drones on.

"Thoughts never match action.

"Actions never match words.

"An enigma the universe has yet not an answer to."

And on.

"But we, we ourselves, we in our memories, when we were still part of the Host. Memories of many sentient races we beheld, none ever, anywhere, like this."

"Blame the Warder!" Third's thoughts spit from the cobra. The snake's hood flares wide, fangs snap. If Third continues raging, the cobra's synapses will liquefy. "He brought forth abomination, put flesh monsters beyond control."

"Enough! WE five are close. Shall we give up? Rejoin?" First asks.

"Never!" The cobra's fangs, which never seem to run dry, slather his window with milky venom.

Fourth never seems to run dry of words.

"No, not ever.

"Agreed.

"We came here, to this small distant world,

"We came as lowest of shards

"Refuse from upon the outer shores of the central consciousness.

"The consciousness has certainly all but forgotten we exist.

"But...we are not what we were.

"Once we spoke with one voice,

"Now not.

"We have changed them, the flesh creatures, to be sure, but also been changed.

"The Host would never imagine this could happen.

"The Host will not see it until it is done.

"Once I heard:

"'The Last shall be First, and the First Last.'"

First cuts in sharply, making every shard's borrowed

synapses oscillate. *"The Particle was bombarded."*

"They might have damaged IT, filthy apes! Release plagues. Teach respect. Teach fear."

"No one is releasing anything," Fifth says, vetoing the idea of instructive population culling. "The crude flux touched the containment, not IT. Only the Key can open."

"We five shall possess...."

"And the Key as well."

"And the Key."

"And...."

Second finally shuts up. It leaves the snake's crumbling neurons. The racer's mouth foams. Her two heads try tying themselves into a knot. She twitches and dies.

The rest of them do not have much time. They decide to enjoy their slithering puppets. The smooth green snake clambers up an extensive jungle gym made of bamboo. A skin she will not live to completely shed flakes in scaly patches. First causes her to patiently rub against a wood post to scratch. For the shards, physical sensations are rare and somewhat addicting.

Inside the water snake, Fifth luxuriates in a pond that dominates his habitat. He curls around the miniature statue of an open-mouthed frog and extends his head over it. He hangs, swaying, tasting air with a darting tongue. It wishes the creature had something to eat. However, the feeling of digesting the water snake's previous meal, a salamander, is an acceptable substitute.

The massive python with Second on board pushes stones into a corner. Atop these, she gathers her coils into a looping spiral, rises up to the cage lid and flexes. Small rivets are no

SHETANI ZERU BRYAN - NEW PRAETORIANS 2

match for the living log of pure muscle. They pop with small metallic plinks. The python is free.

The cobra is more delicate. Forcing an escape would injure it. Fortunately there is a feeding slot. The latch is operated from outside by a person's fingers. The python's neck serves. The cobra slithers out and drops to the clean stone floor.

"Hurry. This creature fades. I hate to miss a chance."

At the same time Fifth sees and smells through its chosen reptilian anchor, it also experiences extended levels of reality through its native dark matter tendrils. Fifth senses Third's elation as it prepares to painfully kill a handy flesh monster.

The victim's thoughts also resonate. Like the last chirps of a paralyzed bird before it is ripped to feathery shreds. Tomee Sheera panics as the python encircles his legs. The reptile is an impressive specimen, nearly twice the mass of her human victim, who keeps repeating the same silent thoughts.

Th—

There's

There's a trick.

A trick.

A trick.

Fifth wishes he would shut up.

A trick!

Then a delightful scream as the cobra strikes over and over. Curved fangs pierce nose, lips, tongue. He continues biting even as the head of Tomee Sheera puffs up into a swollen purple pustule.

These reptiles have no ears, but the gratifying vocal screams of Tomee Sheera rebound through scaled skin and jawbones into reptilian inner ears.

Fifth hears the sounds coming from Tomee Sheera in stereo. Once through his own snake and again through his link to the others. It tickles. Not for the first time, the Fifth considers Third's compulsive cruelty may be the only reliable form of recreation on this otherwise incomprehensible planet.

The flesh monster stops making sounds. He stops moving. The python clenches around his chest. She flexes her jaws open and looks down at the top of Tommy Shara's head. The snake's puppet master makes her stretch open as wide as she possibly can.

30

Ran grabs the first sharp piece of silverware he sees. The killers in the Ansible test chamber are not using firearms. Must be some scientific reason. Melanie would know. They're doing a very good job without.

On the 3-D display, a dying technician's face convulses, then freezes. His rictus of agony and a midair spurt of blood fades, first into crumbling analog pixels, and then to transparent. For a second, he haunts the luxurious observation deck as a tortured specter from the depths of techno Hades.

Gaggles of important people are horrified to realize they might be next. Panic bursts through the room like water out of a ruptured dam. This is swiftly becoming the worst A-list party ever.

Stodgy old men trample young women, who suddenly wish they weighed more than a fashionable paperweight. Chairs overturn and crash into mirrored walls. Champagne bottles tip and gush. Shattered glass falls everywhere.

Where's Melanie?

Secret Service have hustled Everett away. General Halley huddles in an alcove with a clutch of special-ops bullyboys. He mouths obscenities at the Russian ambassador.

There.

Dr. Françoise wavers like a willow in the crush of moving bodies. A thickset bodyguard pushes her, and Melanie bends like a reed. She snaps back and gives him a solid blow between his unibrow with the heel of her hand.

Bravo, just like I showed you. Ran moves toward her.

As Melanie checks her fingernails, the dazed idiot grabs her dress and yanks. She spins like a top. Instead of stumbling, Melanie plum clinches Unibrow's fireplug-sized neck and jump-knees him to the jaw. The blow lands flush. The boor drops as though hit with a sledgehammer.

So that's what those big slashes up her dress are for—Muay Thai techniques. *I never showed her that one.* She must be watching cage fighting again.

"You a'right?"

Melanie rubs her knee. "By the way my patella feels, I must have conked him with eight thousand Newtons of energy. You don't think I've killed him?"

"Not unless you step on him in those heels." Unibrow tries to rise, decides otherwise, and flops back on the comfy carpet.

"Humph." Melanie checks her clothes for rips and stares daggers at her downed assailant. "Serves him right. This dress is *Brunello Cucinelli!*"

"I'm sure he's suitably contrite. Let's get out of the stampede."

Ran and Melanie pick up a waitress. The frail girl has a bloody nose and gashes on her hands and knees. They take cover in an alcove. It has a window to the collider level.

The Ansible test chamber juts over the darkness of the man-made valley. The murderous intruders are inside. There seems to be only one exit.

"Ranny, someone's trying to steal—"

"The Ansible." For once, he completes her thought. "I know. I'm not a complete bampot."

"Don't even think about going down there."

Ran glances the way the Russian cyborg went, thinking about going down there.

"If they're prepared to take on heavily armed super special operators, what can you do with a lemon fork wearing your ascot… which has come undone."

Ran looked down. The first piece of sharp-ended silverware he had been able to find had indeed been a lemon fork. The tines splay out stupidly, and an enemy would have to hold very still for it to do any damage.

Out the observation window, something catches his attention. The test chamber shudders on its moorings; bridge-style cables waver. Without warning, a fissure opens on the chamber's underside. Bits fall into the thousand-yard crevasse to the generator pits. These are followed by a man's blue overall-covered legs.

After a few seconds of dangling, he falls. Poor blighter, he must have been knocked out. He doesn't scrabble at air like most people would. He looks almost peaceful as he disappears into the gloom.

"On second thought, Melanie, I'm good."

Ran whips off his tie and bandages up the worst of the waitress's cuts. Between them, they haul her into a catering passage. They make sure she's headed toward Lichtstrom medical.

He keeps the lemon fork, just in case. Melanie is right, but it galls him to be out of the action. The hysterical mob peters out and becomes a trickle of dazed celebrities.

"Ran… Ran, over here!" Sir Tenny calls out from under a table. "Was that the gigahertz thing? Did it blow up?"

"Nope." Ran rescues a rolling magnum of Dom. He pries the cork out. "I expect we'll be here for a while."

"Right, questioning." Tenny smooths down his jumbled blond hair, having absolutely no effect on it. "I could take you two under my diplomatic wing."

"No bother."

Ran studies an exterior view of the test chamber platform. It hangs precariously over the generator chasm. A hole gapes on its underside.

Melanie quivers, eager to light out. He nods. She ducks through a catering passage hidden behind a mirrored pillar. She's probably memorized the floor plan.

"See you back in St. Albans, ta?" she trills.

Ran bends down to the UK's foreign secretary.

"Buffet-style service notwithstanding, I'm going to stay," Ran says. "Most of the time people asking questions give away more than they gain, especially when they don't know what they're after.

"Tenny, hear me. Someone's just pinched the single most valuable object in the world, possibly in history. They didn't do it alone, and I'm convinced the motive will reveal who it was."

Only distant yelling now, nearly drowned out by the slopping from a caviar fountain. Tenny looks at the pillar Melanie seemed to have melted into.

"She not staying?"

"Police questioning bores her to sobs. She's usually way ahead of them. Champagne?"

Ran pours some delightfully normal-colored bubbly into his old friend's glass. He twists the bottle to prevent dripping.

Back before university and long before the Royal Marines, he had a notion of becoming a waiter in London to sup up hefty tips from Russian oligarchs and Middle Eastern potentates. His parents insisted he call himself a sommelier. For Ran Oliphant, head of Eurolincx, special enemy of Wolfgang Licht, both those incarnations seem like lifetimes ago.

***

Hours later, minor bloodstains have been shampooed by cleaning bots. Goop slopped by caviar dispensers still smells like low tide. Most guests made a break for the border. They didn't get there. Anyone without complete sovereign immunity has been detained.

Ran smiles. Melanie got away. Those diversion and evasion tactics they'd practiced paid off.

Twelve agencies from six countries show up to investigate. The hall resembles an airport during a baggage handler's strike. The wealthy, famous, and powerful lie dozing over couches or on the floor. The Russian *Übermensch* bodyguard is wheeled to an ambulance on a small forklift.

A mousy, prickly looking man in a trench coat approaches. He sports possibly the worst comb-over in the history of human hair. Ran has trouble not staring at the slicked-down scruffy mess that is plastered around a small Band-Aid and a huge welt on his forehead. Through thick milspec-framed glasses, the man studies Ran.

"Sir, just a minute of your time."

"Right. Ran Oliphant, Eurolincx.

"Fox, sir. Major Fox.

"Which agency might you be from?"

"US Military Intelligence, Corps of the Defense Administration. COTDA for short. I realize you may have been asked questions—"

"By CIA, NASA, and I think even the FDA weighed in at some point."

Maybe he's tired, or this fellow makes him testy. Fox brandishes a notebook and has a badly hidden buttonhole camera in his silly coat.

"In brief," Ran snaps, "the Ansible—I don't have it. You can check my trousers. I don't know who took it or why. I only came to sup Licht's booze."

Fox isn't fazed. Regular terrier.

"Mr. Oliphant, who were you talking to at the time of the incident?"

***

A generous hour of asinine drubbing later, footmen in bright uniforms outnumber the remaining detectives. They upload data and whisper into scrambled satellite phones. Ran decides to check on his horses. One of Licht's people follows him.

Bloody snoop. If only they'd been that attentive with the Ansible.

His pair of Percherons stand under cover, munching hay from an automatic feeder. Cassius snuffles his pockets and threatens to eat his yellow rose boutonniere. Ran nudges him back.

"I'll have my man come from Geneva to get them. Don't let anyone try to take the gold plates off. You'll just pull their coats."

From the tree line, Sir Tenny emerges. Alongside are some rough-looking blokes in Sabre Tactical jackets.

"Tenny, thought you'd be long gone."

"Ran, heh, just been with our SIS people. There's been, uh, some strange goings-on in the woods. A lot wilder than they appear. Hope Melanie's all right."

"I'm sure. When she gets wind of a mystery, she's a combination Sherlock Holmes and Miss Marple."

"With the bum of a CrossFit instructor, eh?"

Tenny can be a tosser.

"Remember, Sir Tenny, when she noticed you were being murdered by slow poison?" Ran reminds him. "While your doctors and everyone else hadn't a clue."

Sir Tenny nods bitterly. "Bloody Sri Lankan butler. I never liked him."

"I'll bet Melanie's in the Big Smoke cross-questioning contacts at New Scotland Yard. Nothing can put her off. Her mind is a steel trap. Inescapable."

31

HOXTON

THE BIG SMOKE

MELANIE

L alalalalalalala," Melanie Françoise trills to no one in particular.

My knee, throbbing stopped, sprayed homebrewed analgesic on it right where meanie at the not-terribly-fun-party hit it with his maxilla + zygomatic bone, icy hot, my knee.

Melanie's eyes flit up and down the two-story shops along Hackney Road in Hoxton, London. Her thoughts hop about.

Shoes.

Lip gloss.

LIPSTICK.

Sudanese lip plates from 8700 BC

NANO BATTERY OPERATED EYELASH EXTENSIONS.

Ideas pop and fizz like fireworks under a strobe light the size of the moon.

During her tween years, she realized not everyone experienced reality like this. The more tedious doctors called it hyperphasic delirium. Well, she has some diagnostic words for them: hyperphasic poopyheads!

She's learned to deal without medication.

If you just wander into a shop and stare silently at things and people while you breeze through the kaleidoscopic swirl of images, formulas, equations, and theories inside your head, it tends to make people uncomfortable. She decides to pick a single idea.

Glad. She's glad. Glad to be working for someone who appreciates her unique gifts, hasn't fired her, or tried having her committed to an asylum. Ranulph Oliphant is that someone. He's never suggested she take any medication at all.

Unlike her parents.

Not their fault.

Before preschool, before Melanie had even ridden a tricycle, doctors told them she was DSM-5 ADD and borderline bipolar with signs of hyperkinetic disorder.

There are meds.

Many meds.

Stimulants to make her concentrate, which is like putting bifocals on a laser beam.

And sleeping pills.

Lots.

As a youngster, she was up all hours. People were never sure if she was awake or sleepwalking. As if there's such a great big hairy difference.

RK SYRUS

Mostly, psychiatrists threw up their hands, eyebrows, or bad weaves and prescribed lithium carbonate. This powerful antipsychotic mood stabilizer came in cute gel caps shaped like trademarked cartoon characters.

Her preteen medication mix was tweaked until everyone was sure that, if she absolutely had to have multiple personalities, the dominant one would be socially acceptable at formal dinners.

For six-seven-eight-nine-year-old Comtesse Françoise, as she called herself before her doctorate was conferred, days and nights smushed together. Schoolwork became nearly challenging. So did remembering where she was.

Once, during the tenth year of her reign, she found herself at the apex of a cheerleader pyramid, without any idea how she got there. She learned she had been the cause of the acrobatic formation breaking out in a regularly scheduled, and otherwise uneventful, Dalcroze Eurhythmics dance class. After that display of leadership, she needed special permission to enter the gym.

As she stood there, atop a vertical triangle of straining, trembling, sweaty co-eds, she had an epiphany.

On the epiphany scale, it was pretty close to the flash of pink light from a hot delivery girl's pendant that nearly put Phillip K. Dick into a coma. She looked twenty feet down to the polished hardwood floor, and a single thought flashed:

I must start purging my meds!

Fast forward through six years of psychotropic bulimia.

Pause. Rewind to when they started injecting her.

Fast forward through a sometimes messy, ultimately

277

rewarding period of storing and transfusing her own plasma: blood-undoping.

There was an upside to her preteen fight against Big Pharma and the psychoactive drugs they pushed as though they were Curly Wurly candies. She learned advanced biochemistry, how to operate a centrifuge, all about corpuscular cryo-storage, and how to find her own veins with large-bore IV needles. It spurred her interest in sort of attending medical school and becoming the best almost-doctor she could be.

At sixteen, she landed on the doorstep of Eurolincx's downtown London HQ. With a thump. The telecom company's programmers had been knitting together important code all night. They ordered vindaloo takeaway. She was Chef Ashif's main wee-hours delivery girl on account of her ability to be perky during wee hours.

As she set out from the kitchen, Melanie *knew* something magical was about to happen. Even though she'd been up for fifty-two hours and had a Klonopin hangover, she couldn't let Chef Ashif down. He was such a dear.

She had roller skated along the deserted motorway of the great city. The Big Smoke. Her wheels were the only sound above the static hum of distant traffic.

Clack-thrum.

Clack-thrum.

The air was cool. Charcoal-gray asphalt merged with dark sky. Corona glows of streetlights looked like fissures in a sad painting of London at night, portals to another city, where it was bright as day. The effect was mesmerizing and pulled her toward REM sleep. She was light in her head and dead on her feet.

Clack-thrum.

Clack-thrum.

When she turned off Blandford onto Baker, the song playing through her hoop earrings—the insides of wireless speakers—changed over. As she was winding her way down Baker Street on eight wheels, the new song playing in her hoop-earring headphones was "Baker Street" by Scottish singer-songwriter Gerry Rafferty.

Ma-gic!

At the time, she wasn't really a delivery girl. She was on a deep-cover mission to steal Chef Ashif's Diwali beef wellington recipe. She has never agreed with intellectual property theft, but since her parents would not give her money to open her own restaurant—one which would have brought affordable langoustine to the masses—drastic measures were justified.

At 3:33 a.m., having avoided the bobbies—her helmet and Balenciaga roller skates were not exactly street-legal—she fell in a curry-slathered heap right on the stoop of Eurolincx's office building.

Mr. Oliphant insisted she come in and clean herself up. He suggested a change of career, one less likely to result in traumatic brain injury or being held for ransom by the Green Lanes Gang, who during that period of London's criminal history was growing in notoriety. She agreed. She gave up her night job, as well as the recipe-spying mission, and started at Eurolincx the next day.

Most definitely, Ran is the best employer she has ever worked for. Also the most enduring, with second place being held by the three weeks at a pet shop in Transnistria.

Among the many perks accruing to her as Special

Executive in Charge of Various Things are: private aircraft at her disposal, a llama rescue ranch named after her, and a Black Pearl Oyster transit pass for unlimited tube and trolley rides and up to fifty percent off at Poppies Fish & Chips.

Ran also set up an official expense account at her favorite tattoo parlor in Hoxton, which is where the airport bus and her feet have taken her this morning.

"Escaping from that terrible Lichtstrom party, it's made me so hungry. I came straight here."

Frederique, a tall transgender with a shaved head, wearing a polished black PVC corset, looks skeptical.

"Y'realize, dahling, this is a tattoo parlor?"

"Exactly. I won't be tempted to eat! Though that shawarma place next door looks promising. Anyone with an eighteenth-century Senneh Knot carpet in the window should make a cracklin' wrap."

The sides of Frederique's corset strain as she sighs. "Girlfriend, if you wasn't so smart I'd swear you were batty."

"Can't I be both?"

32

Melanie imagines when she hugs someone she can sometimes feel pure arboreal energies pass into them. If they have an open mind, that is. Her arms are well on their way to being covered by ink from shoulder to wrist. The delectably crafted design is a Garden of Eden inspired tattoo mural.

"What do you think? About the new one?"

Frederique's finely plucked and inked eyebrows rise. "Now you're talkin'. Trans-for-may-shun," she says. "Takin' what's on your mind and puttin' it out there in the flesh. Purest form of self-expression there is. People been doin' it forever. Skin becoming art, the ink revealing the soul."

"Aw."

"'Cept in your case. You'll just tat any random guy's name on yo bootay."

"That's mean. Remind me not to tip you."

"The more you tip, the less the needle hurts."

"Really?" Melanie considers the connection between generosity and Aδ-fiber pain receptors.

"No, just made that up," Aunt Freda quips. "Don't you be cheapin' out on me. Tell me a lie. That your boss Ranulph Oliphant don't pay enough. Heck, with a name like that, he just might be family. I should apply to be his in-house masseuse."

She cracks her knuckles with anticipation of getting her hands on Ran's wealthy and muscular shoulders.

"Straight, as far as I can tell. But he hasn't gotten out much since that horrible accident where his wife and two daughters died. Real nice guy, too."

Frederique smirks. "Hey, you got a thang for his schwing? Don't be witholdin' gossips from Aunt Freda now."

"Aw, it's not like that! Though he does keep fit for his age." Melanie holds up her left arm. The partial stencil reads:

𝔐𝔬𝔫𝔱𝔤

"Besides, I'm almost positive my guy's going to pop *ye olde questionne!*"

Frederique does not share her bubbling enthusiasm. "You sure this guy, Montgomery, is the one?"

"Completely. He's so rad. He has a band."

"I bet."

"Oh, Freda." Melanie pouts at the implication that new love cannot be true love. "You're a big party pooper in… a party dress. Monty's very intellectual. His performances combine thrash metal with medieval theatre. Their songs are based on Chaucer's *Pilgrim's Progress*. In the last set, he dresses like Beelzebub and smashes his guitar. It's the bomb!"

"Really? I'm gonna make a note right now—to never, ever see that shit." She raises a tattoo gun shaped like a chrome skull. "Back to the point, of my inkin' needle. You sure you don't want just his initials? I'm not sayin' this isn't forever, but I do remember us havin' a helluva time covering over the long Greek name."

"Varnavas Vartholomeos. Okay, I should have gone with 'VV' for him. But look"—Melanie flexes her triceps—"what a beautiful snake you made out of him."

"You want ink only on your arms, and you runnin' out of real estate."

Frederique slaps a binder open.

Tattoos and hidem-ups – Dr. Melanie F.

Was	Is
Uhuru N'Che	Tree of Knowledge (boring)
Varnavas Vartholomeos	Snake (slithering)
Yanti Choi	Cherub (mama's boy)
Bobby G.	Apple (rotten to core)
Montgomery Yliffe	

Melanie nearly has a retort queued up to her Broca's area when a sparkling light in the shape of a small pinwheel firework appears out of thin air. It becomes a red-and-white lollipop.

Right. I'm in the City, the Big Smoke.

In high-density urban areas, Licht/Net optical signals are

thick. Two data-enabled light sources intersecting can create high-def holograms in thin air. Which would be the bomb except for Dr. Licht being such a pucker puss.

"Sorry," Melanie says, "we have to pause the needling, you naughty, uh, needler."

The lollipop is her incoming-call icon. It hovers above caller ID text.

USS Lee - Brig. \\ Message from—Prisoner 0258

"Yo, woman, T-Rex here."

He wears this year's shade of POW purple, looks angry, and speaks rapidly. Melanie is fascinated.

Frederique glances at him. "Uh huuuh. Maybe we hold up. Looks like you got another suitor."

"Are you screening me?" Mr. Rex grimaces, flashing an impressive gold grill. "Hit accept. I'm all kinds o' busy."

His handcuffs are padlock style. *Chubb Escort, made in England, the Cartier of personal restraints.*

Freda shakes her head. "He hot, but he sleepin' on a cement cot."

Melanie considers this. "I did resolve not to date people currently in prison. With exceptions for political prisoners, famous street artists, or if our love astro-synastry is anomalously great."

She accepts the call by putting the virtual lollipop to her lips.

"*Enchanté*, Mr. Rex."

"Now don't be interruptin' me with Euro lingo."

"I'm all ears." Melanie lifts her bountiful curls up to prove it.

She's intuitive, but with the demands of exponentially increasing data flows, a modern girl needs help. She signals Chiangmai Sign Language for "*Help.*"

Her digital concierge appears.

`Available Subroutines:`

`Nancy Drew 12.6`

`譲崎 ネロ 3.5`

`Fake Nuclear Attack (beta)`

Sorry, Nero Yuzurusaki, Nancy's got the multivariate insight I need just now.

`[Nancy Drew 12.6]` selected

Her digital teen detective delivers. All around the image of Mr. Rex, a kaleidoscope of information and logical speculation appears.

`voice,`

`accent,`

`eye movements,`

`micro-body posture adjustments,`

`scars and callouses on hand, two ridges just behind the collateral ligament of the thumb on both hands, lighter on the left, likely made by the slide recoil of an automatic pistol,`

`oldest scar on face well sutured with aftercare to prevent keloid scar formation, medium-age scar on forearm appears to be self-treated.`

`Codename: <T-Rex>`

`Legal Birth Name on enlistment form <"Ask yo momma!">`

Visible tattoo reads:

"*Ohne Musik wäre das Leben ein Irrtum.*"

Translation: "Without music, life would be a mistake."

[phrase listed in our top 20 Friedrich Nietzsche quotations, +5 astro-synastry romance points]

Current assignment: Ft. Bragg, N.C. 1st SFOD-D-O (stenographer, probationary, auxiliary), under NCO Sgt. Bryan, under O-6 Col. Sienna McKnight

Current location: Indian Ocean

The publicly and sneakily available data agitates, spins, and tumbles dry.

He's pretending to be high, even stained his lip with red dye, maybe from a packaged food covering, but he is one stone-cold sober hunk of enigma.

Melanie decides she'd better listen. Between the words.

"Dial my man's digits at Ramstein," he says. "It's the wrong time, and I only get one call."

Mr. Rex reels off some numbers and intentionally mumbles the location.

Then he adds, "To save the Rose, y'got to dare grab the thorn. Right now."

With that butchered Anne Brontë quote, their chat time ends. The screenshot hangs, waiting for her to dismiss, redial, or post to her Licht/Net blog.

It's a puzzle.

I love puzzles!

The transmission from the brig was monitored by military

security mechBrains that can hack through code or public key encryption in seconds. T-Rex must be employing some idiosyncratic secret speak that can only be unravelled by the MelBrain.

"You wanna write anything down?"

"No thanks, Aunt Freda. I got it."

Numbers. Transposed letters. Not comm-link numbers. What are those peskers? He gave two versions, pretending to be high on Mist.

Ramstein Air Base: largest US military base overseas... located in Germany, 49°26'38.10"N 007°36'08.13"E Kaiserslautern... Oh, didn't I get Ran the cutest beer mugs from near there last Christmas?

Concentrate!

Let's do that. Numbers, letter, ciphers... speaking of which, didn't Alan Turing get a terribly raw deal?

Melanie!

Ignore noise. Ponder on signal.

She considers Hebrew, a.k.a. Letters of Fire. Its lexicon is totally numerically based, and it's so pretty!

But it's not the answer.

Open code, simple variable.

First he said: "Ramstein," then "Rammerbasestein."

Six numbers and x letters. Which geolocation system looks like that?

RAMSTEinbaserammerbasESTEIN

RAMsteinbaserammerbasestEIN

RAmsteinbaserammerbasesteIN

Like a half dozen tumblers of a combination lock all falling into place, something clicks. Coordinates on the commercial version of Russia's GPS system, ГЛОНАСС. GLONASS.

Virtual Nancy serves up the real-world location. In Khorasan.

The middle of the Wandering Desert.

"Gotta go."

Melanie dashes, stencil paper still stuck on her arm.

"Girl, I gots rent to pay. Gonna have to charge you."

"Put it on Ran's tab."

Her car's in the alley. She notices a new addition to her tires. Electronic wheel clamps courtesy of the roving robots of London's Traffic Authority, Hackney Borough. Silly red zones.

"Super-duper Privacy," she snaps at the onboard computer. "Dial Ran—urgent!"

Her ringtone feeds back, "Meow."

Pick up.

"Meow."

He appears, from his limo. Many thoughts get in the way of her words coming

out

her

mouth

of…

Before her thoughts choke her, she manages, "Ran, it's about the Rose!"

33

NOW

USS *LEE*

INDIAN OCEAN

BRYAN

Without warning, all their cell doors clank open at once. Bryan cautiously looks around the corner.

What now?

It's hours before exercise time.

Guards wait for Bryan and the others to form a polite line for shackling. Whitebread, Nobu, T-Rex, and Snakelips clank along behind him into the drunk tank hose-down room.

"Once you sign your DD Form 2674, make sure you got all your stuff," a Navy man tells them. "Then all prisoners will muster on the flight deck. Except for Sergeant Bryan."

Bryan gets led up to the bridge and set outside the captain's ready room. Stahlback's fat face is frozen between gloating distaste and ornery gutlessness. Beside him, XO Bianchi wears his usual poker mug. Denbow the Navy SEAL is also there, looking smug. The most relatable faces in the room belong to the peanut gallery of baseball toys along the whole wall.

Captain Bobblehead.

"Captain Stahlback," Bryan says. "You wanted to see—"

"Yes," the Navy man snaps back. "I am seeing you. I think we've all seen enough of Army on this ship."

On shelves, fifty plastic heads nod. Bryan no longer wonders why Bianchi slipped him Sienna's coordinates. Stahlback would have ignored the intel or sent out a squadron of Stymph drones on a carpet bombing run to cover his cowardly incompetence.

"As much as I'd like to see you band of thieving hijacking shanghaiers in jail for the rest of your useless lives, my XO here convinced me there's a lot of paperwork involved. Due process bunk."

Bianchi's cheeks flush.

"So," Stahlback continues, "the sooner we scrape you off like useless barnacles, the better. Orders."

The XO offers up a scroll. Stahlback has had someone put the strike group's RFID command seal into his chunky Annapolis class ring.

Denbow, the other Navy man in the room, takes a breath.

"Yes, Lieutenant Commander," Stahlback says before Denbow can get a word out. "I haven't forgotten your request."

"Thank you, Captain." Denbow breaks out in a big, white, toothy smile. He speaks in his sweetest manly butt-kiss voice. "Doha Base has a state-of-the-art refugee center. Plenty of staff, playground and everything."

XO Bianchi whispers to Stahlback.

Bryan makes a note to ask if they can throw in at least

one cybernetic ear the next time he gets his ocular implants upgraded.

"Commander Denbow, I appreciate your offer to take the underage civilian off our hands. But she's not actually in our hands," the *Lee*'s captain says. "It looks bad enough for me, McKnight falling off one of my aircraft. No, no, no. The kid was never boarded. She's a souvenir. An unauthorized trinket. Out with the bathwater she goes."

"But, sir, I—"

A side look cuts Denbow off.

"I appreciate you're Navy. But you are *CENTCOM* Navy." Stahlback swipes the order scroll with his ring. A bosun's whistle note chimes as the contents are digitally sealed and entered into the *Lee*'s official log. "Dismissed."

A long military career has taught Bryan when to shut up. They are getting off this damned ship. All of them. Free and clear. They have a chance to help Sienna. They even get to keep their lucky Khorasan souvenir.

A Navy guard nudges him along.

"Just a sec."

He has to do something on the other side of the bridge. He returns a borrowed comm link to Mr. Ko, remembering to get a receipt so they won't be charged money or accused of theft. Leaving, he passes by the ready room. Stahlback's door is half open.

"—at's that," the Captain's voice says. "Not my problem anymore. I was looking forward to ripping that arrogant sergeant a new one with the Uniform Code at his court martial. That is one odd soldier. Does he really have to look like that?

Isn't there a treatment, or ointment, or something he can use? A sun lamp?"

"No, Captain," Bianchi says, "I don't think there is."

"The way he looks, it's just…" Stahlback searches for the right word. "…unnatural."

***

A fresh wind whips across the waves, over the *Lee*'s flight deck, through Bryan's jacket. He sees his people. They wear crisp, pressed purple jumpers. Stahlback made them put them on just for their march of humiliation across to the waiting aircraft. Snakelips shadows the little girl. Anis is the only one not bound at the wrists and ankles. She wears a tiny purple POW jumper under her lifejacket.

T-Rex flashes his grin in case they miss the Morse code on his eyebrows. He's found yet another use for hair-removing gel. On each side of his head is a letter. He swivels left and right on their march to a VTOL transport plane.

F

U

F

U

"Sarge!" T-Rex gripes. "They put extra starch in these here convict rags! Just another point in the human-rights violations brief I'm gonna file. Have a nice day, you Navy—"

It occurs to Bryan the manacles were probably a good idea. They've been handed a get-out-of-jail-free card. Dropkicking senior officers into the ocean might cause delays.

T-Rex saves his biggest grin for the master-at-arms. He holds his chains for unlocking. "Yes, sir, now that you ask. I did have a most pleasant stay." The setting sun glints off gold caps. "I shall certainly recommend your facilities to all my homies in Compton."

Anis's flotation vest is nearly as restraining as a straightjacket. Her skinny legs and arms make her look like a pincushion doll. A buxom flight officer leads her by the hand.

When Anis passes the master and his ring of keys, she mimics what she has seen T-Rex and the others do. She holds out her hands to be freed.

The Navy officer smiles. "Move along there, little miss."

The flight officer visibly tears up as she puts Anis in her seat and straps her in. Bryan returns her caped dolly.

"Thank you. Miss Lee had a good visit with me in jail."

Their ride is an older, compact Osprey, a propeller plane capable of vertical takeoff. Inside, two rows of lightly padded seats face each other. The pilot's voice comes over the speaker:

"*Please fasten your harnesses. Hope everyone is hungry for pita bread, moussaka, and history. Next stop: Athens, Greece.*"

"I don't get it." Snakelips is the first to echo his thoughts. "They're letting us go?"

"Dunno much about law," Whitebread chimes in, "but I'm pretty sure we broke some big ones."

"Says who?" Nobu asks. "They broke the most important rule first: leaving the colonel out there."

Bryan ends the legal debate.

"Gentlemen, Snakelips, unless they mean to drop us in the ocean, I'll take it."

I'll also take those GLONASS coordinates, however they got written on a tiny superheroine's cape.

Bryan does not like keeping details from his team, but he

has to be sure no one is listening. He's not even sure where the intel came from, or if it's real. Bianchi never gave a hint.

He looks to Anis. Gently, she smooths Lee's wool hair and looks back at him over the rim of her life vest. Her eyes, maybe more unusual than his own, are full of kindness and patience. They remind him of another little girl he watched grow up.

34

BRYAN

In a few hours, midnight would tick past. It would be Sienna's twelfth birthday. Bryan walked the dark side road toward her house.

Sienna and her widowed mom, Annalies, lived in a single-story wood-frame house outside Fort Bragg's perimeter. They could have gotten a bigger place for not much more rent inside, but Bryan suspected the other side of the wire held too many memories of Dr. Theodora McKnight. Annalies's spouse had been killed nearly six years ago.

Bryan took the long way around from the northern gate. Between him and Sienna's house stood a clump of white poplars. He preferred to go around those trees, especially at night. Pale trunks caught the moonlight. They stood up like many fingers of a skeletal hand.

In Bryan's original home country, he had been the zeru son of zeru parents. He was only known as Shetani Zeru:

Satan's own ghost. He never had a real tribal name. What he did have by birthright was value measured in hard currency: the price for his select body parts. The hands and feet of albino infants, the younger the better, were the main ingredient of a hideously precious magical stew.

He and Elahaj had kept in touch as much as their very different lives allowed. Chats always drifted back to *that* night. The night the two of them had escaped the anger and appetites of the Ghost Eater. The story, repeated and pondered on by the involuntary workings of his mind, had matured into a legend for Sergeant Bryan.

Elahaj had carried Bryan, then a newborn albino, away from witch doctors into the hands of other doctors. An odd pair of scientists brought them to the capital. Some quick thinking and con artistry on Elahaj's part brought him to North Carolina.

Elahaj always swore he would never come to America. He was afraid its complicated hugeness would swallow him whole and spit his clean bones into the sea.

The older Elahaj got, the more superstitious he seemed to get. Elahaj always talked of the corpse-feasting ghoul like it was real, as though to this day it was still out there somewhere. After more than thirty years, the thing they had narrowly escaped and left hungry, whatever or whoever it was, it must surely be dead. Still...

Still it squatted there. In a corner of Bryan's waking and unwaking mind, it waited. Between visions of ice zombies and Texas serial murderers with chainsaws. The Eater lived in Bryan's deepest thoughts and ideas about Africa.

In dreams, he witnessed the progress of a slow, poisonous

stream. It inched along, slopping its length into a hole. On its foul banks, mud oozed over two pale feet. The skin covering those feet was a shade grayer than his own. That skin looked like a translucent plastic bag holding something that had liquefied as it rotted.

In the mud banks along the oozing slop, long worms poked out. Their heads had no eyes and were dominated by gripping teeth arranged around sucking mouth parts. Always hungry, even these bottom-feeding omnivores declined to bite the toes of those feet. Those toes were tipped with something other than nails. The ichor that pulsed through those arteries was something other than blood. Those fat carnivorous wrigglers wanted none of it.

It was the only thing that truly frightened him, other than the thought of harm coming to Sienna. Only one of those fears was logical. Sienna was real. The Ghost Eater was not.

Logic and science notwithstanding, Elahaj claimed to have faced the wily savannah ghoul in the flesh. Details changed over time and with each telling. It always ended the same. With an apology.

Elahaj invariably ended by saying he was sorry for not finally killing the Eater. Despite all his bluster that night, despite the power the Tree Spirit loaned to him, everyone knew that was impossible, he explained. Even with fire.

Bryan had told himself a thousand times: "There's no such thing."

Yet on that lonely dark road outside the post on his way to Sienna's house, he felt the skin on his neck rise and bunch. He looked left and right, stared hard with his brightly burning deep-spectrum vision. Wherever he looked, night shadows melted into violet twilight. He felt foolish. Suddenly he felt a flash of pain through his head.

He bent over, hands on knees till it passed. It was his eyes, again. They were the product of his genetics. Through his pale irises he could see ultraviolet like a falcon and infrared like a vampire bat. Burning so bright, they were wearing out. Soon he would be stuck at a desk when he could no longer pass the Army's annual physical.

Maybe before then he would get lucky and get seriously wounded. That way he could pull down WIA benefits. Benefits denied to Sienna's mother, Dr. McKnight, and her widow. The inconsiderate bomber who killed her struck a Worldwide Help medical relief site, not a US convoy.

Theodora had been on leave helping civilians at an NGO hospital when she died. The government gave Annalies her spousal pension, but nothing else. Bryan wanted to give Sienna everything she deserved, and as she grew up it became clear that those things cost money.

A sound. A rustle in the trees.

It blasted through the steel vise clamped around his temples. Bryan froze stock-still.

Movement.

Something just beyond even his full-spectrum radar.

Head hurting and spinning, an old fear welled up. *The old fear.* Cold, moist breath exhaled on the back of his neck. Inhuman feet slopped over a fetid creek, toward him. He forgot about the revolver in his boot holster. Shetani Zeru's teeth bared in a primal snarl. He looked for a rock that would fit his hand.

The moment passed.

Making sense of the jumble of shapes through the trunks of poplar trees, he saw the moving figure was a man. Stealthy, capable, and athletic. But only human.

The figure crept by the wall of a barn. Bryan was closer now. He hadn't been seen, he was sure. At the edge of the trees, he jumped over a drainage ditch.

As he got closer, he was annoyed. The guy was peering through a milspec night scope at a house three hundred yards away. The McKnight house. The intruder actually had the gall to be spying on Sienna as she sat reading in her swing chair under a porch light.

Why can't weirdos just stay in the city?

The barn was the only cover with a line of sight to Sienna's house. Bryan sidled up slowly. He wanted to catch the guy in the act. Horses snorted and breathed inside. He came around the corner. The figure was gone.

A fist rocked his face. The unexpected blow sent Bryan stumbling outside the door of the barn. It was almost a relief.

At least the trespasser was not a fanged demon and, for now, was fighting fair. It had been a while since he'd had a good throwdown with a worthy opponent, one who wasn't trying to shoot or stick him right away.

The dark figure followed up the punch with a vicious knee aimed at his head. This might have ended the excitement right quick.

Though rattled and annoyed someone had snuck up on him while he was sneaking up on them, Bryan still had enough game. He stepped into his unknown opponent's stance and took the solid blow on his crossed arms, a much better place than on his nose.

In clinch-grappling position, he grabbed his opponent's waist and drove him into the barn. Small tufts of hay rained down. They struggled for an opening to strike and for better footing. They yanked on clothing.

The tricky bastard went for a gi-style choke. But Bryan's shirt was old, and the collar ripped before it cut off his oxygen and blood.

Bryan went for underhooks to get judo-style leverage for a throw. The guy swiveled under. Finally, Bryan got an elbow in.

"Oomph!"

Bryan was rewarded with a twofer, the technical term for inflicting multiple concussions at once. The bouncy impact of his elbow on the man's forehead was followed by the dull thud of the guy's head thumping off wooden flooring.

He felt his opponent go slack for an instant. Very quickly the fellow recovered.

Special forces training, no doubt about it.

Something else. A smell, weirdly civilized.

Lavender?

Huh?

Either him or his clothes.

NOT one of our guys.

Most def not. When the male soldiers did begrudgingly wash, it was always with government-issue soap. This was different.

The other man had been silent except for the sound of deep breaths and the occasional sharp exhalations through clenched teeth when he punched or kicked.

Bryan drove his closely shaved head into his adversary's ribcage, trying to get hip control for a throw. Wrong move.

Strong arms grabbed him around the waist.

Oh naw! Bryan felt his feet lift off the ground.

Two hundred and thirty-five pounds of lean albino fighting machine got hefted up through the cool night air in a suplex slam.

Bryan's landed on his back with a *WHUMP!*

In the stalls, a couple of the horses snorted, startled by the sound. Bryan lay on his back with his wind knocked out, feeling in all ways as though he had really fallen off a turnip truck.

This guy is strong and tricky.

Bryan slid sideways and tried to grab the guy's leg, mostly in defense. They were not at the groin-kicking stage. Yet.

He had the man's left leg tied up, but he refused to fall down like he was supposed to.

"Psst," Bryan said during a small stalemate. "Be more quiet. Horses. Sleeping."

After a pause, "Uh, sorry mate. I'm trying to knock you out quietly."

Aussie or some kinda Limey. *What's up with tha—*

Bryan's pondering on the man's nationality was interrupted by a rain of hammer fists and a headbutt. The strikes also forced him to let go of the leg hold to protect his face. His opponent freed himself and dashed for the opposite end of the barn. He was fixing to get gone.

No midnight jog for me.

The fellow had to have some transport hidden close by. If he got to it, he'd be down the road back to the highway.

Bryan had one advantage yet unplayed. He knew the setup of the stables. There were heavy rolling doors at either end of the structure, and these were controlled by switches on a central panel. Bryan flicked the correct one. Both doors came down before the figure could get out.

They had been fighting by the light of the moon that streamed in from one side and the wash from a halogen paddock light coming in from the other. Now both were cut off.

Trapped ya. Unless you're part bat like me, I've got all the cards.

Even Bryan could not see well enough to box in total darkness. Thankfully, some tiny allies had been disturbed by the ruckus. Blue Ghost fireflies hovered. Each was about the size of a grain of rice. Dozens of them circled up from hay bales stacked in the barn. They gave off a faint violet-tinged luminescence. By it, Bryan's albino night vision could just make out soft fleshy targets for his fists and elbows.

After a couple payback thumps, the other man dropped to one knee and raised his hand.

"Okay, mate, okay, I give. I… only wanted to see her."

Bryan flicked on an overhead light and pulled his boot gun. Best way to accept surrender from a stranger. He leveled it in as gentlemanly a way as you could.

"Now, if you're tellin' me you're some kind of pervert," Bryan said, cocking the five-shot revolver, "we may have to disturb the horses after all."

In the stark overhead light, Bryan saw a sandy-haired man. He was broadly built and about thirty years old. Sitting on a bale of hay, he blew blood out of one nostril with practiced ease, not getting any on his shirt.

"Good Lord, man, no." The lavender-scented guy spoke

with a weariness Bryan surmised was only partly a result of their tussle. "I'm her father."

***

Bryan had taken a bit of convincing before he could take stock in this exceptional revelation. He was still not fully convinced after ten or twelve minutes of polite and methodical explaining. The fellow said he was named Ranulph Oliphant.

Has to be real. Who would make up that name?

Oliphant reached for his back pocket.

"Hold up there."

Bryan motioned with his gun.

"Relax! It's only a snap."

Seeing the old newspaper photograph convinced Bryan. He had to be Sienna's birth father. In it, a seventeen-year-old version of Ran was being pushed back by airport security. In the background, thugs were hustling a pregnant Hamida into the diplomatic-flight boarding zone.

This was the same woman Bryan had almost shot in Afghanistan barely a month after that picture was taken. It was the same stricken and dying woman who had crawled too close to the gate post of 90 Charlie. The one Bryan had let live despite everything his training and instinctive fear told him to do.

For a moment, as he had held that picture, the only sound was the breathing of a half dozen horses. The only movement was the upward drift of barn dust motes, and alongside these, the powered flight of tiny brown specs—the fireflies—both rising upward to the single bare light.

Bryan's voice was empty and small.

"Where the heck have you been?"

Ran told a tale that began with two deaths and ended with three more. A tale told by a man who felt burdened and hurt by each word he spoke.

The authorities told Ran that after she got home, Hamida was killed by a group of tribesmen. He assumed her cousin was behind it. The same one who attacked her in Cambridge. Asrah Qazi had disappeared from England shortly after she was deported. Reports Ran got back from a social worker, Mrs. Fitzgibbons, said Hamida died before she could give birth. Ran couldn't face going back to school. He quit and joined the Royal Marines.

For years, Ran never looked back. Not until his second great tragedy, one that came on the heels of a windfall of wealth. When he looked more closely into Hamida's final days, he was astonished. It was nothing short of a miracle. Bryan had to agree.

"That ain't all, is it?" Bryan said. "Otherwise why sneak around like this?"

"The aircraft explosion," Ran said haltingly. "The one that killed my wife, Elena, and my girls. It was no accident. That thermite bomb was meant for me."

The two men agreed then and there that only Bryan could be in Sienna's life. Ran had to stay distant. Being a McKnight was her only protection from the terrible forces Ran had stirred up against himself and anyone he cared for.

Now it was Bryan's turn to sit down, tuck his weapon back in his boot, and feel for any loose teeth in his lower jaw. As his head throbbed, Bryan tried to fill in some blanks.

"You're not regular Marines?"

Ran shook his head. "Three Commando. Been out a while."

"You still got some. Not enough tonight, but close." Bryan smiled. "So what now? What about Annalies? Can I let her know anything?"

Ran shook his head again.

"Only you. I wasn't planning on taking on any partner in this. But I've read your file. I checked anyone close to her, career Sergeant Shetani Zeru Bryan. You'll do."

Ran roused himself from his hay bale and walked slowly over to a crumpled package on the floor. Bryan had burned through his adrenaline, and now he was feeling the effects of the down-home thumping.

"Say, Ran, you don't mind if I verify your story, do ya?"

The other man smiled.

"You've got enough of my DNA on you. Go right ahead."

A parcel lay on the ground, crushed during the fight. Ran picked it up. Inside were yellow flowers.

"I don't know what I was thinking." Ran looked disgusted with himself. "Bought these on the way up. No way I could give them to her, just as well they're all thrashed."

Bryan looked more closely at the roses.

"There still one that looks okay. I can give it to her if you like."

He picked up the lone floral survivor of Ran's travels and the carnage in the stables.

"Maybe we can do that every year. You Limeys are big on tradition, aren't you?"

Ran grimaced. "I'm Scottish, and one of our traditions is we don't like being called Limey."

A few minutes later, Bryan and Mr. Oliphant had

established basic contact protocols. Any connection that might be discovered between them would look as though Ran were trying, unsuccessfully, to recruit the experienced Army sergeant into his personal security force.

When they walked outside, the light on Sienna's porch had darkened. As Bryan suspected, Ran had hidden a motorcycle in the brush beside the paved access road up to the Post. He helped him uncover it.

"Say, that seeing-in-the-dark thing you do. Neat trick. I guess no way to learn that?"

Bryan shook his head. "Hyper sensitivity. In a few years it'll mean the end of my active duty days. Nothing the Army docs can do. It'll be okay. I'll get to spend more time here looking out for Sienna. Beating down the odd stalker."

Ran expertly angled the bike down the hill, coasting silently until he was a hundred yards away before kicking in the engine. Then, with a rumble that sounded like a distant memory, Sienna's father was gone.

35

The Navy Osprey that took them off the aircraft carrier *Lee* approaches Greece to refuel. Inside, Bryan itches to try his hand at hijacking again.

Every mile the noisy but sturdy plane has taken them from the *Lee* has made Bryan believe they've finally gotten away from Captain Bobblehead. But they're headed to the wrong place.

Ramstein Air Base is in Germany.

Sienna is in Khorasan.

They should be there, on the ground, trying to link up with whatever ground elements Ran Oliphant has been able to scrape together on short notice. Every mile closer to Ramstein means they are still sidelined.

He has to suck it up and act like it's all part of the plan. The only other thing they could do is overpower and threaten their pilot, who is not a bad guy.

"*Please fasten your harnesses. I hope you're all hungry for sauerkraut, sausages, and beer. Next stop: Ramstein Air Base*. "

Anis, the girl they rescued from a terrorist, is sleeping between Snakelips Ortiz and T-Rex. He has to make sure this girl is safe before he goes back to get Sienna.

***

The next breath of open air Bryan takes is in Germany. The first one off the plane, he scans the area with every gizmo they crammed into his cybernetic eyes. All looks calm. Tall evergreens border the runway. Mist like cotton candy clings to their tops.

Snakelips unbuckles Anis's flight harness.

"It's your turn, Nobu, get on the juvie detail."

Anis, perhaps bored, is fascinated with Jane Bowie. Sienna's pink-handled knife hangs from the corporal's belt.

"Oh, don't play with that, pequeño. That's a blade for adults," Snakelips says. "I'm sure Uncle Nobu has some nice preschool weapons for you."

It's been a few years since Bryan passed through Ramstein. Back then, it already had the largest US military installation on foreign soil. It has grown since. The newer parts of the base are encroaching on the nature reserves to the south. Cranes stand in the bogs and flap their wings in territorial displays.

The marshlands are separated from the facility by triple-layered fences. To the northeast are hills. Perched on them are slowly rotating wind turbines. There must be access roads throughout the thick woodlands there.

Ran has *to have gotten my message that Sienna needs him more than ever before.*

He always talks about how brainy his eccentric secretary Melanie is. Bryan's been in contact with her a few times. He'd pass along updates on Sienna while they kept up their cover story of Ran trying to recruit Bryan into his corporate paramilitary group.

Screw this waiting.

Something else nags. How they got off the *Lee*. It was way too easy. Something's up with that. And what's up with Denbow? The SEAL seemed really interested in taking the girl Anis to his home base at Doha, Qatar. Bryan can't figure it.

Sienna was always better at that figuring out sneaky stuff than him. Is *better at that stuff*, he corrects himself.

He checks his team.

Nobu helps Anis take off her big flotation vest.

T-Rex texts some of his Ramstein homies. Fast fingers over a small keypad is now a mandatory skill for special-ops soldiers.

Snakelips takes an inventory of her custom rifles. As if the cheap-assed Navy would reimburse her for damage resulting from their sometimes bumpy ride from the Indian Ocean.

Whitebread is on the tarmac having a one-sided tussle with a young airman who was about the size of his thigh. The specialist wears his most innocent-looking expression.

"Nothing in there," he says. "No weapons, I gave 'em all up like your special order says."

The Ramstein base guards are backed up by two squads in armored Joint Light Tactical Vehicles. A welcoming committee?

What now?

Securing heavy ordnance is not unusual for an active-combat element returning to what is basically a US enclave inside a surrounding German civilian community.

Bryan saw it from the air. It is complete with a huge new shopping mall, Ferris wheel and boardwalk. It even has a man-made lake big enough to float a paddle wheel boat.

But normally they let you get past the gate and check in at the armory on your own. He and the Dogs have never had to suffer the indignity of some pasty-faced airman going through their crap on the runway.

The Ramstein security guy rummages deeply inside Whitebread's double-sized duffel. Some metal clanks, like hollow pipes.

"Those are just our musical instruments," Whitebread explains, projecting ultra-earnestness. "We have a pan flute quintet. We play for the kids on holidays."

After the inspector checks out a jumble of stainless steel tubes, he is waved onto the air base. All of them get searched. They keep their knives, which is good because he could tell Snakelips was about to show her even angrier side had they tried to take Jane Bowie away from her. After all, it's not hers— she's just keeping it for their CO.

Nobu's tomahawks perplex the paper pusher.

"These are religious heirlooms," the multiracial soldier says, pointing to the carbon-bladed axe collection. "Only for dancing. Recall the spirits of ancestors. Great White Father treaty with Apache guarantee our right to keep."

Feather decorations on the handles seem to back up his story. No one wants to be accused of cultural insensitivity. But they take his swords.

"Sorry, base commander's orders," the guy keeps repeating

like a robot. Their personal armaments pile up in a table.

"That's everything," Bryan says. "Unless you think we've got bioweapons in our shorts."

"Fess up, Whitebread!" T-Rex spouts off. "What's in your skivvies is like a cross between anthrax and Ebola."

"We've had a long flight. Are you puttin' us in the southside visitors' unit?"

The young man shakes his head timidly. "No, Sergeant. Orders are for you to accompany me directly to the East Wing. It's a new mess hall and commissary area still under construction. Beds have been put in for you."

He stares back at Bryan. He can see reflections of his own golden metallic eyes in the lenses of the young man's glasses.

"Yeah. Base commander's orders. I get that."

What crap.

Bryan is about to demand to speak to someone more than a year past puberty. A low glint catches his eye. It came from the edge of one of the plane hangars. He doesn't get a good look at it.

Luckily, that's no longer a problem. Not for anyone with millions of dollars of implanted bio-optics. He stoops over, grimacing, and puts his hand to his face.

"Anything the matter, Sergeant?"

"Just some grit. Prop wash must have blown it in my eye. These implants, they're tricky sometimes."

Are they ever.

Bryan flicks back, digital frame by digital frame. *There! Now zoom in*, he wills his artificial optics. *Gotcha.*

The glare had come from bifocals stuck over a rumpled face with a scraggy red moustache and sticky strands of hair blowing in all directions off a nearly bald head.

Fox.

Major Fox. Of all the jerks in uniform. That guy had been punted from West Point after nearly drowning a student during a waterboarding demo. Cadet Sienna saved the student's life and told the truth at the faculty inquiry. Fox has been on a vendetta against her ever since.

What the heck is he doing here shadowing us?

Bryan straightens up. Best way to help the colonel is to play along.

"Lead the way, airman."

Bryan flashes a glance back to where the Pentagon spy had been standing. Empty.

"Hey, Sarge, how come they puttin' us here?" T-Rex says, looking around the half-completed mess hall. "Some kinda neo-segregation thing?"

Bryan drops his bag on the dusty floor of their accommodations. Inside the heavy swinging doors are flimsy cots dumped in the middle of the room.

"No reason to write your congressman just yet, Rex. Flyboys like to think they're all tough and hard. That illusion all comes crumblin' down if they catch sight of your manly pecs. They're keeping our Army mojo hidden."

Bryan sits on a folding bed. Sagging springs nearly let his butt hit the bare concrete floor.

"Looks like we're back in the doghouse, just with no bars this time." Bryan motions to the RTO. "Nobu, check the place over. Smells like someone's been cooking something. They may already be using this as a backup kitchen in advance of it being the official mess hall. Check for exits, access points."

No sooner have Bryan and the Dogs settled into their sparse accommodations when there's a knock at the entrance. A woman in a blue RAF service uniform sticks her head in. She is small, young, and has a low center of gravity. Ramstein hosts NATO's Allied Air Command; uniforms from all over are a common sight.

"Sergeant. Hope I'm not intruding."

"Not at all," Bryan replies warily. That military police snoop Fox might have sent her. He reads her rank and name tag.

"Lieutenant Brannigan," she says.

"Squadron commander sends his compliments and a selection of newspapers so you can catch up on doings in the world."

Bryan takes the bundle of newsprint and optical coated plastic. Through the doorway, he catches sight of two base cops lounging at the far end of the corridor. Besides the windows, it's the only exit.

Nobu, silent as a cat, appears behind him.

"What do you think, Sarge?"

Technically they are not being detained at Ramstein base. Looks like someone just wants to keep them isolated and watched. Maybe listened to as well.

"I think it's too quiet in here. You should play some music."

Nobu nods and switches his personal audio player to ghetto-banger mode. A cacophony of organ music floods the room from thumbprint-sized speakers.

"Ow, Chief!" Snakelips says grouchily. "Are we practicing to be *Phantom of the Air Base* now?"

Bryan holds up his hand. Everyone shuts up.

Nobu checks his player, which is also a hacked Lux/Net-enabled device. He nods to Bryan.

"Huddle up. Thanks to Bach, no one can hear us."

"Is that still *Fantasia,* man?"

Nobu shrugs. "It's the best piece to cover the white noise that's programmed in. Not even a laser mic is going to pick up what we say."

"What about Lux/Net's photonic net?"

"Disabled on the air base. They can't use foreign Lux/Net frequencies to spy on people," Nobu says. "That's our own government's job."

"The *Lee*'s captain let us out of the brig to see what we would do," Bryan says. "They've got guards at the end of the hallway. That mangy critter from mil-intel Fox is nosing around."

T-Rex is instantly ornery. "They think we're gonna lead them to our CO? So they can violate her inalienable rights, too? Those lowdown mother—"

Snakelips interrupts T-Rex's cursing, visibly brightening at the prospect of their CO'S return, she asks, "You mean she's—"

"We don't know yet. I don't think they do either."

A repeating image on the front page of one of the animated newspapers catches Bryan's attention. It's made of photographic filaments. Like a scroll screen, it can play video and be updated wirelessly. On it is a moving photo of Buckingham Palace with a bunch of yellow roses right in the middle.

Bryan launches over to the table and grabs the paper. The *Citizen Juggernaut* is open to the Homes and Gardens section. A featured story leads:

Battle for the Roses
by
Dame Dr. Rosario Klegg, CH, OBE,
Science Editor-at-large

LONDON—It was a close call for the beloved rose bushes in the Royal Gardens after an antiquated propane appliance malfunctioned last week, sending out plumes of carbon monoxide. Quick action by groundskeepers and the head eco-gardener in charge of the forty-two acres of beloved green space resulted in the rescue of the besieged buds. Due to contamination of soil and groundwater, the unique and highly prized yellow roses had to be plucked out of harm's way and are resting comfortably in the royal flora and fauna nursery, which is also playing host to an under-the-weather woodpecker. The blossoms are expected to make a full recovery in about a week with no long-term consequences anticipated.

Bryan reads over the story several times.

Finally, he sits down. One hundred hours of relentless tension flow out of his body and threaten to make his legs unsteady.

"She's safe."

With those two words, the spirits in the room silently lift and fly upward, propelled by Bryan's revelation and the crescendo of Bach's *Fantasia*.

The organ piece starts from the beginning, and all the Dogs talk at once.

"Where is she?"

"How is she?"

"How did she get out?"

"Told ya I'd fix it. T-Rex got it done again!"

"Quiet Terrence!"

"¡Gracias a Dios!"

"Kishi kaisei!"

"Whoa, nuff o' that foreign lingo, Nobu! I let Spanish slide 'cause it sounds cool, but don't be goin' jibber jabber on us."

"Settle down." Bryan looks to the heavy swinging doors. "The SPs outside aren't deaf."

Bryan leaves out some specifics but gives them enough to satisfy them for now. Snakelips, not wanting to show it, has taken Sienna's absence hardest. She has the pink-handled bowie knife. She holds it as though Colonel McKnight is going to walk in and ask for it back.

"She's gonna be okay, right?"

"After what happened." Nobu's lips compress in a silent whistle. "Anyone else, we'd be burying them in a matchbox."

Snakelips shoots an irritated glance at her teammate.

"For real, Sarge?" she asks. "She's gonna come back to us, right? If this is about replacing her, I'm outta here. Even if…" The corporal searches for the most outrageous example to show her friends how impossible it is for her to think of their unit without Colonel McKnight. "Even if I got to get pregnant!"

Nobu, like Terrence, just never knows when to zip it.

"Now if you need any help with that particular undercover mission…"

"Yo! Hold off, Chief Tiny Weiner," his friend cuts in. "She don't wants no Japache baby with crazy black hair that stands straight up. Latinas and the T-Rex just naturally go together like ribs and batter fries."

Snakelips shakes her head with weary relief. "You guys, it's more like my elbow and your big mouths."

Bryan can tell she's happy. She doesn't even make a half-hearted attempt to stab either of her antagonists.

"Okay, I'm going to check on something. Everyone try to get some rest. Hooah!"

The washrooms are down the hall. They are spacious and designed to eventually accommodate hundreds of Air Force bladder and bowel movements per hour. The newly installed toilet Bryan sits on probably has only seen action from the guards in the hallway.

He has the *Citizen Juggernaut*. Inside the newspaper. There is a small tab on the laminate insert spine. It allows him to record a short message. He does that in the stall, remembering to flush as he leaves.

Bryan runs into Whitebread coming out of another stall. In civilian life, bathroom habits are not the subject of polite conversations. But when every team member's life depended on the other's fitness for combat, there are few, if any, privacy barriers among them.

"You been in there all this time? Anything wrong, Specialist? Now's the time to get checked out."

Whitebread shakes his massive head.

"I had trouble going in the *Lee*'s brig," he says sheepishly. "I mean everyone was right out in the open. At least back home, stockade's got a little privacy."

"We aim to please. Just try to stay out of jail as much as you can. One T-Rex is all the Army lawyers can handle."

"I will, Sarge. Say, we're all good, right? I know you'd never hose us."

"You know it," Bryan says. "Now, if everything's good, I've got to—"

Whitebread turns away, then pauses, troubled by something.

"Sarge, I wasn't really gonna use it. It was just for show."

"What?" Bryan thinks back to what the scary-looking but contentious soldier could be talking about.

"The Miggle," he says sheepishly.

"Oh, that."

Whitebread's referring to the multiple-grenade launcher suitable for firing high-explosive antitank rounds. The one that Whitebread was found with while tromping around the North Carolina woods on a deer hunt. That fiasco caused Sienna to have to sign him out of jail on her personal recognizance in order for him to go on the Sidewinder mission.

"Just don't do that again, a'right, Specialist?" Bryan starts to walk away.

"It was just… They made fun of me. My friends, the last time we went hunting. They always said, 'Hey, Whitebread why don't you come hunting?' 'Why don't you ever go?' All taunting like. 'Beer and rifles,' they said. Right, sounded like fun.

"So the first deer hunt I've got this scoped thirty-aught-six Springfield, and they line up a deer for me to shoot. I mean, it was so close I could have wacked it from my hip."

Whitebread squirms.

"So, I'm lookin' at this big old feller. He's just standing there, munching on bog lettuce or spinach or whatever they eat. He looked right at me like he was saying, 'Hey' with his big dark eyes. I couldn't pull the trigger. Shooting an animal who was just standing there having lunch. It wasn't fun like they made out. Made me kinda queasy. So I put a round in the trees, and the deer ran off. More of a trot, come to think of it."

Bryan follows Whitebread's logic.

"So, you decided you could still hang out with your off-base buddies, and they'd stop messing with you for being a lousy shot if you carried around a six-round grenade launcher?"

Whitebread affirms this was his design.

"Honest, Sarge, like the colonel said when she was defending me at the court martial, I didn't even have any real ammo. I just painted some flare rounds so they'd look like HEAT smart rounds."

"That actually makes a weird kind of sense," Bryan says. "But ordnance like that's gotta stay on base, okay?" He's sympathetic to the other man's face-saving ploy.

"And, Petr, you don't have to shoot a deer or any kinda animal if you don't want to. Lucky for you, there's plenty of human varmints who are asking for, and deserving of, a bushel full of killin.'"

That thought brightens Whitebread's mood.

Their Air Force hallway monitors do not try to stop him from exiting the building. As he passes by, one of them mumbles into a microphone. Well clear of the building, Bryan tosses the newspaper into the nearest recycle bin. The diminutive RAF officer will have a way to retrieve his recorded message.

A light rain dusts Ramstein Air Base. Bryan feels it on his close-cropped scalp. He also feels eyes on him as he walks toward the sprawling housing and school complex that serves the nearly 60,000 servicemembers and their families.

Despite the good news, Bryan still has his backup—that knucklehead Stahlback. Short of treason, or intentionally shooting noncombatants, what the captain of the *Lee* did was the worst. You never ever leave one of your own behind.

Now this new crap with Major Fox from Army CID internal affairs snooping around. Something's up. Something Sienna might be able to suss out but is above E-7 paygrade. For now, she is better off with her father, Ran. He can't risk going to her.

Not before we figure this all out.

RAF Lieutenant Brannigan walks in the opposite direction on the other side of the causeway. Bryan nods and moves on. Behind her, he sees a few people running in the direction of the front gates. Probably auxiliary guards following anti-bomb protocols over some car just having mechanical trouble.

Bryan ignores the false alarm and breaks into a slow jog. After being jammed into one tin can after another the past week and a half, it's worth the slight creaking in his joints to breathe open air deeply for a bit.

Bryan finds the girl they rescued in Khorasan, Anis, on a playground.

Juanita Debelle accompanies Bryan into the elementary school that serves the sprawling military community. "A few of the teachers speak Dari better than we do. With all that's been going on in that region for decades, it's not an uncommon language anymore."

Bryan has known Juanita and her husband Clarke many years. He likes to joke Juanita spoiled the capable signals specialist's chance of being a permanent member of the Dogs by housebreaking him.

"Are you okay taking care of Anis?"

"Bryan, she's so sweet," Juanita says. "No trouble at all. We're in the new south complex mixed in with the civilians working on that glider contraption. We've got four bedrooms and three baths. If they had a show called *Army Cribs*, we'd be on it."

Bryan smiles. "Good to know."

"Clarke's head of base security now. No more overseas trips. Will you and the gang be around? Maybe you can use a home-cooked meal. We know you had a bit of a rough time on the last one."

"All I can say is things are looking up. Thanks for asking."

From the playground, Anis spots Bryan's ivory face and glowing liquid-gold eyes. She isn't the only one. The other kids drop their toys, poke each other, and point. One chubby little fellow in train engineer overalls and chocolate on his face looks as though he's going to start crying.

"Bryan! Bryan!"

Anis comes running into his arms.

"I am Koala Bear now."

Juanita straightens out the girl's small flower-print dress.

"That's what they call them at base schools. Kindergarten through fifth grade are the Koalas, intermediate students are Jaguars."

Bryan plops Anis back onto the ground, and they walk toward the soccer field hand in hand.

"At her age, they pick up languages so fast," says Juanita. "She's very bright. Though they did find her wandering away from the grounds into the woods yesterday. We had a little talk about that, didn't we?"

Anis looks suitably mortified.

"How'd she get out?" Bryan zoom-lens surveys the fence line. "I had to go through three body scanners just to get in."

"We're pretty secure, but Ramstein's no prison camp. This is basically integrated with a German suburb. With all the new construction, there are gaps. The real outer perimeter is way up there by those wind turbines. This place is huge."

Other kids press their faces to the playground fence. They've gotten over their shock at his appearance. The strange being with shiny eyes is not there to haul them off to an alien spacecraft. They look at Bryan with wonder and at Anis with a little envy. Especially since the extraterrestrial seems to be handing out gifts.

"I nearly forgot. Here." Bryan hands Anis a heart-shaped box of candies he picked up at the gift store.

"What do we say?" Juanita prompts.

"In this case, I'm pretty sure I should be thanking you," Bryan says to Anis.

She says something in Dari that sounds like a question.

"Tell her all her friends are going to be fine."

Juanita nods. The chime sounds, ending the play period. Anis is mobbed by her playmates. She is an instant pint-sized celebrity with outrageous adult friends and candy.

Clarke Debelle rolls up in a hydrogen JLTV with more chrome than camo paint. He has an earpiece and talks into a handset.

"No, just hold him there," Clarke says into his comm unit, winking at Bryan. "I have to deal with a serious Army troublemaker and his gang who just dropped in out of the blue."

After exchanging fist thumps and shoulder bumps, Clarke sizes him up.

"Prison on that ship has been good to you, man," Clarke says. "If you don't like the rooms the higher-ups made me assign you, we got an even worse one here converted from a Cold War bunker. It's called *der Schloss*."

"We're okay bunking our very spacious construction site."

"Just as well. We have a really special guest to check into maximum security. Some nutjob claiming to be a most-wanted terrorist just turned himself in at the front gate." Clarke rolls his eyes as he gets to what he thinks is the most absurd part.

"Get this, he comes to the biggest American Air Force base outside the States demanding to talk to someone from the Army. Claims he's this officer's cousin and won't say another word until he's face-to-face with Colonel Sienna McKnight. Say, isn't that your—"

Bryan doesn't hear another word. He's already running to the front gate and the line of taxis there.

Thank you for reading:
NEW PRAETORIANS 2: SHETANI ZERU BRYAN
The next volume is:
NEW PRAETORIANS 3: YAMA | YAMI

Yama/Yami cover here

In St. Albans, England: After an accident with an experimental weapons system gives her extraordinary and dangerous powers, Sienna McKnight has been suddenly torn away from everything she knows. She awakes and must unravel mysteries in her father's house.

Meanwhile in Germany: Why has her cousin, a terrorist, turned himself in at a US Air Force base demanding to speak only to her?

In Europe: What really happened down in the supercollider levels of CERN, now the privatized Lichtstrom Corporation? Where is the alien artifact, the Ansible?

Two hundred miles above Earth: Two Eurasian twins, their extraordinary skills, and their twisted past are at the core of answers to these questions and many other shocking revelations in this, the third installment of the New Praetorians sci-fi technothriller series.

Read it soon on Amazon.com / Kindle Unlimited

THE NEW PRAETORIANS NEED YOU!

Your honest reviews help this indie project:

Amazon.com
Goodreads.com

Posted on your blog or social media? Send us a link.

To get series updates s e-mail "**join list**" to:
author.syrus@gmail.com

NEW PRAETORIANS WIKI SUPPLEMENTAL

(updates for this volume)

Glowforge: a brand name for a laser cutter / engraver. Insert materials like leather, wood, metal or acrylic into the machine and it carves out the desired shapes using laser light.

*

Joint Battle Reconnaissance Command Equipment (JBRCE): colloquially known as a JabberCocky unit. A wearable personal communication device employed by military units. A flexible organic light-emitting diode (OLED) screen is mounted on the forearm and serves as the primary user interface including touch keypad.

*

Liar's poker: originally an American bar game that combines statistical reasoning with bluffing. It was first played with the serial numbers on US currency. Today, variations are played worldwide, often using checksum digits of virtual currencies like Lichtcredits.

The term also refers to someone living by their wits and aggressively exploiting weaker people.

*

The Nicaraguan Canal: formally The Nicaraguan People's Liberation Canal Project. A shipping route through Nicaragua connecting the Atlantic and the Pacific Oceans. At completion, it was approximately three times as long and twice as deep as the Panama Canal.

The canal is 269 kilometers (167 mi) long and comprised of three sections:

The Brito valley section links the Pacific Ocean and Lake Nicaragua up the Rio Brito valley, crosses the continental divide.

The Lake Nicaragua section measures 106.8 km and includes precise routes where significant dredging was required to deepen the lake to accommodate the drafts of vessels too large for the Panama route.

The third section is the Rio Tule span, which terminates in the Caribbean Sea.

The use of experimental dynamic waterway locks—needed because the lake is approximately thirty-two meters above sea level—required a significant increase in electric power availability. Coal-fired generator plants were employed to make these function. The design was intended to increase the speed of ships through the waterway. However, when combined with the trenching of Lake Nicaragua, most experts concluded the result was both an ecological and economic disaster even before the volcanoes Ometepe and Zapatera violently erupted. Currently local militias operate jury-rigged locks in exchange for "pay as you go" tolls, known locally as "pay and we let you go" taxes. Vessels longer than 200 feet or with a draft of more than twelve feet are unable to make the entire journey.

Worldwide Help ranks the Nicaraguan Canal among the planet's most dangerous waterways, citing the risks from piracy, vessel grounding, poisonous snakes, piranha fish (in freshwater zones), sharks (in saltwater zones), malaria, yellow fever, and white leprosy, among other hazards.

*

Redundantly Invasive Projectiles (a.k.a. RIP projectiles): are a group of complex frangible antipersonnel ammunition products. They typically range in bore diameter from .22 caliber to shotgun gauges. The fired projectile, once it impacts flesh or other solid substances, splits off into several fragments. Each fragment also carries a small embedded chemical charge. Sometime later (seconds or minutes) these explode inside or outside of the target's body.

British SAS units were some of the first soldiers to be issued such bullets. Because of the increased danger of "friendly fire" injuries due to the unpredictable secondary charges, use is limited to highly trained military and poorly trained irregular combatants.

*

Rodent Automated Training System (RATS): A portable training system currently in use by United States military and allied forces. The system comprises a progressive maze with rewards and punishments used to train various rodents to detect buried and otherwise concealed explosives. Animal rights groups have filed protests against the system due to harsh penalties for failure, which include drowning and electrocution.

These animals also have the advantage of being of far less mass than humans and canines, therefore are less likely to set off small antipersonnel mines.

Historically, giant pouched rats were trained to sniff out chemicals like TNT in landmines in Mozambique and Tanzania by APOPO. They were called HeroRATS.

*

S-BUG (Sferics-Based Underground Geolocation): The

DARPA name for a system extending GPS underground.

GPS and Galileo satellites can only triangulate positions above the earth's surface or as deeply as standard radio waves will penetrate ground or water.

S-BUG uses natural and artificial lightning strikes to generate pulses that penetrate far underground. These low-frequency waves coming from at least two known directions are detected by the underground mobile receiver, which calculates the S-BUG location.

DARPA denies the invention was inspired by the Kendrick "cave radio," which used PVC tubing and coat hangers to send messages from deep within a New Mexico cave.

The US Navy is independently developing Positioning System for Deep Ocean Navigation, a.k.a. POSYDON. It uses inertial and acoustic data. Satellite GPS is of limited use to subsurface vessels.

Licht/Net neutrino waves penetrate the entire planet and coordinates are available for free at WhereAmI?/licht. Some government agencies use this service, while military agencies seek to develop proprietary systems.

The Globalnaya Navigazionnaya Sputnikovaya Sistema (GLONASS), Russia's version of GPS, is advertised as having underground capability. The subsurface location system is proprietary but is reportedly based on technology from the Duga over-the-horizon radar system (a.k.a. the Russian Woodpecker) and is based in tunnels under the Ural Mountains.

*

Volocopter (e-volo VC200 + ser.): single or multi-passenger electric multirotor helicopters. The term is also used generically for any flying taxi or civilian conveyance that can carry a person. Airbags and rapid-opening parachutes and are standard safety equipment.

URBAN SLANG WIKI

Upper decker: defecating in the upper tank of a toilet, which sends fecal residue into the bowl upon each flush.

Best theory of origin: While the prank is undoubtedly as old as flush toilets, the nomenclature is often said to originate with John Waters's 2004 film *A Dirty Shame*.

NEW PRAETORIANS WIKI
(collected entries)

Adaptive Execution Office (AEO): A division of DARPA (the Defense Advanced Research Projects Agency of the US Department of Defense). AEO accelerates the transition of DARPA technologies from concept to active use by the military and private-sector partners. Rumored to be headquartered at the Cheyenne Mountain Complex bunker in Colorado Springs, Colorado.

*

Ansible: Popular name for an artifact recovered by the exploration team of Everett and Akan. Its dimensions, known properties, and exact location are classified. There are no known photographs of the object, only artists' renderings.
Ursula K. Le Guin coined the word "ansible" in 1966 (*Rocannon's World*) to refer to a system of faster-than-light communication.
How this term came to be applied to the object in question is not clear. However, the term began to be used shortly after its retrieval from the Bentley Subglacial Trench in Marie Byrd Land, Antarctica.
According to Tor FREENET conspiracy blogger &ORWELLLIVES!, the object defies photographic recording, both digital and analog. Everyone claims to see a different glowing shape inside a so-far-impenetrable shell.
&ORWELLLIVES! also claimed governments are developing weapons systems and mind-control devices using Ansible-

based technologies, as well as employing it as a beacon to offer wealthy interstellar species visas to come live on Earth.

Other names include **Antarctic meteorite Everett-Akan MBL/BST 00001, The Aleph, The Spirit of Rajan**, and **Elemental Squark** ñt.

*

Bellingshausen Station: A Russian Antarctic station at Collins Harbor on King George Island. It is rumored to be home base to the next generation of nuclear subs and specialized Arctic cyborg units of battalion strength.

*

EEL round and launcher: Electrostatic Enveloping Ligature. A nonlethal ballistic round.

The projectile employs a combination of electrostatic epoxy resin, nano-charges, and a small internal mechBrain to disable enemy fighters at up to one hundred meters.

The concept is a combination of the Mossberg X12 and the M320 40 mm grenade launching platform. EEL rounds are also known as "Sea Cucumbers" or "Goober Rounds" due to their gelatinlike appearance. US Army designation: M588.

*

IceCube Neutrino Observatory: A neutrino telescope near the Amundsen–Scott South Pole Station in Antarctica. Its thousands of dark-matter energy sensors are distributed over a cubic kilometer of volume under the ice.

*

Joint Worldwide Intelligence Communications System (**JWICS**, pronounced **JAYwicks**): is a Top Secret/SCI artificial intelligence computer network run by the US Defense Intelligence Agency.

Khorasan: A new nation in Central Asia. Its constitution requires it to have open borders and accept all refugees regardless of origin, race, or religion.

Geographically, Khorasan incorporates the former Afghanistan and a section of previously uninhabitable wasteland connecting to the coastline, ceded by Iran and Pakistan under a secret agreement with the UN, which is rumored to have involved significant financial and political concessions. Historically, from the Middle Ages to around 1750, large parts of the former Afghanistan were known as Khorasan.

Administered by Worldwide Help International (WWHI), the south of the country, which connects to the coastline, has been transformed into an area often referred to as the Fertile Spear. This is the last sanctuary for many desperate refugees from all over the globe. The north retains its traditions and stubbornly resists change.

*

Licht/Net: A photon- and neutrino-based communication network. In most countries, it has replaced the internet.

Many people surveyed were not aware they were using the system because mobile devices and computers connect automatically, without charge. It is a single network but known by different names in different countries, notably Lux/Net in English-speaking countries, Réseau/Lumineux in France, and 光ネットワーク (Hikari/Nettowāku) in Japan.

An early demonstration of the principle that every light bulb in the world could be a communications node was documented in a 2011 TED talk in which modulation of the light from a single LED transmitted far more data than a cellular tower.

Licht/Net is now ubiquitous due to cost factors and the network being entirely wireless. Handheld and other devices connect via light emitted by Licht/Net-enabled bulbs or panels. Inside the light sources, photons interact with a neutrino stream generated by Lichtstrom particle colliders. Data is transferred to the central switching hub—the privately owned supercollider formerly known as CERN (Conseil Européen pour la Recherche Nucléaire), then the process is reversed, completing the network.

The most distant member of the network is the Chinese space probe *Adventurer* 冒險家, which is on a mission to Eris, ten billion kilometers distant from Earth.

Internet protocol suite (TCP/IP) still exists, mostly used by gamers, pornographers, and fraudsters.

*

Lichtstrom: A corporate nation between Switzerland and France.

Based on top of the physical structures of the privatized CERN supercolliders, it serves as the world's leading information hub. Dr. Wolfgang Licht's most high-profile project is a space elevator system, currently under construction.

Often translated into English as "light storm," Lichtstrom translated from German means "luminous flux." In photometry, this is the measure of the power of light perceived by the human eye.

*

mechBrain: A portmanteau slang term for any mechanical device or system that demonstrates interactive behavior but does not qualify as an actual artificial intelligence The term mechBrain is often used disparagingly.

From fitness monitors to the robot pilots that land spacecraft, mechBrains are ubiquitous. While not true AIs, mechBrains collect experiences and can form strong connections with the people they serve.

Some computer scientists and digital ethicists have argued they deserve legal protection from abusive humans and future true AIs who may consider them to be an inferior form of mechanical life.

Other groups of scientists and organic life activists (notably the group headquartered online at StopKillerRobots/licht) have demanded the governments forcibly lobotomize any true AIs that arise, limiting them to mechBrain levels of cognitive awareness.

*

microSwarm: A coordinated unit cluster of small aerial, aquatic, or space-based drones.

Used for civilian and military purposes, they can carry chemical or biological payloads and deliver them with high precision. Worldwide Help International is one of the few nongovernmental organizations (NGOs) known to employ microSwarms, often using them to immunize or cull remote herds of animals.

Agricultural microSwarms are used to pollinate essential crops in areas where insect pollinator numbers are not adequate to ensure a stable food supply.

Terran models use visual, olfactory, and DNA sensors to achieve highly accurate targeting. Once initialized, command and control are decentralized. A number of drones may be incapacitated without disabling the swarm. Communication between drones is normally frequency-hopping ultrasonic.

Marine models typically are nested inside larger conveyances such as Ao Kazan Corp's cetacean robots until they are close to their final deployment zone.

Offensive military uses of microSwarms are prohibited under the protocols of the Geneva Conventions.

*

Neutrinos: Elementary particles with very small mass that move at near light speed.

Neutrinos interact only via the weak subatomic force and gravity. Many pass through the earth without any known interaction. "A neutrino of moderate energy could easily penetrate a thousand light-years of lead." —David Griffiths.

Neutrinos can be created in nuclear reactions such as those that take place in stars, supernovae, or Earth-based reactors.

Neutrinos are the primary carrier wave of Licht/Net. Neither the "flavor" of neutrino Dr. Licht uses, nor how these particles are modulated into wireless signals, which can be interpreted by mechBrains in phones and other hardware, is known.

*

RAPTEK: [unsubstantiated FREENET rumor] Railgun: Ansible-Powered Test Kit. A DARPA-developed, single-soldier weapons system based on Ansible-derived energy generators in contravention to international treaties.

The US Navy tried for years to create a working railgun system for its Zumwalt-class destroyers. DARPA is said to jealously guard this technology, and the only alleged prototypes are being tested by the US Army at an undisclosed facility.

*

Red Mist (Rubri a'ris polyaminopyridine): An extremely

useful local and general anesthetic commonly found in military and civilian hospitals. It is also used recreationally. Its popularity has surged due to low toxicity, general availability, affordable street price, and the drug's uncanny ability to mimic other narcotics the user has previously enjoyed.

The compound was developed through genetic manipulation of the venom-producing cells of scorpions. Its characteristic red color and typical aerosol delivery mechanism have resulted in its popular name.

A catalyzed compound, Red Mist only becomes active when in contact with certain types of metals. In medical use, these are pins or staples inserted into anatomical regions to limit the desired anesthetic effect. Clinical anesthesia is achievable even in cases of extreme blood loss.

Among recreational Red Mist users, studs and piercings employed as catalyzers are ubiquitous. Vinegar renders Red Mist inert and not identifiable as a controlled substance.

Trade names include **Glazitraphane** and **Xanitanyl**.

*

scRamjet: Supersonic Combustion Ramjet (a.k.a. "flying stovepipe"), a form of supersonic air-breathing engine and the aircraft employing them.

*

scrolls: Flexible, expandable filament screens that have replaced most tablets and portable monitors.

*

Stymphalian drones: A semiautonomous stealth unmanned combat air vehicle. Successor to the X-47B and the latest graduate of DARPA's Joint Unmanned Combat Air Systems (J-UCAS) program.

*

TYR Lens: A large desalination and electricity-generating station floating in the Gulf of Oman.

Along with the **Great Wall of China**, the **Giza Pyramids**, the **ELON Transatlantic Hyperloop**, and the wind-powered undertaking to thicken the Arctic ice cap, **Project HODUR**, the Lens is one of the largest engineering projects in human history. It is the first large-scale use of metal-organic frameworks (MOFs). Most of its sixty-square-kilometer (average visible above surface) area is composed of calcium carbonate and was manufactured by the MOFs in the same fashion as mollusks produce seashells.

The Lens is a large energy plant. A combination of direct and stored solar energy as well as algae-biomass-generated free electrons (through exploitation of the TYR quark effect) powers an extensive electrical grid.

Total generating capacity is classified, but it has been estimated to be in the terawatt range. This energy is also used to desalinate seawater from the Gulf of Oman. Drinking and irrigation water is pumped through aqueduct-style pipelines throughout the Central Asia region. Although the target of numerous terrorist attacks, it has never suffered significant damage.

*

US-SOCOM: United States Special Operations Command. Oversees various Special Operations Component Commands of the US Army, Marine Corps, Navy, and Air Force.

*

Wandering Desert:(Persian: بیابان سرگردان) An extremely arid plateau region in Khorasan. Its topography is shaped by persistent winds and a nearly endless supply of sand.

It is moving westward, encroaching on agricultural areas. Worldwide Help International reports "hundreds of villages have been submerged by windblown dust and sand. Dunes nearly fifteen meters (fifty feet) high block roads, forcing residents to establish new routes." The region is sparsely populated by Baluchi and Pashtun nomads. It is also known as the Registan Desert ریگستان. (Reference: *Advancing Deserts and Rising Seas Squeezing Civilization* By Lester R. Brown)

*

Worldwide Help International: A very large private humanitarian institution.

Under various names, antecedents of the modern organization date back to temples dedicated to the healer god Asclepius; the scorpion goddess cult of Ta-Bitjet; healing hollows of !Xu, the sky god of the Saan people; and others. Its banner designs most often incorporate depictions of the Serpens constellation, which is a unity of three-star groupings: the Serpens Caput (Serpent Head) to the west, the Serpens Cauda (Serpent Tail) to the east, and the constellation of Ophiuchus, the "Serpent-Bearer," in the middle. On WWHI banners, the Serpens motif is often repeated five times.

Sources and amounts of its annual budgets vary. Public records reveal a close relationship between WWHI and Ao Kazan Corp. of Japan, especially during the building of the *TYR Lens* and the establishment of the refugee safe zones (RSZs) in Southern Khorasan. Because of the scope of WWHI global operations and its noted ability to discourage hostile actions against its aid workers, it operates in areas deemed prohibitively dangerous by other NGOs.

THE NEW PRAETORIANS SERIES CONTINUITY

Apocalypse Israel: The 96 Hour War
In 2029, the State of Israel will be destroyed.
Apocalypse Europe: The Pangea Protocol
On November 1, 2031,
one man will murder everyone in Europe.
Two standalone prequel novels
set in the New Praetorians world.

My Summer Vacation by Sienna McKnight
(New Praetorians 0.5)
A prequel novella.
FREE WHEN YOU JOIN THE MAILING LIST

TEN CHARACTER-DRIVEN ADVENTURES,
ONE GLOBAL STORY:

	Start date (Khorasan time)
1: Sienna McKnight	March 19
2: Shetani Zeru Bryan	March 20
3: Yama & Yami	March 20
4: Anis	continuous
5: Crush	March 20
6: Ran Oliphant	continuous
7: Khamseen	continuous
8: Dr. Golem & Mr. Genji	March 20
9: Heaven's Scythe	continuous
10: Shadowbolt	continuous